MAGONIA

MAG

ONIA

MARIA DAHVANA HEADLEY

HARPER
An Imprint of HarperCollins *Publishers*

ISBN 978-0-06-232053-7

Typography by Ellice M. Lee
16 17 18 19 20   PC/RRDH   10 9 8 7 6 5 4 3 2 1
❖
First paperback edition, 2016

FOR CHINA
{{{{   &,&,&   }}}}

PROLOGUE

I breathe in. I breathe out. The sky's full of clouds. A rope is looping down from above, out of the sky and down to earth. There is a woman's face looking at me, and all around us, hundreds upon hundreds of birds. The flock flows like water, surging up and into the air, black and gold and red, and everything is safe and cold, bright with stars and moon.

I'm tiny in comparison, and I'm not on the ground.

I know everyone has dreams of flying, but this isn't a dream of flying. It's a dream of floating, and the ocean is not water but wind.

I call it a dream, but it feels realer than my life.

My history is hospitals.

This is what I tell people when I'm in a mood to be combination funny and stressful, which is a lot of the time.

It's easier to have a line ready than to be forced into a conversation with someone whose face is showing "fake nice," "fake worry," or "fake interest." My preferred method is as follows: make a joke, make a half-apologetic/half-freaky face, and be out of the discussion in five seconds flat.

Aza: "Nothing really majorly wrong with me. Don't worry. I just have a history of hospitals."

Person in Question: "Er. Um. Oh. I'm so sorry to hear that. Or, wait, *glad*. You just said that nothing's really wrong with you! Glad!"

Aza (freaky face intensifying): "It's incredibly nice of you to ask."

Subtext: It isn't. Leave it.

People don't usually ask anything after that. Most are polite. My parents, my family, not so much, but the randoms? The substitute teacher who wonders why I'm coughing and having to leave the room—then having to go to the nurse's office—then having to have a nice 911 call to summon an ambulance to spirit me back to my white linoleum homeland?

That sort of person doesn't typically want to remind me of things I no doubt already know. Which I very much do. Don't be stupid. Also, don't think I'm stupid.

This is not, like, *Little Women*. Beth and her nice, invalid Beth-ness have always made me puke. The way people imagined she wasn't dying. The way she blatantly was. In that kind of story, the moment someone decides to wrap you in blankets and you accidentally smile weakly, you're dead.

Hence, I try not to smile weakly, even if I feel weak, which I sometimes secretly or unsecretly do. I don't want to make myself into a catastrophic blanket-y invalid.

Bang, bang, you're dead. Close your eyes and go to bed.

Side note: *invalid*. Whoever invented that word, and made it the same word as not-valid? That person sucked.

So, right, the question of death comes up in my presence on a regular basis. Adults don't want to talk about it. Seriously, it's not as though I want to talk about it either. But other people my age do.

DEATH DEATH DEATH, everyone's thinking, like we're in our cars, driving slowly past accidents on the highway all day long. They're grossly fascinated.

Some of us, the ones actually dying, are maybe less fascinated than others. Some of us, maybe, would rather not get stuck in rooms where people are regularly talking about celebrity death-y things, whichever kind you want, the OD, the car crash, the mystery fall-apart . . .

People my age enjoy crying and speculating dramatically over how people our age could die. Take it from one who knows. Take it from one whose role has been, for years, *The Girl I Knew Really Well Who Tragically Died One Day.*

Not that I've died yet. I am still totally here. Which is why all the artistic, goth morbidity is a bummer.

Adults want to talk about death way less than people my age do. Death is the Santa Claus of the adult world. Except Santa Claus in reverse. The guy who takes all the presents away. Big bag over the shoulder, climbing up the chimney carrying everything in a person's life, and taking off, eight-reindeered, from the roof. Sleigh loaded down with memories and wineglasses and pots and pans and sweaters and grilled cheese sandwiches and Kleenexes and text messages and ugly houseplants and calico cat fur and half-used lipstick and laundry that never got done and letters you went to the trouble of handwriting but never sent and birth certificates and broken necklaces and disposable socks with scuffs on the bottom from hospital visits.

And notes you kept on the fridge.

And pictures of boys you had crushes on.

And a dress that got worn to a dance at which you danced by yourself, before you got too skinny and too breathless to dance.

Along with, probably, though this isn't worthy of huge thinking, a soul or something.

Anyway, adults don't believe in Santa Claus. They try hard not to believe in Santa Claus in Reverse either.

At school, the whole rare-disease-impending-doom situation makes me freakishly intriguing. In the real world, it makes me a problem. Worried look, bang, nervous face, bang: "Maybe you should talk to someone about your feelings, Aza," along with a nasty side dish of what-about-God-what-about-therapy-what-about-antidepressants?

Sometimes also what-about-faith-healers-what-about-herbs-what-about-crystals-what-about-yoga? Have you tried yoga, Aza, I mean have you, because it helped this friend of a friend who was supposedly dying but didn't, due to downward dog?

No. I haven't tried yoga to cure my thing, because yoga isn't going to cure my thing. My thing is a Mystery and not just a Mystery, but Bermuda—no sun, only Triangle.

Unknowable. Unsolvable.

I take handfuls of drugs every morning, even though no one is entirely sure what the thing that's wrong with me actually is. I'm rare like that.

Rare, like bloodwork and tests and things reaching down my throat. Rare like MRIs and X-rays and sonograms and swabs and never any clear diagnosis.

Rare, like my disease is standing onstage in a tuxedo belting out a torch song that has a chorus along the lines of *"Baby, you're the only one for me."* And then the disease just stands there, waiting for me to walk into its arms and give up resisting.

Rare, as in: so far, I'm the only person on earth who's been diagnosed with this particular precision awesomeness.

Maybe I sound like I'm exaggerating. No. My disease is so rare it's named *Azaray Syndrome*.

After me, Aza Ray Boyle.

Which is perverse. I don't want a doppelgänger in disease form, some weird medical case immortality, which means medical students'll be saying my name for the next hundred years. No one asked ME when the lab published a paper in *Nature* and gave this disease my name. I would've said no. I'd like to have named my disease myself: the Jackass, or maybe something ugly, such as Elmer or Clive.

None of the above topics, the death and dying topics, are things I actually feel inclined to talk about. I'm not depressed. I'm just fucked up. I have been since I can remember. There's not a version of my life that *isn't* fucked up.

Yes. I'm allowed to say that word if I feel like it, and I do. I feel like swearing about this. It's me in this body, thank you, snarled and screwed up and not going to make it; let's not go on about things we can't revise. I'm an edited version of a real live girl, or at least, that's what I say when I want to tell you something and I'd rather not talk about it but have to get it out of the way so we can move on to better topics.

Yeah, I totally know I don't look well. No, you don't need to look concerned. I know you wish you could help. You can't. I know you're probably a nice person, but seriously? All I really want to talk to strangers about is anything other than this thing.

The facts of it, though? Basic, daily of Elmer /Clive/the Jackass/Azaray Syndrome? I have to live in rooms kept free of dust. This has been true almost since forever. When I was born, I was healthy and theoretically perfect. Almost exactly a year later, out of nowhere, my lungs stopped being able to understand air.

My mom came into the room one morning and found me having a seizure. Because my mom is my mom, she had the presence of mind to give me mouth-to-mouth and breathe for me. She kept me alive until they could get me to the hospital. Where they also—barely—kept me going, by making a machine do the breathing. They gave me drugs and did things to make the oxygen density of the air less, rather than more. It got a little better.

I mean, a lot better, given that here I still am. Just not better enough. Early on, I slept for what felt like centuries inside a shell of clear plastic and tubing. My history is made of opening my eyes in rooms where I didn't fall asleep, the petting of paramedics, the red and white spinning shriek of sirens. That's a thing that just is, if you're the lucky girl who lives with Clive.

I look weird and my inner workings are weird, and everyone's always like, huh, never seen *that* shit before. Mutations all over my body, inside, outside, everywhere but my brain, which, as far as anyone can tell, is normal.

All the brain chemical-imbalance misery that some people have? I don't. I don't wake up riddled with apocalypse panic, and I don't feel compelled to do anything in the category of biting my own fingers off, or drinking myself into a coma. In the scheme of things, having a brain that mostly obeys your instructions is not nothing.

Otherwise, I'm Aza-the-Exhibition. I'm the World's Fair. (All I want, ALL I WANT, is for there to be a *World's Unfair Exposition*, preferably in a city near where I live. Booths full of disappointments, huge exhibits of structures built to fail. No Oh-My-God-the-Future-Will-Be-Amazing Exhibits, but the reverse. No flying cars. Cars that squinch along like inchworms.)

I try not to get involved with my disease, but it's persuasive. When it gets ahold of me, the gasping can put me on the floor, flopping and whistling, something hauled up from a lake bottom. Sometimes I wish I could go back to that bottom and start over somewhere else. As some*thing* else.

Secretly, as in only semi-secretly, as in this is a thing I say loudly sometimes—I think I wasn't meant to be human. I don't work right.

And now I'm almost sixteen. One week to go.

School Nurse: "You're a miracle! You're *our* miracle!"

Aza Ray Boyle: (retching noises)

Because I'm still alive I'm thinking about having a party. There's that thing about sixteen. That big-deal factor. Everything changes and suddenly you're right in the world, wearing a pink dress and kissing a cute boy or doing a dancey-prancy musical number.

I clarify, that's what happens in movies. In this life? I don't know what happens from here. Nothing I majorly want to think about.

Who would I invite? EVERYONE. Except the people I don't like. I know enough people to categorize the group of people I know as everyone, but I like maybe five or six of them, total. I could invite doctors, in which case the group would radically grow. I said this to my parents a couple of days ago, and now they hover, considering my questionable attitude. Which they've been considering since forever.

But I ask you, wouldn't it be worse if I were perfect? My imperfections make me less mournable.

Nobody enjoys birthdays. Everyone in the house is nervous. Even the plants look nervous. We have one that curls up. It isn't allowed to share a room with me, but sometimes I visit it and touch its leaves and it cringes. It's curled up now into a tight little ball of Leaves Me the Hell Alone.

Get it?

Leaves? (Oh, haha. Oh very haha.)

High school. First bell. Walking down the middle hall. Past a billion lockers. Late for class. No excuse, except for the one I always have.

I raise my fist to bump with Jason Kerwin, also late, who doesn't acknowledge me with his face, just as I don't acknowledge him with mine. Only fists. We've known each other since we were five. He's my best friend.

Jason's an exception to all rules of parental worry re: Hanging With Humans Other Than Parents, because he knows every possible drill of emergency protocol.

He's allowed to accompany me places my parents don't want to go. Or *do* want to go, but don't want to spend hours at. Aquariums, natural history museum bug collections and taxidermy dioramas, rare bookstores where we have to wear masks and gloves if we want to touch, back rooms full of strange butterflies, bone and life-size surgical model collections discovered on the internet.

Et cetera.

Jason never talks about death, unless it's in the context of morbid cool things we might want to hunt the internet for. Aza Ray and the Great Failure of Her Physical Everything? Jason leaves that filth alone.

Second bell, still in the hall, and I raise one casual relevant finger at Jenny Green. Pink streak in her hair, elbows sharper than daggers, tight jeans costing roughly the equivalent of a not un-nice used car. Jenny has pissed me off lately by being. I mean, not by basic being. Mean being. We have a silent war. She doesn't deserve words at this point, though she called me some a couple of days ago, in a frenzy of not-allowed. Calling the sick girl names? Please. We all know it's not okay.

I kind of, semi, have to respect her for the transgression. It's a little bit badass, to do the thing no one else has ever dared do. Lately, there's been this contagious idea that I resemble a hungry, murdery girl ghost from a Japanese horror movie, so Jenny came to school in blue lipstick and white powder. To mock me.

Jenny smiles and blows me a kiss full of poison. I catch it and blow it back through my today very indigo lips, thoroughly creeping her. I give her a little shudder gasp. If ghost girl is going to be my deal, I might as well use it to my advantage. She stares at me as though I've somehow played unfair, and takes off at a repulsed run for her class.

Insert meaningless pause at locker. Slow walk. Peer into classroom windows, through the wire mesh they put in there to discourage people like me from spying on people like them.

My little sister, Eli, senses me staring, and looks up from her already deep-in-lecture algebra. I rock out briefly in the hallway, free, fists up, at liberty like no one else is this time of morning. Sick-girl privilege. Eli rolls her eyes at me, and I walk on, coughing only a little bit, manageable.

Seven minutes late to English and it's Mr. Grimm, eyebrow up. *The Perpetually Tardy Mizz Aza Ray*, his name for me, and yeah, his name is Grimm, really. Blind bat eyes, thick-frame glasses, skinny tie like a hipster, but that look's not working for him.

Mr. Grimm's muscle-bound, though he never rolls up his sleeves. He has the kind of arms that strain against fabric, which fact tells me he has no actual life, and just veers between being a teacher and drinking protein shakes.

He'd seem as though he belongs in the PE end of the building, except that when he opens his mouth he's nerdtastic. I also think he has tattoos, which he's tried to cover up in various ways. Pancake makeup. Long sleeves. Not too smart to get a skull/ship/naked girl (?) permanently marked on you. You have to button your cuffs all the time.

Mr. Grimm's new this year. Youngish, if you can call thirty

young. But the tattoo is interesting. I can't tell exactly what it is because I've never seen the full extent of it.

It makes me want tattoos. I want one that's worse than whatever his is.

He's got a constant complaint going that I could work up to my potential if I'd only pay attention instead of burying my face in a book while he lectures. He can't lament too successfully, considering that I am one of, oh, what, four people in this school who read.

And I know that's trite. Yes, I'm a reader. Kill me. I could tell you I was raised in the library and the books were my only friends, but I didn't do that, did I? Because I have mercy. I'm neither a genius nor a kid destined to become a wizard. I'm just me. I read stuff. Books are not my only friends, but we're friendly. So there.

I don't need to pay attention to Mr. Grimm's lecture. I read it already, whatever it is, in this case, Ye Olde Man vs. Ye Olde Sea.

Obsessed guy. Big fish. Variety of epic fails. I have to wonder how many generations of sophomores have been oppressed by stories about this same damn thing.

Why? Which of us is or will one day be engaged in a death struggle with a big fish? What is the rationale?

I've read *Moby-Dick*, another version of Obsessed Dude, Big Fish, and taxonomies of sorrow and lost dreams.

I know, whale = not fish. Mammalian cetacean. Still, whales have always been the prototype for Big Fish Stories, which makes all kinds of sense given how wrong humanity always is about everything.

I even read the *Moby-Dick* chapters that no one reads. I could tell you anything you need to know about flensing. Trust me on this, though, you don't want that information.

Ask me about *Moby-Dick*, Mr. Grimm. Go on. Do it.

He did do that once, about a month ago, thinking I was lying about reading it. I gave a filibuster-quality speech about suck and allegories and oceans and uncatchable dreams that I then merged into a discussion of pirate-themed movies, plank-walking, and female astronauts. Mr. Grimm was both impressed and aggravated. I got extra credit, which I don't need, and then detention for interrupting, for which punishment, in truth, I respect him.

I glance over at Jason Kerwin, who is ensconced in his own book. I eye the title. *Kepler's Dream: With the Full Text and Notes of Somnium, Sive Astronomia Lunaris.* It looks old and semi-nasty, recycled hardcover library copy. Big picture of the surface of the moon on the front.

No clue: me.

I slink my hand over to his desk and snatch it to read the flaps. The first science-fiction novel, it says, written in the 1620s. An astronomer tells a story of a journey to the moon, but also he attempts to encode in the novel a defense of Copernican theory, because he's looking for a way to talk about it without getting executed for heresy. Only later did people realize all the fantasy bits are pretty much Kepler's code for astronomy and equations.

I thumb. There's a flying alien witch.

Awesome. Kind of my kind of book. Except that I'd prefer it if I could write one of my own. This is always the problem with things containing imaginary languages and mysteries. I want to be the cryptographer. I'm not even close to being a cryptographer, though. I'm just what used to be called "an enthusiast." Or maybe a hobbyist. I learn as much as I can learn in like fifteen minutes of internet search, and then I fake, fast and furious.

People therefore think I'm smarter than they are. It gives me room to do whatever I want, without them surrounding me and asking questions about things. It keeps people from inquiring about the whole dying situation. I invoke factoid privilege.

"Give," Jason whispers. Mr. Grimm shoots us a *shut-up* look.

I consider how to pacify my parents about the birthday party. I think they have visions of roller-skating and clown and cake and balloons—like the party they had for me when I was five.

That time, no one showed up beyond two girls forced by their mothers, and Jason, who crashed it. Not only did he walk a mile uninvited to my birthday party, he did it in formal dress: a full alligator costume left over from Halloween. Jason didn't bother to tell his moms where he was going, and so they called the police, convinced he'd been kidnapped.

When the squad cars showed up outside the roller rink, and the cops came in, it became immediately clear that Jason and I were destined to be friends. He was roller-skating in the alligator suit, spinning elegantly, long green tail dragging behind when they demanded that he show himself.

That party was not all bad.

For birthday sixteen, though, I'm drawing a better vision in my notebook: a dead clown, a gigantic layer cake from which I burst, a hot air balloon that arrives in the sky above me. From the hot air balloon's basket dangles a rope. I climb. I fly away. Forever.

How much pain would this solve? So much. Except for the pain of the dead clown, who died not according to his own plan, but mine.

Apparently, Mr. Grimm hears me snort.

"Care to enlighten us, Miss Ray?"

Why do they always use this phrase? Rest of the class is taking a quiz. They look up, relieved to be legitimately distracted. Jason smirks. Nothing like trouble to make a day pass faster.

"Do you really want enlightening?" I ask, because I'm working it today. "I was thinking about dying."

He gives me an exasperated look. I've used this line before in Mr. Grimm's classroom. It's a beautiful dealbreaker. Teachers melt like wet witches when I bring it up. I kind of enjoy Mr. Grimm, though, because he sees through me. Which means he's actually looking. Which is, in itself, weird. No one looks at me too closely. They're afraid my unsustainability is going to mess them up. That plastic bubble I lived in when I was little? It's still there, but invisible now. And made out of something harder than plastic.

"Dying, in the context of which literary work, Aza?" he asks. No mercy.

"How about *The Tempest*?" I say, because there it is, on the syllabus, looming. Everything is ocean this semester. "Drowned twins."

"The drowned twins who don't really drown are in *Twelfth Night*, not *The Tempest*," he says. "Try it again, Ray."

Embarrassing. I'm at a loss, unfortunately.

"Play it again, Sam?" I say, illegally using Mr. Grimm's first name. Then I embark on my traditional method: one-fact-that-makes-them-think-you-have-all-the-facts. You can learn the oddest little items from a wiki page.

"Except that that's a misquote. 'Play it, Sam,' it should be, but people want it more romantic and less order-givey."

Grimm sighs. "Have you even seen *Casablanca*? Ten more minutes till pencils up. I'd do the quiz if I were you, Aza. And don't call me Sam. It's Samuel. Only people who don't know me call me Sam."

He's won, because he's right. I so haven't seen *Casablanca*. That fact was all I had. I cede the field and pick up my pencil to navigate old man and marlin.

Samuel. Who names their kid Samuel these days? I consider making a remark about pen names: Samuel Clemens, Mark Twain, and *Life on the Mississippi*, recently read, but I don't. Last time we did this it became a duel, and there's something about my chest right now that makes me uncertain whether I can properly duel without coughing.

There's a storm kicking up outside, and trees are whacking against the windows. The blinds are rattling like crazy, because this building is a leaky, ancient thing.

Jason flips a note onto my desk. Mr. Grimm is vigilant about phones buzzing, so we go low-tech. *Giant squid*, it says. *Tomorrow, five o'clock. Your house.*

We were supposed to watch the footage a couple of nights ago, but I was coughing so hard I had to go to the hospital. Which sucked.

I had to have a scope and when I revived all the way from the anesthetic, the surgeon was looking at me with the usual whoa, never seen that before look.

Mutant, I scribbled on the notepad they'd given me in case of complaint.

The surgeon looked at me, and then laughed. "No," he said. "You're a special young lady. I've never seen vocal cords like yours before. You could be a singer."

If I could breathe, I wrote, and he had the grace to look mortified.

In solidarity, Jason didn't watch the squid footage without me, though he attempted to convince them to put it on in the ER. He couldn't get permission from the nurses. They're hardcore in there.

Speaking of ocean and big fish in it. This is the first footage of a giant squid ever taken in which the squid is swimming around in its own environment. Imagine this sea-monstery unbelievable thing with eyeballs the size of a person's head, and a body and tentacles twenty-five feet long. As long as a school bus. Now, realize that no one's ever seen one moving around down there before. It's a pretty huge miracle, and if this exists, maybe there are things in Loch Ness too. Maybe there are things everywhere, all over the place. Maybe there's . . . hope?

Because every time someone finds a new animal, or a new amazing thing on earth, it means we haven't broken everything yet.

Up till now there's only been video of really dead or really sick giant squid, but a scientist went down in a submersible and found one and filmed it.

Someone Jason knows has a hack on Woods Hole, the oceanographers in Massachusetts, and he caught wind of expedition communications. He snatched the video from a server four days ago, and hasn't stopped crowing since.

I look over at Jason to smile at him, but he's deep in his book. I lower my head to get down to the quiz, when out the classroom window, over the top of the iguana terrarium, I see something in the sky.

It's only for a second but it's weirdly familiar, something I dreamed, or saw in a picture, maybe.

A mast. And a sail.

More than one sail—two, three. Tall-ship style. Big, white, flapping. And out of the storm comes the prow of a ship.

Which . . .

I've hallucinated before, but nothing in this category. I read something recently about mirages in the sky, *fata morgana*, that's what they're called.

Someone once saw Edinburgh hanging in the sky over Liverpool for half an hour. But what's this—this boat reflecting from? We're inland. Deep inland.

I reach out and tug Mr. Grimm's sleeve. He looks at me, irritated. I point.

He looks, and for a moment, he doesn't move, staring hard out the window. Then he takes off his glasses and glances again.

"Shit," he says.

"What?" I say. "You see it? Do you see it?"

He shakes his head.

"Storm," he says, and yanks at the blinds.

As the blinds clang to the bottom of the sill and the room goes back to just being a room, I hear a whistle, long and high. Not exactly a whistle. More than a whistle.

Let me correct that. *Much* more than a whistle.

Aza, it says, the whistle. *Aza, are you out there?*

CHAPTER 2

None of this is real, Aza Ray Boyle, it is not real.

That's what I'm muttering to myself.

This is a new one, this kind of bad. The kind having to do with my brain.

My mom looks at me over the kitchen table, rumpling up her blond-gray ponytail and wrinkling her forehead.

"Are you sure you're okay? You don't sound okay. Remember last time you hallucinated? You had a fever."

Once she looks at you, you're done. There's no room for fake around my mother. She's spent all day in her lab. She's an immunologist, and most nights she's out late and involved with mice.

Today, she's home relatively early, eleven thirty. Her experiments have been miserable recently. She has no tolerance for the thing she refers to as "flimflam," in this case, me telling her I'm fine and don't need to go to the doctor.

"Greta," I say. "I'm as fine as I ever am."

"Greta," she says. "Is not what you call me, Aza Ray."

"You don't have to call me *daughter*," I say. "You're allowed to call me by *my* name."

She doesn't even dignify that, but starts calibrating dosages, then sticks a thermometer into my mouth.

"Okay, *daughter*," she says, and smiles at me as though I deserve it. My mom has a smile that is simultaneously loving and blistering. The dominant emotion is just a matter of degrees.

So—I'm getting away with nothing in the realm of faking fine.

"You're a hundred and two," she announces. "So, there's your skyship."

I usually have a fever to some extent or another. I'm used to it. Clammy or boiling. Whatever. My mom wraps a blanket around my shoulders. I shed it as fast as I can. (Death-foreshadowing blanket? No, thank you.) I tug my particular million-pocketed hoodie on. The snick of the zipper is not allowed to remind me of a body bag.

"Take a breather, Aza," says my mom.

I give her a look. "Breather? Really?"

"Take a breather on your freak-out, because freaking out helps nothing, and here's a pill," and even as she says it, the pill's in my mouth, and I swear, I'm apparently a dog, because she gets it down my throat before I notice she's literally pilling me. Other hand has a glass of water at the ready, so bam, I'm washing the pill down.

That's Greta for you. She's quick. What's the point in resisting?

Besides, the pills seem to help.

They said, when I was two, that I'd be lucky to make it to six. When I was six, they said I'd be lucky to make it to ten. When I was ten, people were bewildered, and so they said sixteen.

And here comes sixteen, moving swiftly toward us.

So now, when I'm rushed to the hospital, my family has a full procedure to deal with things we're unwilling to talk about. We actually wrote them down, just in case. My mom thinks this will make it somehow less problematic, the whole major-concerns-over-dying thing.

I have, for example, a written apology from her for the time she spanked me when I was five and I gasped and wheezed my way into a brief coma. I forgive those things. They aren't even things. But she insists I have to carry the paper if I need to go to the hospital anyway.

My mom has a written apology from me for the entire category of brutal sarcasm. Eli has one entitled *Excessive Bitchiness, Hogging of Parental Attention by Repeatedly Being Sick Unto Death but Not Actually Dying*, and Variant Category: *Theft of Clothing*.

The one to my dad runs more along the lines of *Things I Wasn't Very Interested In, Parts 1–36*.

My mom's been—for the past many years—doing a side project along with her normal work. She's breeding a mouse, a kind of super mouse, which in theory will be invulnerable to various inhalable environmental toxins. It's based on an original badass Chicagoan lab mouse, which had a breathing mutation. The plan is that the new mouse breed will have a mutation that makes them able to flip their nostrils closed and reduce their need for air, at least temporarily, combined with some various invulnerabilities to all sorts of plague vectors.

The mouse is meant to be a drug-developing step. It's supposed to help drug companies end up with a drug that might make people who can't breathe normal air very well figure out how to deal with it better. People like me, obviously. But there are other applications, which at least have made people willing to fund the research. If someone, for example, sets off a bomb with nerve gas? This mouse should be able to react fairly calmly, for an hour or so, which may or may not give the gas time to disperse. Originally my mom tried to make a joke about war-mice, riffing on the dormouse from *Alice in Wonderland*.

War-mouse. Joke fail.

My mom isn't a supporter of war anything. She never wanted to do military applications for her research. Because obviously, for everyone you'd protect with a war-mouse drug (civilians, kids, teachers, anyone who is stuck in a war zone and at the mercy of a chemical attack) you're also creating a version in which the attacking soldiers could potentially make themselves invulnerable to poisons they were pumping into the civilian air.

Which is to say, my mom is in massive conflict all day long. All she wanted was to create some kind of asthma drug, done large, something that would help the entire category of lung problems, emphysema, asthma, Azaray. But instead, she's stuck developing the war-mice.

Eli's also at the table, snipping off the bottom one-eighth inch of her hair with a pair of scissors she's sharpened herself on the knife sharpener. She's precise. I don't know how she manages it, but when she's done, the whole thing hangs like a smooth blond sheet of paper—her ends impeccably straight.

We look nothing alike. My hair's black and knotted and my eyes, though blue, are navy blue with some gold and red swimming beneath the surface. Eli's are the color of a barely-there sky. If this were a fairy tale, she'd straight up be the good sister, and I'd be the wicked one.

"Item One," Eli says, without bothering to acknowledge my

elder-sister superiority. "You heard thunder. We *all* heard thunder. I heard it from algebra. Item Two. You saw clouds. Which we all also saw. It was a storm. Item Three. You hallucinated a ship, because you're basically side-effecting and fevery.

"There's no way the storm spoke to you," she concludes. "Also, there was no loudspeaker yelling your name. Just FYI."

Possibly I got somewhat high-pitched in Mr. Grimm's class. Possibly a scene was caused. Possibly I am known for drama. Possibly Eli is known for her amazing unhysterical nature. Even though she's fourteen and has every right to be out of control with wrath and what used to be known as humors.

No. Even-keeled, Eli. She got her period last year and was like, *Right, fine.* She went straight to ballet class in a leotard, and there were no problems.

I myself have never gotten my period, which I'm actually not too upset about. Postpone the misery, I say. It's because I'm too skinny, and have no luck gaining weight.

Clarification: by "too skinny," I don't mean Sexy Goth Girl in Need of Flowery Dress and Lipstick to Become Girl Who Was Always Secretly Pretty but We Never Saw It Till Now. I mean: dead girl walking. Corpse-style skin, and sometimes when I cough, it's way gross. Just saying.

I'm not sure what happened today either. My dad had to come and fetch me from the principal's office after I screamed a couple of words regarding liberty and self-determination and window blinds. Mr. Grimm gave me a look, and told me I knew where to go. Nurse's office or principal's office. I rotate.

My dad met me, sympathetic even as we were both chided. There is an attempt being made to treat me not like a freak, but like everyone else. Meaning no special anything.

Beyond the special everything already in place.

For example, there's a buddy system, which means there's presumably always someone sideways-watching my progress through the halls in case I fall down choking. I have no particular faith in this fail-safe. Couldn't tell you who was on Aza Duty today.

Lecture mode, though, is actually relatively typical.

Principal: "Ms. Ray, you know better than to create a disruption in the classroom."

I want to say, "Define 'know.'"

Because sometimes I find myself doing things I "know" better than to be doing, but that doesn't stop me. The activities in the corners of my brain call to me, and they're strong. On a daily basis, I have to actively not think of them, if I want to retain focus.

In eighth grade, I lost vigilance, and an hour later, I'd turned my copy of *Grapes of Wrath* into a circus of a hundred and thirty-four origami animals, ostriches and elephants, train cars with actual wheels, acrobats.

There was a bad period in third grade when it was all I could do to leave the aquarium alone. I kept feeling sure the fish were looking at me. And then again in sixth, when my classroom had a canary. That time, I swear, it *did* talk to me. Not in words. It just sat on its perch, staring hard at me and singing, incredibly loudly, so loudly that it actually had to be moved to another class, because it disturbed everyone.

Birds. I've never not had trouble with birds. I'm the person who gets dive-bombed by whatever's flying by. I wear hats when I'm outside.

Anyway, principal's office.

Aza: "I saw something weird in the sky."

Aza's Dad: "I apologize for my daughter. Her medication—"

Aza (disliking hallucination implications): "No, you're right. I got bored. So I made it up. Leave it."

Principal (eyeballing to see if he's being mocked): "Just no more, Ms. Ray. No more of your antics."

Antics is pronounced like a dirty word.

Upon extrication from the principal's office, I pressed my face to the window in the stairwell to try to see whatever it was I'd seen before. But no, nothing. It was gone.

Now my dad looks exhausted. He cooked. Tonight, some sort of noodle casserole with desperation sauce. Peanut butter involvement. He swears it's legitimate Thai, but there's no macaroni in Thai food. Nor jerky. I'm pretty sure there's jerky in there.

"She did see *something*," my dad tells my mom.

My mom looks at my dad, who regularly gets into trouble for believing things that defy logic. He's a passionate imaginer. My mom and Eli are the house realists. My dad finally shrugs and turns back to the stove.

"She hallucinated something," my mom says. "Not saw."

"She has a *vivid imagination*," Eli says, and snickers at the stupid phrase, which has been used on me for as long as I can remember.

"Whatever," I say. "It's over. Leave it."

I've already been out again, staring up at the sky—which is dark, plus a skinny slice of moon—and there's nothing whatsoever unreasonable about it. It's just itself, the sky, and there, the North Star.

I like the sky. It's rational to me in a way that life isn't. Looking at it doesn't suck the way you might think it would, given all the dying-girl-stares-at-heaven possibilities. I don't think of the sky as any kind of heaven item. I think of it as a bunch of gases and faraway echoes of things that used to be on fire.

The proper name for the North Star is Cynosure, named after a nymph. It's a *scip steorra*, "ship star," for navigation. In some of the old stories (give it up for the many peculiar and awesome philosophers of the 1600s—in this case, Jacques Gaffarel, and no, I can't explain how I happened upon him, except that at some point, deep in the library, I saw a circular diagram of the sky, and the stars looked like breeding fruit flies in a petri dish, and I was So Obsessed), the patterns of the stars form letters. Celestial alphabets. Writing that gets rewritten as the earth moves. If you look at the sky that way, it's this massive shifting poem, or maybe a letter, first written by one author, and then, when the earth moves, annotated by another. So I stare and stare until, one day, I can read it.

When I was little, I tried to sneak out at night to get my fill of the stars. I had a plan involving bedroom window, drainpipe, up instead of down. My mom busted me as I was dragging the blanket onto the shingles, but she surrendered and took me up at four in the morning, accompanied by all kinds of just-in-case breathing equipment. We looked at the sky together, wrapped in my comforter, with a thermos, a flashlight, and a book of constellations. We just sat there in silence, and periodically, my mom would show me one of the star pictures and explain its meaning.

So when I complain? I complain with this context. My parents are the kind of parents people wish they had. They had no problem setting up a lamp with a shade poked full of holes that project the entire Milky Way onto my bedroom ceiling when I turn the light on.

Imagine if you could see all the stars we can't see anymore. If the lights all got turned off, all over the world, the sky would be blazing and crazy, the way my lamp makes it look.

I don't know how to navigate by any of the stars, but I read once about someone who took on the entire ocean on a little handmade raft, from South America to Polynesia. The *Kon-Tiki*, his raft was called. He was a Norwegian explorer named Thor.

I kind of wish my name were Thor. It implies warrior-ness. But, no. Aza. Named after what? No one.

I didn't even start out being called Aza Ray. This is the name they gave me after the breathing problems started. Before that, I was called Heyward. (Heyward was a great-uncle. Eli is named after a great-uncle too. I'm not sure what's wrong with my parents. Could they not name us after our aunts?)

I'm still Heyward on official forms, which, Tell Not a Soul. But—

Mom: "That day, after we thought we were going to lose you, we suddenly knew your name was Aza. You were meant to be named after the full spectrum, *A* to *Z*. It was perfect."

Dad: "It just came to us. It was weirdly spiritual. We figured, who defies that?"

This Aza-ness, though, contributed totally to my freaki-tude. For part of grade school, I went by Ava, because some teacher screwed it up, and I let her. Eventually, I was busted in a parent-teacher conference.

Aza. For years, I thought that if I had to be a palindrome, make me *kuulilennuteetunneliluuk*. Which is the Estonian word for the part of the gun a bullet whizzes through on its way to kill you.

If you're gonna go there, go there all the way. Right?

Instead, I'm the alphabet. Depending on your worldview and knowledge of the history of the alphabet, there could also be a silent & in there. The ampersand used to be the twenty-seventh letter. You'd recite your alphabet and at the end, you'd say *X*, *Y*, *Z*, &. So if you're doing my name, it's an alphabet loop, and that means that between *Z* and *A*, you get to add in an & too. Az(&)a.

There's an awesome thing about having that & in my name, as follows: the symbol itself is the Latin word for "and," as in *et*, with its two letters twisted together. So, there's an invisible extraterrestrial in my name.

Jason and I discovered this five years ago and we were obsessed with my internal ET.

I mean, how could you not be? "Phone home" and all of that.

Do you see how I'm making this awesome and not just weird? Do you give me credit? This makes me feel slightly better some days. Other days, not so much.

Today? Today sucks.

There's a rattle in my chest right now, and I'm pretending there isn't, but something about the misery of maybelikelyprettydefinitely hallucinating again, something about the fact that I'm a test case for every new drug the market invents, puts me into such a miserable place that before I know it I'm sitting at the kitchen table with my entire family, crying my eyes out, and coughing simultaneously.

They pack me off to the shower, where I sit on a stool in the steam, naked and bitter, inhaling water and trying to forget about the ship I saw, the words yelled out of the sky, trying to forget about everything, including sixteenth birthdays and parents and sadness.

"You know you're just special, baby," my mom tells me as she's closing my bedroom door. "We're in this with you. You're not alone. We love you."

"Even if I die?" I say, because I am weak. "Will you still love me even if I die?"

My mom stands in the doorway. I see her trying to calm herself down enough to answer me. I can see her wanting to say "You're not going to die," but she doesn't let herself, because that would be full-throttle lying.

She's making herself meet me in this stupid messed-up body that has not enough time and not enough stability. Greta's gripping my doorframe hard, but her face says, *Don't worry*. She swallows, and then smiles at me.

"Even if you die," she says. "Okay? We'll love you forever and forever. Until the end of time."

Because I feel very very shitty, I think about saying "You won't. When people die, you forget about them eventually. You have to. Time passes. Nothing's *that* important," but I don't say it.

My mom walks away, quietly.

She thinks I don't hear her crying in the hallway for an hour after I'm supposed to be asleep.

She thinks I don't hear her start the car and drive back to the lab because that's all she knows how to do, the slow-research fix, inventing a cure for something no one even understands.

I'd like my parents to not have to be constantly thinking about me and my issues. I have a vision of my mom and dad at a beach, drinking things with umbrellas in them.

We've never been to a beach. They've never been on a vacation by themselves, because: me.

So now I'm thinking halfheartedly about hitchhiking to some other city. Or stealing the car and driving there. I maybe-semi-kind-of-know how to drive. I learned three months ago, my dad beside me in the passenger seat, and my mom in the backseat, and both of them swearing they trusted me, even as I crashed into our garbage cans.

My Mom: "Don't worry. Nobody ever died at two miles an hour."

My Dad: "Snails?"

My Mom: "Lemurs."

My Dad: "Shrews. Wait. How fast do shrews move?"

My Mom: "Shrews move incredibly fast. They're predators. They take emergency ten-second naps, and the rest of the time, they hunt. You lose."

My Dad (grinning): "You win."

Me: "Um. Should I start the car again?"

I haven't actually gotten my license. But I know how to drive at top speed, because they showed me that, too, in the middle of the night, illegal on the highway, far out of town. I've never done it alone, but I did it with my parents. I drove really, really fast.

If I could drive really fast to another town, I could die there. Possibly in a hotel. And save everyone the catastrophe of watching me go.

Eli, I think. *No matter what I do, this is going to utterly disaster her.*

And all night, I'm thinking about how whatever I heard

coming out of the sky, it wasn't English, and it wasn't even really words. But it was familiar. I felt it in my bones, in the strangest way.

I felt like something was ringing me like a bell.

I wake up at 4:30 a.m., sweating, panicked, heart pounding, coughing. My skin feels tight enough that I'm not sure it's not ripping. I walk shakily to the bathroom and look in the mirror. I look like me. The in-pain version.

I dream for the rest of the night, weird faces, and feathers, and I keep feeling smothered, as though something's pressing against my mouth and nose, and like there's something in my lungs. I wake up again, and it's seven. The sun's rising, and I'm convincing myself not to freak out.

I can't get rid of the feeling of my skin pinching too close to my bones, snagging on itself. My mouth feels weird too. My cough's epically worse than it was last night.

So, no school. Instead, doctor, where I put on my own backless white gown, with name embroidered—small perks—and my own slippers.

I've been known to pretend things about these events. Usually, it's the Black and White Ball. Truman Capote. My backless white is a gown constructed of silk and petticoat, and maybe some nice netting made of Audrey Hepburn's soul. (Audrey was invited, but did not attend.) Except that at that famously glamorous party, I don't think anyone's gown was bottomless. No joy like the feeling of frozen upper thighs against an examining table.

This is a children's hospital, though, so there are things worse than me. I've seen curtains pulled shut suddenly, and on the other side the unmistakable sound of parents sobbing. I've seen the Make-A-Wish people roaming the hallways, costumed and ready for action, and sick kids looking like the world has flipped over and given them everything they ever wanted at the last possible moment.

What they want, inevitably, turns out to be things made of trying to be the same as everyone else. Once I saw a certain floppy-haired teenage singing idol in red leather pants shambling his way down the hallway to make someone's wish come true. A while later, I saw him leave, looking brain-broken.

Classic mistake: he'd shown up convinced he'd make the blind see and the dying live. It doesn't work that way. Famous people aren't magic. Despite their thoughts to the contrary.

A kid comes tearing around the corner, hairless and bleating like some kind of very hungry, quite large baby bird. He's chasing a clown, though, not running from a doctor, so it's not terrible.

The clown pauses in my exam room doorway and juggles her rainbow pom-poms. The three-year-old patient claps his hands wildly and looks at me with huge, excited eyes. Despite my bad mood, I end up smiling too.

Even though this is blatantly in violation of my rules against befriending fellow victims of the unimaginable, by the time my doctor arrives, I have the kid in my lap, and the clown is alternately blowing soap bubbles, and playing "Over the Rainbow" on a harmonica. Not a good song choice, in my opinion, but one I've regularly been exposed to over the years. Some people think it's comforting to imagine being flung over a rainbow when you die, grabbed by your ankles by a bluebird, and swung into the void.

I mean, fine. There are obviously more upsetting possibilities. The kid's humming happily along. Neither of us is the worst thing that could happen. We're walking, talking, and coughing almost like regular humans.

Dr. Sidhu arrives and the clown carries the kid off into the labyrinth of hospital. My doctor begins her usual procedures of chest knocking and listening, as though she's a neighbor trying to spy through a locked door.

Except that Dr. Sidhu is the kind of neighbor who can see through the walls. Her face doesn't change expression. It's the not changing that tells me something's wrong.

"Huh," she says.

"What do you mean, 'huh'?" I ask.

I've known Dr. Sidhu my whole life. She never says "huh." And this is my body we're talking about. My organs are in strange places.

There's a theory that things in my chest cavity got shifted during that early period of really, really not being able to breathe. One of my lungs, for example, is tilted far toward the center of my chest. My ribs are more flexible than they should be if I were anyone other than Aza carrying around a disease named Clive.

Clive the Jackass makes me flat-chested, pointy-ribbed, and lung-tilted. Otherwise, I'm totally awesome.

"There's an unusual sound. Stop talking."

I don't want to stop talking, but I do, because Dr. Sidhu looks up at me and makes a dangerous face. She has little patience for the likes of me, yammering on through my appointments. She lassos her stethoscope around, and considers my heart. (Heart. Also misplaced. It's never had quite enough room. We deal with this shit, we deal, we do, but bless any intrepid doctor who ever tries to listen to my heart, beating where it isn't. I've let some doctors try it, just to watch their faces when they think momentarily that I'm somehow walking and talking, heartless. Entertainment.) She takes me to X-ray, and disappears briefly to peer at the results.

"MRI," she says.

Great. I can feel my dad, outside the door, dreading.

"I'm okay," I tell him as I hit the waiting room, wheelchaired (hospital policy). Into the MRI tunnel, where they give you earplugs but you still hear things popping and clicking and hissing and singing out as they ping along your insides.

Sometimes while I'm here, I pretend I'm a whale, deep down, listening to the singing and dinging of my whale family. Today I hear something more along the lines of: *Aza, Aza Ray.*

It's like I'm hearing something coming from outside again. Or is it inside? No matter what, I hate it.

"Hold your breath," says the tech. "Try not to cough."

I try not to cough. I pretend "giant squid" instead of "whale." Lights flash. Things whistle and pop and extremely beep and make me feel as though I ought to be listening to something else. I read a thing once about deep ocean creatures and how the noises of earth are messing with their sonar. Whole lot of lost whales beaching themselves in cities—things like that. I read another one about sound-chaos, how nature is supposed to be harmonious, but human noises are screwing everything up and now people are going wacko due to atonal everything. Maybe I'm already wacko.

Aza, go outside.

I press the call button.

"Do you hear that?"

"Hear what? The obnoxious noise? You know what this sounds like, darling, you've been here a thousand times," says the tech, Todd, who is a friendly person.

Todd always gives me an extra heating pad before I get rolled in here. I love him, because he moonlights in a laser hair-removal clinic, dealing death to follicles. He has some very happy stories involving vanquishing unwanted whiskers from women's faces. The patients in the hair-removal clinic are totally grateful all the time. Here, people tend to grumble. No one really likes getting an MRI, and everyone's sick. "We're almost done. Are you okay?"

So not, it turns out, because the moment I say I'm fine, and the whistling begins again? I hear: *Azalistenlistenazaaza azalistencomeoutside.*

I clench my teeth, don't cough, and stand it. It is not easy to stand it.

When I get out of the thing, everyone's looking at me, like *What the hell?* That isn't the usual look that people give you when you come out of an MRI. Todd sighs, and pats me on the shoulder.

"You can't say I said, but basically, there's a feather in your left lung."

"As in, I grew a feather?"

Of course I'm not growing feathers. But it's the first thing I think.

Todd clarifies. "As in, we think you aspirated a feather. Which would explain the coughing."

Except, no. It's the sort of thing you'd notice. If you snorted in some air, and with that air came a feather big enough to show up on this scan? You'd so, sO, SOOOO know.

They give in and show me, and yes. A feather the size of my little finger. This feather can only have come from a pillow, and feather pillows aren't allowed in my room. Whoever put a feather pillow on my bed is in trouble. (Eli, obviously. My dad is as appalled as I am.)

I don't think about the voices I've been hearing.

I don't think about the sky.

I don't think about how everything feels apocalyptic all over my life. Apocalypse, we all know, is a sign of brain betrayal, and my brain's the only part of me that's ever been okay.

"Is there any explanation?" my dad asks, but the techs have nothing for him.

"Doctor Sidhu will call you in for a follow-up," says Todd. "Seriously, don't tell her you saw this."

I have, of course, seen scan results for years. Everyone shows me everything. It's that way when you're a lifetime patient. I've been interpreting MRIs longer than Todd has. That does not mean this doesn't totally freak me out.

Todd's freaked out too. I can tell. He's whistling under his breath, in a way that's meant to make me feel more comfortable but actually makes me panic.

His whistling, of course, does not have any sort of words or patterns of words hidden under it. It doesn't, except that I'm hearing words in *every* whistle. Everything sounds sentient to me now, and I can't help myself. The squeaks of the floor. The creaks of the doors.

I put my clothes and various metal things back on. Earrings. Necklace. Unnecessary bra.

Aza, come outside.

The fact that I hear that combined with some kind of birdsong?

Is not relevant to any of my fears, any of my bad dreams, any of the things I've been worrying about.

It's meaningless.

It's nothing at all.

It's amazing that we're allowed to leave the hospital, but we are. Back tomorrow for little pinchers down my windpipe. I've had worse. At least it's not a full-on surgery. I try not to think about the fact that it's a feather, not a swab; the fact that everything is wrong; the fact that my birthday is only five days away.

I don't think about the center of my chest, where my ribs come together, and how that might look, opened up wide: French doors into someone's poisonous overgrown garden.

That's not how surgeons get into the lungs anyway. But something about this seems not-just-lungs. My ribs rattle like a birdcage. There's nothing in there that's not supposed to be in there. I swear it to myself as we walk across the parking lot.

The sky's full of huge storm clouds, which I very emphatically don't look at. I have no urge to see any more ships. That's where this wrongness started, and I want it un-wronged. I shiver, even though I'm bundled up.

"Alright. I'm the one you tell," my dad says. "Give it up, Az. Have you been smoking?"

I give him a look.

"This is serious, Henry. You act like it's not serious."

"I'm Henry, now? No, you can keep right on calling me Dad. Cigarettes? Pot? Hookahs?"

Hookahs. He really asks that. As though we are, where? There are hookahs in the world, yes. I've seen the parlors in the university district, people in there, smoking and looking kind of queasy and too excited, but really? The only place I can imagine anyone actually smoking a hookah is in *The Thousand and One Nights*.

"I don't have a thousand and one nights left to smoke in, even if I wanted to, which I don't, because no one smokes hookahs unless they're in a story, and unless they're completely not me," I tell him.

"You *do* have a thousand and one nights," my dad says, sounding sure. "You have two thousand and one. You have three thousand and one. You have thirty thousand and one."

He's smiling like he's telling me the truth.

When I was ten, my dad carried me up onto our neighbor's trampoline, and we jumped and jumped together. This was supremely not allowed, but he did it anyway, against doctor's advice, against my mom's rules. We jumped. And when we were done, he put me down, did a backflip, and bowed for me. He looked as though maybe he'd pulled something crucial, but he was grinning.

"Right," my dad said then. "That was someone who shouldn't flip upside down flipping upside down. In case you were wondering how that'd look."

"Don't worry about the feather," he tells me now. "I can see you worrying. We'll get through this. I'm a master fighter. If it turns out Big Bird's hanging out in your bedroom, I'll slay that bird."

This is actually weirdly comforting for someone who's pretty sure that she's about to die. Having a dad who's willing to declare war against an institution as deeply rooted as Big Bird is not nothing.

"Even if the bird goes Hitchcock?" I ask him.

For a moment, my dad and I sit in silence in the car, imagining *The Big Birds*, a sky horrifically full of big, yellow, leggy birds, dive-bombing us. At first, it's funny, but then, more worrying than you'd think.

"I don't care. I'd still fight them for you," he says. "I'd pluck them into oblivion."

I'm actually semi-laughing as we pull up to the house.

Jason Kerwin's waiting for me on our front steps. It's only two o'clock, which means Jason isn't where he's supposed to be—namely, school. My dad notices this at the same time I do and sighs.

"Do you need me to call attendance?" my dad asks him.

"Seriously?" says Jason. "What do you take me for? It's covered. I'm at a dentist appointment. Routine cleaning that'll turn into a small gum surgery, with a couple of days of recovery time." He turns to me. "I'm coming with you to the hospital tomorrow."

How he knew anything about me going to the hospital tomorrow is anyone's guess.

Jason has long been a collector of information. He's also an entrepreneur with three patents, one of them for a chemical compound that can be sprayed on clothes, dry-cleaning them in seconds. It comes in a tiny can the size of a battery, and can be hung from a key chain. He invented it for people who don't want their parents to know they smoke. Jason doesn't smoke, because you don't smoke if your best friend has a mortal-terror lung disease named after her, but he saw a market.

He has another patent for a small piece of plastic that attaches to hotel—or hospital—fitted sheets, kind of like a shoehorn, and enables people to make beds in half the time it previously took. These bits of plastic are manufactured in a small place known as the Kerwin Factory, in New Delhi. Jason runs the whole thing from his phone. We've had discussions about labor and questionable policy regarding outsourcing, but I haven't won. There are parts of Jason that are more OCD than even I can penetrate. His vision of a factory trumped my utopian idea of handcrafted things made primarily of wood. So, he's not perfect. He sometimes does things just because he can—and not the way he necessarily should.

He's killing time in high school. He barely passes his classes because he says he's proving a point. He plans to graduate at the bottom and then take over the world. Better for the inevitable, eventual biographies, I guess.

Jason is notoriously frustrating to all teachers. He doesn't work up to his genius potential. He merely looks at you, blankly, and conquers.

"A feather in your lung," he says. "Really? You snorted a feather? Going for an Icarus thing?"

When we were ten, I did go for an Icarus thing. Jason built the wings, from plans drawn by Leonardo da Vinci. Turns out that canvas and balsa-wood Renaissance wings don't cut it when you're hopping from the top of the garage. He broke his arm, and I broke my leg, and that was the end of Icarus. Our parents were relieved. It was one of our few displays of semi-normal. They told everyone the story of the wing fail for years, with these hopeful voices, an *oh, kids, they do the craziest things* tone. All the while not itemizing any of the other craziest things Jason and I did.

When we were twelve, we stole Jason's mom Eve's Pontiac, and drove it three hundred miles in order to acquire the correct feathers for the taxidermy of a hoax griffin. We paid a weirdo in cash, got back onto the freeway, and drove home, busted by Eve in Jason's driveway. The Pontiac had a trunkful of dead turkey and roadkill lynx on ice, along with assorted talons from vultures, and a serious stash of superglue and glass eyeballs. Eve, to her credit, had an expression of *hell yeah* on her face when we opened the trunk, because Eve's the kind of person who'd build a hoax griffin on a moment's notice, but then she had to pretend parental upset. Carol, Jason's Mother Number Two, went to bed for four days.

Jason and I did normal things, too, knee-skinning things, bug-capturing things. But it's the griffin-building that sticks in everyone's minds.

Jason will either be recruited by the CIA or he'll live a life of crime. No one is sure which. I mean, like those are opposites anyway.

"What?" I ask him. "Do you really think you get to have an opinion about me snorting feathers?"

I sit, despite the frost on the step. My dad sighs, takes off his coat, and buttons it around my own.

"Five minutes," he says. "Then I'm coming for you."

"Don't snort that," Jason says, pointing to the coat, though of course it's fake down, not really feathers.

We sit a minute in comfortable quiet, except that today has sucked so much nothing's comfortable.

"There's an increased likelihood of something," I say experimentally.

"Of?"

"You know. Soon. Very soon."

"You've been dying since forever," says Jason, who doesn't respect the rules. "If they think things are accelerating, they're wrong. You look good."

He glances at me.

"For you, you look good."

His face tells me I don't. The fact that he suddenly takes off his scarf and wraps it around my throat tells me I don't. Jason doesn't normally seem nervous, even though he's spent his entire life on a constant loop of calculation, stressed about everything.

"How are you?" I ask him. "You seem weird."

"Good," he says, talking too fast. "I'm fine, I mean, I'm not the one we need to be worried about, obviously. So stop worrying about me."

This version of Jason doesn't bode well.

"Did you take your pill?"

"Stop," he says. "Of course I did."

I'm suspicious. Also guilty. Because if Jason's this worried, it's my fault.

My dad makes us come in, but he leaves us alone in the kitchen. Jason begins speedy work on baked goods. I watch him from behind as he pushes up his sleeves and puts on my dad's apron. His hair is the color of the chocolate he's melting. He has freckles on the back of his neck, five of them. His most distinctive feature is the serious furrow between his eyebrows, which he's had since we were nine and he realized we definitely weren't immortal.

I don't know how someone who's a genius might have

thought we'd live forever, but he'd been working on some kind of chemistry compound related to both starfish and tortoises, and he was pretty sure, up until it exploded in his garage, that it was totally going to be a Thing. I think he was trying to grow me some new lungs, but he's never admitted it.

Jason looks like someone recently emerged from a sealed city. Last week, he wore the T-shirt top of a pair of ancient *Star Wars* pajamas to school, with his grandfather's suit jacket over the top of that. The pajamas dated from when he wasn't the height he is now. The sleeves ended not far below his elbows. The shirt was tight. He didn't care. I saw girls looking at him all day long, not with the expected look of horror, but with happy surprise.

It was like he'd grown boobs over the summer. Well, except not, but you know. He'd become stealth hot or something.

Jason, however, didn't notice the girls. I mean, he's straight, but he's never cared whether anyone knew it or not. He has two moms. The last time anyone commented critically on that, he gave that guy a black eye. Jason's right hook, and the resultant bruise, startled everyone, including Jason, I think, because it isn't like Jason normally punches people.

When he feels inclined, he's been known to make chocolate éclairs. Today he feels inclined. If I weren't already worried, this'd worry me. Chocolate éclairs are for birthdays. If he's making them early, I must really look bad.

Yeah. I think I'll avoid the mirror.

"I'm home, aren't I?" I say. "They'd never have let me come home if things were that awful."

Jason just looks at me with his particular hazel-eyed stare. The stare claims he doesn't give a shit what I say, and that nothing could possibly surprise him. He'd pull it off, if not for the furrow, which is especially deep today, and the rapid way he's stirring.

Maybe it's that furrow, maybe it's me, also feeling worried, but I tell him everything. The whistles, the ship, all of it. The way it just drifted out of the clouds. Hunting.

Hunting?

I don't know why I think of it that way, but that's how it felt. Hunting. I tell him about Mr. Grimm, too, who acted weird, in my opinion, though maybe that was me acting weird. For a second, I was pretty sure Mr. Grimm saw the ship, too, but then he pretended not to.

Jason puts the pastries in the oven, whisks their filling for a moment, and considers, as though he's rifling through papers inside his brain.

"Ship was a cloud formation. Basic answer."

I start to protest.

"Stay with me," he says. "Unexplained visual phenomena. Green ray starts UFO panics all the time."

I raise my hand.

"People understand like half of why light does what it does," Jason continues without answering my question. "There's a whole category of mirage where people see ships in the sky. Some people actually think the *Titanic* sank because a mirage made the iceberg invisible."

I'm researching while he talks, on my phone. Boy's a Wikipedia sinkhole, though he's doing it without any internet connection. He's just whipping the éclair filling, casually fact-ing me into oblivion.

What I saw, though, was not any of the things he wants to

make it. I feel bitey. He should believe me. He's the person who always believes me. I count on him to be my primary enabler of Vivid Imagination.

"You looking it up? Pissed off with me for not swallowing your story without questioning anything? Well, how about spooklights?" he says. He turns around and grins at me, which disgruntles. "UFOs, black helicopters, phantom dirigibles. All those things."

Then he says one more word, and for some reason it stops me dead.

"Magonia."

"Magonia?" I repeat, feeling twitchy.

The word isn't unfamiliar. I try to joke it out.

"Is that a disease? A kind of architecture? A poisonous plant? If it's a disease, I don't want to know, I warn you right now. I'm not in a disease textbook mood—"

"We're not talking about diseases. We're talking about mirages. Check the *Annals of Ulster*," Jason says, and sighs his long-patented Sufferer's Sigh.

"Ulster. Like blisters crossed with ulcers? Leprosy of some kind?" I blather to disguise the fact that the word immediately haunts me. I feel a memory lurking somewhere in the black holes of my brain. Maybe I read about it somewhere. After all, everything I know, I read about.

Jason snorts.

"Don't tell me you haven't read the *Annals*."

"I've read them." I lie, because maybe I have, maybe I haven't. I cough, part fake. I don't know why I'd even try to lie to Jason. When someone hangs out with you every day since you were five, they pretty much know what you've read, and they definitely know when you're emergency-skimming internet synopses beneath the kitchen table.

The *Annals of Ulster* are Irish histories, according to the wikis.

"No one's read them. But I studied the relevant sections today. Mass hallucinations. About seven forty-eight AD, there's this: 'Ships with their crews were seen in the air.' Does that ring any bells? Anything at all?"

Nope, nothing. He goes into his favorite mode, fast-talking, clipped words, robot boy.

"Basics. Not the *Annals*, but part of the same story. Eight thirty or so AD. France." He grand-gesture sketches out the date and place in the air with his hand, subtitling his documentary. "This Archbishop of Lyons reports four messed-up people in his town, three guys, one woman, insisting they fell out of the sky. Fell from ships. In. The. Sky. Are you hearing me?"

I'm hearing him. So hearing. I pretend I'm not.

"The bishop goes to a public meeting where these four are in the stocks—"

I interrupt.

"Do not tell me you're doing the universal hand gesture for 'in the stocks,' because that doesn't exist, no matter how hard you just tried to make it a thing."

He has the grace to blush and remove his hands (and the precariously tilting bowl of éclair filling) from "dude trapped in the stocks" position.

"—and getting screamed at for being crop thieves. They've been dumb enough to claim they've been stealing crops from earth using little sky-launch boats. The people in the town agree with the idea that they're crop thieves, because, duh, they're having harvest problems anyway."

I am so annoyed at the randomness of Jason Kerwin. He's a mutant memorizer. He has no apologies for that, and never has.

"*MAGONIA*, they say—all of them. We fell out of Magonia. People in town start to freak out."

Jason whisks the filling so hard some of it splatters on the fridge.

"Then what?" I ask.

"Yeah, so I can't remember if the Magonians ultimately got hanged for being witches, or if they got run out of town, but I doubt it was a fantastic outcome for them, given that they'd already said they didn't belong on earth and wanted to go home with all the village's corn."

"Jason," I say eventually. "You are Not Relevant."

"All I'm saying is, if you're hallucinating, you're hallucinating in an old tradition," he says. "Congratulations on the quality of your visions. Want more Magonia?"

"Nope," I say. "I want chocolate."

I can't believe I didn't know everything about this Magonia stuff already. It's totally my kind of thing.

"*Maganwetar*. That's Old High German for 'whirlwind.'"

"Jason," I say.

"Calm down. I don't speak Old High German," he says.

"You'd better not," I tell him. "Because that would be a big lie. The secret learning of Old High German without me."

There's no shaming him.

"Some people think that's where the word 'Magonia' comes from. If you're from Magonia, then, you live in a whirlwind. That's what Jacob Grimm says, the same guy who wrote the fairy tales. He also says that it might refer to magicians, like *magoi*, Greek, hence Magonia would mean 'Land of Magicians.'

I prefer whirlwind. Plus, a land of magicians would be boring, because the whole point of magic is that not everyone can do it. Otherwise it's just normal life. It'd be, basically, Land of Mechanics."

I'm head down in my phone. There. Some archbishop named Agobard grumbling about how the people in his town believed hail and lightning were made by storm-makers in the sky.

"But I've heard rumors of crowds, nay, entire villages of people overwhelmed by gullibility, turned to such fools that they insist there is a kingdom named Magonia, where the sky is sea, and where ships sail the clouds. These ships harvest the leavings of our crops, our fields broken by weather and trampled by hailstones, and they carry them up into their own storehouses. Payments are made by the sky sailors to storm-creators, and thus are our own crops stolen from us. I am shocked to discover that my own town has lately been so blind and certain of the existence of this Magonia that four prisoners have been displayed in chains, one woman and three men who claim they are citizens of the sky, fallen from cloud ships. The townspeople voted at meeting that these crop-thieves be stoned."

I look up from my phone. "So Magonians are crop thieves?"

Jason's smug. "I don't care about crop circles, but you know how the UFO people are. Are you at Gervase of Tilbury yet?"

No. I'm scrolling through reams of Irish history. Things about anchors being thrown from cloud ships.

"I'm in *Annals of Ulster* now," I say and sigh, because of course he doesn't have just one reference. Even his text messages come with footnotes.

"Gervase tells a story about how a whole bunch of people

come out of church one day. They see an anchor drop out of the clouds and get stuck in a rock in front of the church. A moment later, a sailor comes *swimming through the air, and down the anchor rope*, trying to untangle it. How awesome, please, is that?"

I'm Googling. "This happened when?"

"Twelve hundreds. The townspeople cut the rope and kept the anchor. Made it part of the church door."

"That's a fairy tale." Something occurs to me. "What does he say happened to the sailor?"

Jason looks at me.

"The sailor drowned," he says.

I meet his eyes.

"In the air. He drowned *in the air*. So, keep telling me about the 'not-relevant' situation. You haven't been drowning for six-teen years in air or anything."

I feel shivery. There's something stressfully specific about that anchor story.

"Actually, I'm pretty sure what I saw outside Mr. Grimm's window was a helicopter."

"Right. That's why you freaked out. It's not like you don't have personal experience of helicopters. You definitely *never* got life-flighted out of a field trip in fifth grade, because you stopped breathing at the fake safari theme park."

I roll my eyes.

"There are more things in heaven and earth, Horatio," Jason Kerwin says, at which point he's busted for Trite.

"Hamlet. Really?" I say. "I'm not Horatio. This is med side effects, feather in lungs, early death."

"*Hamlet* is *all* about hallucinations and meltdowns and

early death. Not that you're dying. Because you're not."

He spins around and stirs some more.

I'm now even grouchier than I was. I feel shaky, like a dog wanting to whirl and get loose of water. My skin feels like Spanx. I don't really know how Spanx feel, but my mom has a pair, and she tells me they're torture devices specifically designed to cause women to lose circulation all over their bodies. My skin? Feels exactly that way.

"I don't get it," I say finally, after I bite the insides of my cheeks for a while. I don't quite know what I'm upset about, but I feel inclined toward slapping and also toward collapsing. "Are you saying you think I'm hallucinating?"

Jason just considers me.

"Or are you saying there's actually a ship in the sky looking for me? From this, this—Magonia place?"

I test that out by mumbling it.

"I'm saying you must have read some of this stuff somewhere, and it's been rattling around in your brain, and now it's showing up. You saw a cloud formation, and your brain filled in the gaps." He pauses. "A ship in the sky isn't the worst hallucination you could have," he says. "You could be hallucinating everything on earth being on fire. That happens to some people. After the drugs kick in."

"Please tell me more about drug side effects," I say. "I know nothing about drug side effects." I can't shame him. He doesn't believe me. I don't believe me either. Why don't I want to be hallucinating? Hallucinating isn't horrible. It's absolutely a more palatable idea than ships in the sky yelling your name.

"Sometimes people hallucinate even worse than that," he goes on. "You—the stuff you're hallucinating? It's like, a Disney movie. It's some kind of *Peter Pan* plus *E.T.* hybrid."

I'm disgusted by the implication I'm having a children's hospital hallucination.

"So you think this is brain melt," I say to Jason. "Fine. Whatever." I say something mean. "You're one to talk about brain melt."

"I am," he says, so calmly I feel instantly bad. "I know about what brains do when they get screwed up."

"How do you even *know* about Magonia?" I wish I didn't sound whimpery. "You didn't read the *Annals of Ulster* for fun."

"Remember when I was building the UFO? Magonia's an early version of UFO stuff."

"Your moms would have hated that UFO."

Jason's mom Eve is a biologist who used to be an ecoterrorist. She would say anti-ecoterrorist, because she thinks people who ignore the damage they do to the environment are the terrorists. But regardless, she was once a person who chained herself to trees and in at least one case, for which she was arrested, seriously damaged a bulldozer, using a wrench. You wouldn't think this looking at her. She looks like a mom. I guess that's how it works.

She now writes academic articles about farming practices, and the way we're messing the world up in order to make an economy out of food-buying. An essay she wrote about the irresponsible farming of bananas actually made it so I don't eat bananas anymore.

"The UFO would have been made of recycled materials," Jason says. "They wouldn't have minded that. Taste this."

The éclair's full of hot air, and it burns my tongue. I'm staring at Jason with a bit more wide-eyes than I'd prefer. He's pleased with himself.

"Yep," he says. "Not much I don't know about UFOs." He pauses, then takes pity on me. "Also, when you got busted in Mr. Grimm's class yesterday, swearing about ships in the sky, I Googled 'ships in the sky.'"

I swear again. This time at him. With relief.

"Basic search. On my phone. You'd have done it if you weren't quote, *side-effecting*, unquote, to no clear purpose. You don't usually invent things out of nowhere, Az. I tend to believe you when you say you're seeing a ship sailing through the clouds." He's not looking at me. "So, yeah, I think you saw . . . something."

I'm flooded with relief again, a lot more of it. And something that I guess must be gratitude.

"You didn't see it, did you?" I ask, a just-in-case plea. "No sails? No masts? Or hear it?"

He shakes his head. "Doesn't matter. We'll figure it out, Az."

"Are you sure?"

Jason spoons filling into the éclairs, pours chocolate over their tops, and is done.

"Yeah. Happy birthday." He sticks a candle messily into the top of one of the éclairs and lights it.

"It isn't my birthday yet," I say.

"So what? Your wish is here early," he says. "If you don't blow out that candle, I'm doing it."

I look at the candle some more. It's dripless.

"I'll take your wish and wish it myself," Jason warns. "You don't want what I'm going to wish for."

"Which is?"

"You'll end up in an alligator suit," he says. "Roller-skating. Trust me. I could make that happen."

I smile in spite of myself. I close my eyes.

"Wish," Jason says, like I'm going to forget to wish.

I wish. I blow. I look at Jason.

Jason looks at me. He's chewing on his bottom lip.

"I have a present thing for you," he says.

"Give," I say, and I'm suddenly filled with hope, because this hadn't even occurred to me. Maybe this whole ship-vision thing was something he did. "Did you hire projectors or something? It's a hoax, right?"

He just looks at me. This isn't his usual. Normally he'd shove something across the table, grinning wildly. Last year, he gave me a terrarium containing a flea circus. He'd bought them from some sad guy who'd spent his life training batch after batch of them. They died pretty soon after, as fleas do, but before they did, they did a lot of crazy amazing backflips.

"What is it?" I ask him. "Where is it?"

I poke his shirt pocket. Nothing there. It suddenly feels deeply weird to be prodding his chest and I snatch my hand back like I've just burned it. I try to pretend I have a cramp in my fingers. I can feel his body against my hand still, solid and warm and oh no, no, very no.

"I'll give it to you while we watch the squid video," he finally says.

I'm taken aback. I'd totally forgotten about the squid footage, but Jason's bringing out his laptop.

"Dark," he says. "This demands dark."

"Basement," I say.

Usually, this would be super normal. We spend most of our time in the basement or in the garage.

But he's looking at me in a way that makes me wonder if he's invented the whole giant-squid-footage thing completely, and he's actually going to do something weird—pour water on my head when I walk through the basement door, or present me with immortality ointment. I don't think about any other kind of thing he might be wanting to do with me, because he's Jason, and I'm me.

We plant ourselves on the couch, almost as though we're regular teenage creatures and not two people about to watch stolen raw footage of cephalopods illegally downloaded through back channels.

Jason sets up the laptop and cues the video, and then pulls out his notebook, scribbles something, and folds up the paper. He hesitates, and then passes it across the couch to me.

I open it, and see what he's written inside.

I { } you more than [[[{{{((( )))}}}]]].

Just parentheses and brackets with nothing in them. I look up at him. He looks away.

"Okay. So. That's my list," he says. "In case there ever needs to be a list. Which there doesn't." He pauses. "Right, so that's settled."

He lifts his fist and bumps mine. But then he lets his hand stay there. I feel his knuckles. I feel myself turning red. With my bluish skin, that probably makes me lavender.

For a long time, we're watching a black screen. We can see a little bit of something glowing—squid bait.

I think of the note.

I want to say *me too.*

I want to say *I know.*

I want to say *I can read the gaps in your sentences. I can read the space between your letters. I know your language. It's my language too.*

I want to say that.

Instead, I stare at the screen, and say { } for a good minute and a half while Jason's fingers and my fingers lace together like we're not attached to them.

The squid appears, a constellation coming into being out of a night that previously contained no stars at all. It unfolds, this silver, twirling thing, and it's there. Swimming past the camera, alive and impossible. Its eyes, its tentacles, its hugeness. It explodes into visibility, this thing we've only really seen dead or dying.

Alive.

We don't look at each other.

We're both definitely crying.

I can feel him next to me, his arm against mine, his knee in his jeans, right there next to my knee. I can smell the lemon peel he scrubs his hands with to get rid of most of whatever toxicities he's been touching, the charcoal in the soap he uses to get rid of the rest, the smell of pencil shavings and graphite. All I've got is { }.

Jason's fingers are running up and down my hand, and his other hand is petting my wrist and, and, and.

&,&,&.

!!!!

I can't look at him.

Finally, in the silence of the giant squid footage, as it swims away, back to its own world, I manage to say, "Don't you want to know what I wished for?"

Like he doesn't know. I think he wishes the same wish I do.
Both of us are very good at pretending we aren't superstitious
about these things, but we *so* are.

"I don't need to know," he says, then looks at me and grins a
crooked grin that is in danger of not being a grin at all.

"Aza," says Jason, and leans in. I want to lean into him, too,
I want to, and I start to, and I can't breathe, and I'm me and he's
him and we're best friends and what is this? Kiss the sick girl?

No, no, this is Jason, an inch from me. He's still crying, and
so am I. I'm leaning in and he's leaning in, and

Lightning.

White, sizzling, hair standing up all over our bodies, ozone.
OMG, it's striking in my backyard. Outside the basement windows. Right outside them. Ten feet away.

We jump, instinctively, away from each other.

AZA! screams a whistling voice. *AZA COME NOW.*

CHAPTER 6

{AZA}

Rain starts to pour down the window, and then hailstones the size of Ping-Pong balls. Wind banging hard.

Jason grabs me, and keeps me from falling off the couch.

"Did you hear that?"

"What? The thunder?" he says. "Yeah, that was close."

"No, THAT," I say. "Like a million birds. Like a million birds screaming at me personally."

Jason has his arms around me. I am as stormed by that as anything.

There's another sonicboomjetenginethundercrash of a noise, and that noise screams, in a lot of different voices:

AZA.

I hear more than that. Individual voices, flickering across the wind, humming wire voices. Everyone—who?—is shouting, singing, shrieking my name.

AZAAZAAZAAZAAZAAZAAZAAZAAZAAZAAZA

I grab Jason's shirt, and stare at him. He listens for a second, then shakes his head.

"Crazy," he says.

"Crazy what?"

"Weather. And birds. A lot of birds."

I pull back from him, adjust my shirt, fold up the paper he gave me, and put it in my pocket.

"Maybe," I say. I pretend my fingers aren't shaking.

Shit, shit, shit. I'm losing it. This is a whole new level of wrong.

Jason's staring at me. I try not to think about how one day I walked into my room and looked at the flea circus and all the fleas were just dead in their spangles.

"You okay?" he asks.

"Not so much," I say.

"Because of everything," he says slowly, "or because I just screwed up?"

I shake my head. That's all I can do. "Give me a second," I say at last.

He looks hard at me, and then nods, folds up his laptop and its miracle squid, and goes upstairs. I sit on the couch in the dark, trying to hold myself together. I want to cry and laugh at once.

We almost—

But no.

And—

After a few minutes, my heart goes back to being a heart, and I head upstairs.

"You okay?" He's at the sink, doing the dishes. We are made of awkward.

"Better," I say.

He clears his throat. "Back to Magonia?" he says, not looking at me. "More proto-UFO theory?"

I stare at his back. Shoulders = too high.

"Maybe," I say. And then I'm insanely brave because I keep talking. If this is it for me, if this is the last day I'm going to be alive? Why *not* be brave?

"I want to go back to what we were doing before," I say. "It was me who screwed that up."

I'm forced to blurt out the rest as fast as I can.

"All-right-do-you-want-to-start-over-even-though-I'm-a-disaster?"

Jason's shoulders relax. His face softens. "You think you hold horrors for me . . . ," he says, which is what he always says when I utter anything in this category.

"But you hold no horrors," I say, which is the correct response.

Jason leans over the table, and I get myself ready to change our status, because OMG, I think I would desperately like to change our status, but Eli chooses that moment to bang her way into the kitchen, looking disgusted.

It's okay.

I didn't need to kiss him.

I hadn't been imagining kissing Jason under the surface of my brain for years or anything.

I feel a flash of rage at Eli, whose fault it isn't.

"Weather out there sucks it," she says, and then looks at us, assessing, coolly. "Weather in here kind of sucks it too. I got rained on. Did you see the lightning?"

She flicks a drop of rain off her shoulder. Only one. Possibly she just walked between raindrops. Me, I get drenched anytime there's even fog.

"Eli?" I say. "Do you think you could—"

She must be reading my mind, because she's instantly defensive.

"This is my house too," she says. "You can't order me out of the kitchen."

"I wasn't," I say, cringing that she's about to comment on what she almost walked in on.

"You were about to try to," she says, psychic, and sits down at the table. "It's not happening. I'm hungry."

I leave Eli and Jason to eat éclairs. I go coughing into my freezing room.

There are eleven hours until my procedure. I'm not counting them. I don't need to count them because I'm totally not dying tomorrow.

I take the piece of paper Jason gave me out of my pocket and stare at it. He's not allowed to make me want to stay alive this way. *I {   } you more than [[[{{{((   ))}}}]]].*

and I'm both grinning and stupidly kind of crying—

When the window opens. I put the note back, weirdly embarrassed.

My mom was cleaning in futility and didn't latch it, maybe.

I look out. It's starting to snow, completely wrongly, right after that rain; it's only November. The back lawn is covered already, a thin dusting of it, and it's the kind of glowing dark-ish afternoon that snow makes happen. Like the snow is the surface of the moon. Like we're here, and at the same time, in outer space. Which of course, we are. We're all untethered, all flying around in the dark, the same as Mars and Venus, the same as the stars.

I'm definitely not going to cry.

The window creaks.

I think about celestial junk. Maybe every planet in this solar system is discarded by giant hands. Each star a crumpled ball of paper, a love letter lit on fire, a smoldering bit of cigarette ash.

A robin picks its red-breasted finicky way across the yard, considering the blades of grass sticking up out of the white. It cocks its head and looks at me for a long time.

I turn forcibly away and rummage in my closet, packing my hospital bag. I can hear Jason and Eli blithering on in the kitchen, something about a hailstorm where the hail turned out to be, actually, a rain of frogs, each one frozen into a ball of ice. A rain of frogsicles is so Jason's kind of thing.

I hear a chirp much closer than it should be. When I turn around to close the window, the lawn is covered with birds. Maybe fifty of them. Robins, crows, and blue jays, seagulls, chickadees, and swallows.

On my windowsill, there's a bright yellow bird with a black beak and wings spread like it's wearing a cape made of marigold petals.

This is the one chirping.

Here, it says. *She's ready.*

No, it definitely does not say that. It's a bird. It opens its beak and shrills, and the other birds look expectant. I try to shoo it off the sill. I have my fingers on the sash when all the birds turn their heads and look at me.

Not just in the direction of me. No, there's a flock of birds, out of season, sitting patiently in the snow, watching me. A hawk lands. An owl. None of the rest of the birds even look at them.

And it's insanity, right there, rain of frogs insanity, except that it's rain of birds, and I'm shaking with cold and also with something else. The bird on the sill doesn't move. It just looks at me.

"Fly away!" I yell, coughing, freezing, but none of them move. They start to sing.

To speak.

All of them.

Aza Ray.

Inside my chest, I feel a weird rattle and then there's something I can't explain, a giant gap, inside my lungs. The little yellow bird looks me in the eyes. I cough.

And then, out of fucking nowhere, the bird flies into my mouth.

I can feel its tough little bones, its claws scratching at my teeth. I'm trying to scream but my mouth's full of feathers. It's pushing and its wings are opening in my mouth and then in my throat and I can't breathe, and then it's down my windpipe and speaking from inside my chest.

Got her, sings the yellow bird. I can feel it in my left lung. *Got her. I'm in. We're ready.*

I scream. I can feel it whistling, beating its wings.

Bird in my lung? BIRD IN MY LUNG? I'm hyperventilating.

Out the window, in the clouds, I'm seeing—

Oh my god, sails over the tree line, and rigging—dark figures on a deck. I'm crying and holding my chest and I don't know I don't know I don't know what to do.

Readyreadyreadygo the bird in my chest whistles, and out on the lawn the rest of the birds look at me as though I have a clue what's happening, and I'm thinking this is it this is dying and why didn't anyone in any of the near-death books ever say there'd be a crowd of birds seeing you off? Where's the white light? Where's the peace and calm? Where's the voice of God and the angelic-ness and the—

A rope loops down, down, down out of the clouds and clearly I'm dreaming. It's swinging through the sky outside my window, and there's no air in here, no air anywhere—

Readyreadyready my chest sings. The sky is full of hail and snow and wind. The birds on the lawn are taking flight, and they have the rope in their talons. I'm dizzy. I'm gasping. I'm—

I come to in redwhiteandblue emergency lights, wrapped in heat blankets, snow coming down hard outside the windows. I'm in the back of an ambulance with my dad, Jason, and Eli.

I try to sit up but I'm strapped down. I have a mask on my face. I want to cough. I want to talk. I want to tear it off.

"You had a seizure," the paramedic tells me, speaking slowly, as though I'm not me, as though I don't know everything about this already. I'm a professional patient, even if I have no idea how I got here, no idea who this paramedic is, no idea where the ambulance is taking me, or why.

My chest is still.

The *bird* is still?

"There were birds in your room—a lot of them," Eli says, her voice shaking. "I heard them screaming, so I came in." She looks completely terrified.

Jason's fingers are wrapped around mine very tightly.

What just happened?

I can't really feel my hand in the real world at all, but I can feel Jason's. I want to shake my fingers out of his grasp. I feel like he's holding me somewhere I don't want to be. And that's not okay. It's Jason. I *want* him to hold my hand.

My dad's crying. He's got my other hand.

"Don't worry, Az," he says. "They're helping you breathe. That's why you had the seizure. You're okay. It's okay. Mom was at the lab but she's on her way."

Everything looks as though I'm seeing it from the bottom of a swimming pool.

"It was like you were drowning," Jason says, so quietly I almost don't hear him. "You were completely blue, and you weren't breathing. Your chest was . . . spasming and making this sound I've never heard before. I gave you mouth-to-mouth."

I look at his mouth. It touched mine. I think about the note he gave me. It's still in my pocket.

I blink a couple of times for yeah, I get it. But I don't. I remember the *bird*—god, the bird—and I jerk and try to sit up again. I have to get it OUT.

Am I having a heart attack? My lungs feel crushed and full of something all at once.

"I have the letters in my backpack," Eli says, her voice not quite her voice. "The I-love-you lists, and the apologies. But I never made mine. Now I will, okay? I'm making one for you right now, because I'm sorry for all the times I pretended you weren't my sister and said we weren't related, and the time I stole your sweater and the time I made fun of you because you coughed so hard I told people you swallowed your phone—"

I look at Jason. I look at him and I don't know how, but for a moment I forget the bird and I say {   }.

"Aza, are you listening?" my dad asks me, and there's panic in his voice. More than panic. "CAN YOU HEAR ME?"

I look at Eli, and say {   }.

"I'm sorry, Aza! I didn't mean any of anything I ever did wrong!" Eli is crying now, and talking as fast as she can. She's apologizing for things she didn't even do.

I look at my dad, and say {{   }}. I try to give him extra for my mom.

My dad is fading out. All I can see are my own eyelashes and my own eyelids, and somehow, also, my own brain, all the pathways inside it, everything dark and narrow, and getting narrower, bookshelves closing in, books crushed, falling into muddled piles, pages crushed, words mangled, and me, running through it all, trying to get out before the walls collapse.

I feel the entire inside of my body folding up, some kind of awful origami. I thought it would hurt, but the pain I've been feeling forever and ever is actually something that's ceasing to matter to me, just like my bones no longer matter to me, and I inhale, and exhale, and

Bird in my chest

Bird in my chest

Ships in the sky

Last moments before dying

Like this, the last moments of this, storm, bird, confused, cold can't talk can't tell anyone I love them can't—

How far are we from the hospital?

I stretch my head and try to look into the front. The driver has red hair. He glances at me.

We swerve.

I hear Eli sobbing. I hear Jason talking fast to me. I can feel his breath on my ear. I'm watching the driver, and the ambulance skids, and I see the guy twisting the wheel. Shoving it hard.

We spin slowly in a circle in the middle of a frozen road.

Everyone's screaming but me, because I can't. I'm trying to breathe, to stay, but I'm not staying.

I'm going.

The windows of the ambulance are freezing over, and here's my family, and here I am, on this gurney, and it doesn't matter as much as I thought it did.

Life and death aren't as different from each other as I thought they were. This isn't like walking into a new country. This is walking into a new room in the same house. This is sharing a hallway and the same row of framed family pictures, but there's a glass wall between.

I'm right here. And not.

If this is *it*, then I'm ready. I'm dark matter. The universe inside me is full of something, and science can't even shine a light on it. I feel like I'm mostly made of mysteries.

Inside my chest, I hear the whistling of a little bird, something singing me to sleep.

The ambulance is stopped, lights and sirens still on, ice beneath our tires, and the EMT in the back with us radios for a helicopter, her voice panicky, "Emergency . . ."

The red-haired medic runs out and looks up at the sky. "Signaling," he shouts. He goes into the white, and all around him is a halo of snow.

I'm an ocean with a giant squid inside it. There's a bird buffeting, flying around and banging hard against my ribs.

"Pneumonia," the paramedic says.

"Aza, don't," my dad says, an order. "DO NOT DO THIS."

I want to listen.

I look at my dad. I'm looking at myself, and what I was is

starting not to matter to me at all.

Where am I going?

Readyreadyready says the bird inside me. And someone outside answers *Readyreadyready.*

Something hits my chest, hard, and then it's gone. My chest? Is it even mine? Then, no, I see, it's the medic using crash pads on my heart.

Jason says, "You don't have to die."

Eli's talking fast into her cell phone.

"Mommy-you-have-to-get-here-now-right-now-hurry-I-don't-know-I-don't-know-what-happened-it's-really-bad—"

I hear my mom through the phone, telling Eli it'll be okay, and she sounds so certain that I almost think it will be, that there's something I don't know, but then Eli says, wailing,

"But it's already not okay!"

Readyreadyready

The crash pads hit me again, hard, at chest level. Eli's put her phone to my ear.

I can hear my mom.

I hear her take a deep breath. I hear her pushing words out, and I can almost see her, for a second, the look on her face, her hand pressed to her own heart, the other in a fist.

"You can go if you have to go," my mom says, and her voice shakes, but she's solid. She says it again, so I'll know. "You can go if you have to go, okay, baby? Don't wait for me. I love you, you're mine, you'll always be mine, and this is going to be okay, you're safe, baby, you're safe—"

I'm hearing my mom talking, feeling her in my ear and not in my ear at the same time.

There's a blast of cold air and the redheaded medic comes back in.

"Chopper's coming," he mutters to the other paramedic, and pushes himself into the space beside me. "Get the girl's family to move back."

He pushes the other medic away, too hard. She winces. His hands are working on me in ways that make no sense.

I feel something slide into my skin, near my left lung. It's a cut, but it's different from any cut I've ever felt before. Pain or release? I feel myself dividing, right where my tilted lungs are, right where my ribs have always been wrong.

"What are you doing?" I hear my dad say.

"Sir, you're getting in the way of an emergency procedure. We're trying to keep her breathing. Stay back."

"Calm down," the female medic says. "It's okay, it's going to be okay."

She's trying to keep my dad from looking at what's happening, but I catch a glimpse of his face, his eyes.

I have no voice. I'm trying to say no.

The man's tying a rope to me, I can feel it, around my chest, but I can't see it.

"I'm making an incision for her to breathe. Please, sir, move back *now*," the medic says.

"This isn't it," Jason says urgently. "This isn't happening. Don't let it, Aza. They're going to find a way to— Oh my god."

He sobs. The paramedic's looking down at me and I'm looking up at him. He's has his hand in my shirt pocket, and he's taking something out of it. The note—

There's pressure on my neck and there's still no pain. There's a splitting, something falling off, and that feeling of a rope around my chest, and my body is halfway on the gurney and halfway with me, standing up, watching.

"I'll find you," Jason says, and I hear him. I hear him. I trust him.

The lights flicker. I hear a giant impact up in the sky, and there's an explosion, fire, the smell of smoke and ozone. Something snags me and pulls hard, out the ambulance doors, outside, and my dad is swearing, and Jason's still telling the girl on the gurney he's not letting her go, and Eli's screaming, and then

the

    s

      i

        r

          e

            n

              s

                S T O P.

And after that? There's nothing.

CHAPTER 8

{JASON}

3.14159265358979323846264338327950288419716939937510
5820974944592307816406286208998628034825342117067 98
214808651328230. One day, two days, three days, four days, five days later.

This is what I want to do: I want to pick up my phone and call Aza. I want to hear her voice.

"Why are you calling me?" she'll say. "I hate the phone. Text or show up. How long is this gonna take? Are you here yet? Get here."

But this is what Aza's new number is like: 66470938446095 50582231725359408128481117450284102701938521105559644 62294895493038196442881097566593344612847564823 37867 83165271201909145648566923460348610454326648213 39360 72602491. Onward infinitely, no answer. Dial, dial, dial.

I'm back to old habits. Recite, recite, recite. Not so that anyone can hear.

This is an old thing, and supposedly conquered.

Not conquered, turns out.

41273724587006606315588174881520920962829254091 71

5364367892590360011330530548820466521384146951941511609433057270365759591953092186117381932611793105118548 0744623799627495.

I know more pi than that. She knows even more than I do. But at some point in the memorization of pi I'm definitely going to pass the place she stopped at. It'll be the same as driving past her on a road, not seeing her hitchhiking. Which is about as crap as anything I can think of, in a universe of, at this point, unimaginable crap.

I'm not sleeping. I'm not fine. There are things I'm never going to want to talk about.

Things like what happened in that ambulance. Things like: I saw that medic cut Aza open.

Things like: We called for a medevac. The medic from our ambulance jumped out to try to wave the copter down. I heard the helicopter coming, toward the storm cloud above the ambulance. Then there was an impact. The clouds caught fire. Four people died that day, the pilot and the medic on the copter, and also one of the medics with us, who was out trying to signal for the helicopter when it exploded. I only have grief enough for one. I'm barely holding it together.

Things like—I can't even—

We waited on the highway for an hour, and then the ice got covered enough with snow that we could keep going, Aza's dad driving. By then it was way too late.

I rode in the back with her.

All I've wanted to do since then is press my head against a wall and feel it on my forehead.

If I were in the living room right now, with my moms,

they'd sit me down and have a sympathetic and nervous discussion with me about how she's "gone." Turns out, I hate that word. Also "we lost her."

In the past few days, I've lost lots of things, just to check and see how losing feels. For example, I keep losing *it*.

I hit my head into the wall and bruise my forehead. I smash a window, with my fist wrapped in a T-shirt. Some kind of movie plan for fixing pain. Did not help.

People keep saying infuriating things about fate and chance and bad luck and how she had an amazing life despite it being only fifteen years, eleven months, and twenty-five days long. I don't feel like this is amazing. I feel very, very unamazed.

I stay up at night staring at screens.

Since Aza, I kept looking for some analogy, something to explain this, some version of *lost* that made sense, but nothing was right. Then on a middle-of-the-night internet wander, I found something from 475 BC, a Greek cosmologist called Anaxagoras. At that point, math hadn't thought up the concept of nothing. There was no zero. Hence, Anaxagoras had extensive ideas about the thing that was missing, the something that wasn't.

This is what Anaxagoras said about *lost*: "What *is* cannot *not* be. Coming-to-be and perishing are customarily believed in incorrectly by the Greeks, since nothing *comes-to-be* or *perishes*, but rather it is mingled together out of things that are, and is separated again. Thus they would be correct to call coming-to-be '*being mingled together*' and perishing '*being separated.*'"

That was the first time something felt accurate when it comes to me and Aza. I tried to explain to Carol and Eve that Aza being lost wasn't just her being gone, but ME being gone too, that I was half-dead along with her. This created concerns that I might be planning to perish.

"Suicidal ideation," said Carol, "is what that sounds like." I could feel her dialing a therapist in her head. She wasn't wrong. It did sound that way.

"Straight up, kiddo, are you thinking of offing yourself?" asked Eve, clearly using unserious words to ease her way into talking about something serious.

"I'm fine," I said. She looked at me, her eyebrow raised.

"You don't have to be fine. If you were fine, that'd mean you had no human feelings. I'm not fine. Neither is Carol. We loved Aza. But know that if you ever thought it'd be a plan to kill yourself, we'd come and find you and kill you all over again. Just so you know. So do NOT. If you're thinking about it, come to us. We'll figure out a better choice."

"No," I said. "This isn't about suicide. This is about philosophy."

They looked at me, with no intention of believing anything was about philosophy. Which, okay, I was touch and go. I'm still touch and go.

"Pills?" said Carol. "I notice you're looking a little—"

"A little what?"

"A little pi," says Eve.

I try not to make eye contact with her. A little pi. How does she know? I've been quiet.

"Yes," I told her. "I'm taking them." Anti-anxiety. Which do not work. Anything working right now would be a miracle.

Carol's been trying to get me to see a therapist. Eve's been trying to send me to yoga, the practice of which has semi-calmed her wrath about the state of the universe. I got her to desist by doing a brief, not-too-shabby, I-already-know-about-yoga crane pose. Aza made fun of yoga. It drove her crazy when I did that pose. That was the main reason I learned to do it—to crack her up.

FYI, that shit *is* as hard as it looks.

"I don't blame you for that," Eve said, looking at how I was all twisted around my own arms. "I'm mad about things I can't fix too. Yoga doesn't fix anything. It only dulls the aggravation. Ice caps, Burmese pythons, and floodplains are still a mess. . . ."

And she was off. I briefly, briefly felt a little bit better.

Right now, it's three a.m., and Eve comes into my room. The moms are on guard duty.

She puts a mug of hot milk down on my desk. I look at it, minorly tempted. Hot milk is one of the lesser evils, but it's still an evil.

"Honey," she says.

"I'm busy," I say. "I promise I'm not falling apart."

"You seem like you are," she says. "And even if you're not right now, if you don't start sleeping, you will be soon."

"What if Carol died?" I say. "How would you sleep?" I regret it the moment I say it.

Eve looks stricken. "I'd be awake," she says. "For years."

"Well," I say. "It's the same thing."

"Yeah, but you *can't* be awake for years," she says.

"Even though you just said you would be."

"Even though." She's whispering.

"I can be awake for three days, and I slept before that. I slept for four hours on each of the days after it happened," I say. "I'll sleep after tomorrow. I'm on it. I'm working."

What I'm working on: I'm planning Aza's funeral.

After a while, Eve goes. I feel mean. I send her a text telling her I'm sorry. I hear her phone buzz down the hall. After a second, I get a message back from her.

Don't die, she says. *Dying won't help.*

Sometimes Eve is exactly the right mom. There's no "pass away" or "lose" in that.

She sends another text. This time, a guilty one.

And if you *really* don't want to fall asleep, I wouldn't drink the milk. Carol made it.

Carol loves me, is worried about me, and is a doctor with access to sleeping pills. I move the milk off the desk. I'm not done thinking, but I turn off the overhead light for a minute.

Aza must have done what she did to my ceiling a week or so before she died. It doesn't show during the day. Pretty sure the moms don't know about it. I didn't either until I turned out the lights for the first time, two nights after she died. Glow paint.

AZA RAY WAS HERE.

Except that the last *E* got smudged due to Aza apparently falling off my headboard or something. So, it actually reads AZA RAY WAS HER.

I look at that for a minute, trying to get myself together. I'm a fucking mess of rattling pi and things I never said.

I spent the past ten years talking. Why I couldn't say any of the right words, I don't know.

I want to install a better version of all the things that happened right before she died. All the crazy stuff, beginning with the skyship, right through the feather in Aza's lung. The storm when we were in the basement—the whole town should have been rain, and lightning, and it was only Aza's block.

Yes. I know people die. I know that when people die, the people they leave behind always think something insane happened, because death, by its nature, feels insane. It's part of how humans have always dealt with dying, as though it's somehow special, as though every person who dies is a hero. We want to die spectacularly, not just "perish."

I keep trying to make it make sense.

In the ambulance, the medic cut into her like she wasn't even a person. Aza made a choking noise. Her back arched. Her heart stopped again. The medic used the crash pads to start it. Twice.

And I heard a sound from her chest, this song. A bird, whistling, shrieking.

I'm not crazy.

There wasn't even really a feather in her lungs. The coroner didn't find anything in the autopsy.

There was an autopsy, yeah. I haven't seen any results yet. But I'll get them. I need to see them, and make sure—okay, I *know* Aza died. It felt like she took off running without me. Her fingers clenched on mine. Then they relaxed, like she'd lost all her bones.

When the driver called for the life flight, I was already sure she was dead. Which makes it even worse what happened to the helicopter.

The thing about Aza and me is that we've spent every day since the day we met knowing she was going to die, and pushing that knowledge over to one side. No one knew what was wrong with her, not really, so a few years ago I decided I'd be the hero who figured it out.

Aza didn't know. I went through a ton of medical journals.

It's amazing what you can learn to make decent sense of with the right motivation. I've got articles going back to the 1600s. If you want me to diagram a lung, I could do that for you. I could maybe even do it blindfolded.

But whatever I was doing, I didn't do it fast enough. I'm not a miracle worker. I'm not even a scientist. Some days I'm just sixteen, and sixteen isn't what I want to be.

Aza's mom had the same idea as me, a lot earlier than I did. She's been trying to figure this out for almost fifteen years, since Aza started having trouble breathing, but the meds she's been trying to get testing cycles for keep getting rejected.

I know things Aza didn't know about what her mom's been doing for her. A few months ago, I ran across some really promising data that had come out of the lab Aza's mom works in, and so I asked her about it. Her mom was on an asthma project at the time, on mouse trials. When Aza came down with this, by whatever freakish coincidence, the mouse stuff was almost to human testing, and then it got turned back, because it didn't actually work on asthma without major side effects. It wasn't useful for anything. Except, apparently, for Aza.

"I had a little bit of serum in the house, for severe asthma. I don't know why it works even a little bit, but she was dying, so I gave it to her," Greta told me.

Whatever Aza's mom used was the X factor. Aza kept getting sicker, but it slowed down. According to all medical opinions, lungs that could barely send oxygen into her bloodstream should have killed her, but whatever Greta did probably saved her. It's been part of her daily meds ever since. Despite the fact that it is completely illegal.

This is pretty much the only big secret I've ever kept from

Aza. Her mom begged me not to tell her. She wanted to keep working on it, she said, and if people knew, she'd get yanked. It felt all wrong to know something Aza didn't know.

She died anyway.

I look at the ceiling and try to imagine what happens to someone when they die. *Perished = Being Separated.* All the things that were you and all the things that were her, flying apart, an explosion. Dispersed into everyone else.

Morning. Funeral. Sunglasses. Suit.

Carol supervised, and it makes me feel like I'm a scarecrow. The sleeves are strangely loose, which I guess means it fits. I'm used to my grandfather's jacket, which I wear over everything. It came from my dad's side and even though I didn't know my dad, don't even know who he was, my moms gave it to me. It has about a thousand random pockets. Every pocket has a tiny embroidered label to say what it should contain. There are pockets labeled "opals," "pitch pipe," and "bullets." My grandfather was either James Bond or a traveling salesman.

I'd never wear a suit to Aza's funeral, unless it was that suit, and I'm not allowed to wear that, so.

I'm not calm. I'm not ready. But I'm getting in my car, a bag full of things seat-belted into the passenger seat. Her seat.

I change clothes in the bathroom at school. I walk into Mr. Grimm's class, past the first period warning bell, and sit down.

Everyone looks at me. The whole room is dressed in parent-picks, black dresses, black tights, black suits, and ironed shirts and ties.

Keep looking, I want to tell them. *I'm not finished.*

"Mr. Kerwin," says Mr. Grimm. I look at him. He looks at me. His face softens.

"I can't say that I blame you. Take the top part off and you can stay in the room, but I can't teach you like that."

I put the top on the empty desk beside me. It has graffiti on it. *Aza Ray Was Here* it says, in silver nail polish. Mr. Grimm kept saying he was going to make her clean it off, but he didn't.

I never thought this would happen.

I thought this would probably happen.

I knew this was coming.

I didn't see this coming.

How can anyone keep reciting an endless number when you can't see the next digit? But I keep going. 673518857527248 91227938183011949129833673362440656643086021394946395 22473719070217986094370277053921717629317675238467481 84676694051320 0056812714526356 08277857713427577896.

At noon, the bell rings, the special one that says *Here we go to do something completely terrible*, and I walk out. The flag's half-mast. It's not the school's doing; they didn't even think of it. It went down this morning at around three a.m. I know the janitors.

Kids start pouring out of the building behind me. A lot of them are crying, which makes me both pleased and angry. I think having a dying kid in a school means, in people's brains, that no one else will die. That slot's taken. Everyone's crying over her anyway, even though, to them, she was only the Dying Girl, not glow-painting, hoax-making, squid-watching Aza.

Looping. Some days are so dark I can't see anything but a miserable fog of number after number, word after word, clouds of verbs and nouns and none of them the ones that will make time go backward.

Some of us, I name no names, haven't actually *cried* since the night Aza died. I can feel it wanting to happen, but if I do it, all of me will drain out. So I don't.

> *since feeling is first*
> *who pays any attention*
> *to the syntax of things*
> *will never wholly kiss you;*

That is Mr. E.E. Cummings. He gets that part right. I spent too many years paying attention to everything but the fact that time was slipping away from me. The middle of the poem involves not wasting time while you're alive, but instead kissing the people you're supposed to kiss, loving people you're supposed to love. So much for that. He gets the last line right, too, which is:

> *for life's not a paragraph*
> *and death i think is no parenthesis*

People recite it at funerals in a kind of seize-the-day way, but in my opinion, at this present moment, as a person who failed, it's a non-optimistic poem about not getting what you want, not a good-feelings poem. Aza liked E.E. Cummings. Hence, me liking E.E. Cummings.

I pull out of the lot and start honking my horn. Everyone follows me, first the whole school, and then, as I move onto the highway, the town. Or at least, that's how it feels.

Aza told me a long time ago what she did anytime she had an MRI. She'd imagine the beeps and clicks were whales.

I'm doing my version. Our cars are whales talking to one another. In a kind of fake-o Morse code. (Yes, people who memorize all the facts about everything are also people who create fake codes, because we sometimes enjoy a little chaos. A little *controlled* chaos.) The cars are honking my list. Also, it's fake Morse because I don't need everyone to know what I want to say.

The first time I saw Aza she was sitting on the floor playing with a piece of paper, snipping at it with a pair of (I later learned, stolen) scissors. I got up off my mat, but she had nothing to say to me. She only looked at me once, and bared her teeth.

She was something found underneath lake ice after the spring melt. I know she hated how she looked, which. Oh. World, you are stupid.

YOU LOOK LIKE NO ONE ELSE ON EARTH, I honk. The town honks it in echo.

I felt like the doll belonging to Julie next door, the doll that, when you (um, experiment?) cut off a leg, had a hollow body. Aza stole that doll and stuffed it full of crickets. I glued the leg back on. Julie was fairly freaked out when her doll started to Jiminy.

Aza wasn't nice. She had a way of looking sideways at me and then solving me like a too-easy equation.

"Give me something worse," she'd periodically say. "Make it harder." I didn't succeed in bullshitting her very often.

YOU HAVE SPIKES ALL OVER YOUR HEART, I honk.

When she walked away that first day, I picked up what she'd been working on. A paper ship, masts and sails, tiny people climbing the rigging. A sea made of clouds, which she'd cut using little curls of paper, so that it tossed beneath the ship. An anchor chain made of paper loops, anchor weighted with her gum.

Yeah, welcome to Aza, age five.

Jason Kerwin: file under Done.

Aza Ray Boyle: file under Everything.

I chased after her, and recited the alphabet backward in a frenzy, but I never thought she'd listen. She's the only person who's ever made me feel so far behind.

Again she looked at me, this time with maybe pity, so I tried the Greek alphabet. It wasn't as though I could read Greek—I was little—but Carol had taught me the phonetic version, and I'd memorized the letters like I was memorizing a song. I thought I saw a spark of interest in her eyes, but she just sighed, tore another piece of paper out of her notebook, and started snipping.

"I'm *working*," she said, in the most judgmental tone.

I looked down at her hands.

Oh, just a model of the solar system. When she was done, I picked Saturn up off the floor and considered my problem.

There was no way I could live another moment without Aza Ray knowing my name.

Later that first day, Aza had a huge coughing attack and an ambulance came. I saw them loading her in. I tried to get myself loaded in too.

Eve and Carol got summoned to the school, and I got in trouble for being overly intense. Overly intense = Kid Who Occasionally Has an Episode of Frustrated Head-Banging.

So, I'm still the guy who chases the ambulance. This time, at least, I got to go into it with her. Let's call that lucky.

I've never understood why some hospitals won't let the people you're with in the door with you. It's horrible. Twice, I've had to pretend to be Aza's brother. My moms know I have a fake ID that has Ray as my last name.

They don't have room to judge me, really, if we're talking obsession. My moms met because Eve lived in the top of a redwood for seven months, in a hammock. Carol was the doctor who had to do the distance assessment of Eve's mental and physical well-being. Carol was on the ground, and via megaphone, she fell in love with Eve and Eve fell in love back. Neither of them has ever been able to explain it to me. I've seen pictures. Eve has braids and leaves and muck in her hair, and she's tanned to the color of the tree. Carol looks like Carol. Back then, Carol ironed all her clothes, including her jeans, and she totally did not understand what Eve was doing living in a tree.

They're still in love, as far as I can tell.

And so, me being irrational about Aza? I think my moms actually saw it as karma. They remembered how their parents felt when the two of them met, which was, basically, *WHA?!*

They looked at me, and Aza, and said the exact same thing. But they couldn't tell me not to do it.

Other people watch TV. Aza read about cryptography and sailors' knots. We had an ongoing competition over who could give the other the best "piece of weird" they'd never heard about before. There was a tally, and I was winning, but only by one point.

Last year, Aza signed up for the talent show and came onstage, clicked play on a beatbox MP3, and started doing the strangest whistles over the top of it. I sat in the audience, dying.

Afterward, she said to me, "How's your Silbo?" and cackled. Turns out Silbo is a whistled language from the Canary Islands. She won that round, though not the talent show. I still don't know what she was saying. She wouldn't translate.

I turn left at the cemetery and get in line behind Aza's

parents and Eli, in their beat-up blue car.

I honk: I CAN'T BELIEVE I KEPT FORGETTING YOU WERE DYING.

Aza's dad is driving. He flashes me a sign, and then he honks his own Morse, actual Morse, carefully done.

FOREVER. He told me he was going to do that. I honk it in repetition, and so does everyone else. They don't even know what they're saying. But her dad and I do. Aza's mom and Eli do too. I can see them in the car, trying not to break down.

Brief pi recitation.

So, back to me showing up at her birthday party when we were five, thinking my Halloween costume would make me invisible. It kind of did. I walked a mile, this really small alligator by the side of the road, and nobody busted me. I was on a mission.

No one liked Aza back then. She'd already resigned herself to it, no friends, mostly stuck inside at recess. Everyone said she was gross and contagious.

I don't really need other people. Well, I need *one* other person, and she's gone and ~~shitshitshit~~.

I honk my apology list. It's not much of a list, really. Just one huge item.

Aza's family, with input from me, decided to do this graveside, because the whole memorial thing works better if you can scream it, and that's what we're all about to be doing.

Crazy wind. All these people surrounding a hole in the ground, like something's going to come out of it, rather than go in.

We thought her making it to sixteen mattered. Why? What does sixteen even signify? Nothing. It's this nothing notion. It's not even a prime number.

I look at everyone from school, Jenny Green and company. The whole past few days have been full of people getting passes to get out of class, at which point they smoke behind the cafeteria. Historically, Aza and I would've made fun of them, grieving for someone they didn't love.

Aza didn't especially believe in grief. This is inconvenient. I thought I didn't believe in grief either, but now me and Aza have another divide, another difference. I see Mr. Grimm standing off to the side wearing sunglasses and a hat. He looks as though he's been crying too.

My moms walk up behind me. Carol sighs in a way that says she was fervently hoping I wouldn't be wearing what I'm wearing.

"Really?" says Carol. "Couldn't manage to keep the suit on, huh?"

"You knew he wouldn't," says Eve. She even smiles.

"I thought he would," Carol says. "I even called the costume place. They said the alligator was still right there in the stockroom."

What Carol doesn't know is that the costume place has two alligator suits. One my size, and one Aza's. It was part of her birthday surprise.

"It's Aza's funeral," I say. "She'd have liked it."

I put the head back on. Eve gives me a little thumbs-up, but I catch Carol looking at me. Just when I'm honestly a little worried, thinking she's 100 percent not on my side, she says "Wǒ ài nǐ," which is "I love you" in Chinese, followed by "Nakupenda," which is the same thing in Swahili. We learned to say *I love you* together in what felt like a thousand languages when I was little. That's the kind of mom Carol is.

"Even though you're trouble," Carol says, her voice going a little sobby, "you don't need to be sorry for what I bet you said you were sorry for." I'd forgotten I'd told her about the apology lists. "It wasn't your fault Aza died. You know that, right?"

I look at her from inside my alligator suit. No, I do not know that.

My mom presses her hand to the center of my chest and goes quickly to her chair.

When I first realized that Aza wasn't going to live as long as me, I told Aza all the classic things people tell people who are dying. I said, "I could get hit by a bus tomorrow," et cetera et cetera.

Aza was like: "True, except how often, seriously, Jason, do people get hit by buses and die?" Then she cruelly handed me stats. Not that often, as it turns out.

Aza's mom throws her arms around my alligator self, and I walk Aza's parents to their seats. Both of them lean hard on me.

The grave they're going to put Aza in is really small.

09173637178721468440901224953430146549585371050792
2796

When it's my turn to talk, I take off the alligator head, and recite a little chunk of pi. Then I say, as fast as possible: "So, you may or may not know that people keep finding more digits of that number. I wanted to give Aza all the digits. I tried that, the first time we met. I found out later that she knew more digits than I did. I was trying to give her something that wouldn't ever end."

People look at me. There is a collective adult sympathy noise that makes me want to puke.

"That's it," I say. "That's all. I'm fine. No, don't worry."

People make the faces of a comfort army. In my head, I'm frantically pi.

Aza's family does their thing.

Aza's Mom: "She was sick, but would I have traded her for someone who wasn't? If it meant I'd lose the person she was? No."

Aza's Dad: <shakes head, can't talk>

Aza's Mom: hugs him and passes him a piece of colored paper. I can't see the I Love You list she's given him, but he looks at her for a second, his face saying she just saved him.

Eli: "Last year someone gave me a valentine and Aza claimed she hated it. I liked it. She did too, but she kept pretending she didn't. I'm going to give it to her now."

Eli gets some confetti out, and we throw it into the air. It's heart-shaped. It glitters as it falls.

I think: Why did I never give Aza a valentine? I didn't know she liked confetti. I didn't know she liked hearts. She would've made fun of me. She would've told me I was sappy. But maybe I—

Looping.

I get the balloons. There're a couple hundred of them. It's like we're at a Party Palace, and we're all five years old. Except it's a Party Palace where some of us are dead.

Everyone attaches notes to the strings. Eve objected to these, because questionable materials. I had to go in several directions and find biodegradable. I feel momentarily like I'm getting it right.

It's raining hard now. Some of the balloons pop the moment we let go, but others get up into the sky the way they should. That's what always sucks about balloons. In your hand they're big, but once you let them loose, they're instantly tiny.

Mine's a huge green one, because it has to carry a long letter, inside of its own waterproof tube. I wanted it to get as close to outer space as possible. Therefore, it's a reinforced weather balloon, spray-painted to evade Eve.

And then—

Thunder.

Lightning.

People are fleeing to their cars as quickly as they can without being disrespectful.

Where am *I* supposed to go, exactly? Aza's in a little box in the ground.

The grave is too small for me to get into it, scrunch my knees up to my chest, and let them cover me up. But how can there be a rest of my life?

Trees are leaning over. A branch cracks off and hits the ground not very far away, and my moms are trying, not subtly, to get me to come with them.

I look up, and I let my balloon go. As I do, I see something gleam—

a flash of white sail billowing, and a bright spot of light, something blazing out of the darkening clouds. I see *something*, ropes, the pointed prow of a—

An object falls down out of the clouds, and I hear Aza's voice. I swear I do.

I hear Aza screaming my name.

CHAPTER 9

{AZA}

"Aza Ray," says someone, way, WAY too loudly. *"Aza Ray,* wake up."

I put my head under the covers. Absolutely not. There will be no waking up for me, because it is clearly five a.m., and this can only be cruel night phlebotomy. I have a spinny, achy head, left over from whatever got me here, and yes, I remember some of it, and yes, some of it was bad, but it's been bad before, and here I still apparently am, so it can't have been *that* bad.

I've been sleeping like the dead. That's a joke I'm allowed to make. Whatever drug they've got me on, it's working. If they ask me, I can say pain scale zero, which has never happened before, not in my entire history of hospitals.

The voice gets sharper. This nurse has no sense of nice. Her voice is both way too loud and way too high-pitched. I yank the covers higher over my face.

"AZA RAY QUEL. It's time to wake up now!"

Something sharp pokes me. My bed shakes.

I reluctantly open my eyes and I'm looking at—

An owl.

A HUMAN-SIZE OWL, a, what? WHAT? A WORLD-CLASS HALLUCINATION.

The owl stretches long yellow fingers and runs one over my forehead. It clacks its beak at me.

"Still fevered," it says.

Oh, oh, no no no. Hallucinations in my experience don't talk, though who knows, because I seem to be an entirely new Aza lately, someone who hallucinates ships and gigantic birds and—

"HELP!" I scream. I don't care if I'm breaking hospital rules by freaking out. This is me giving up on my carefully cultivated hospital-patient-since-forever coolness. "SOME-BODY HELP ME!"

The bed swings so hard I get instantly nauseous. I'm tangled in ropes and twigs, and wrapped in a blanket made of—feathers?

The bird thing has a beakish nose *and* lips. It's not a bird. It's not human. It's neither. It's both.

This: you don't know what real hallucinating is until you're doing it. It's a gigantically big deal.

At least everything's not on fire, Jason says in my head. Yeah, except everything kind of *is* on fire. Bent brain, boiled brain, broken brain. The owl's wearing clothes, but also has plumage. She's covered in feathers and stripes. She has wings AND hands and she stretches her fingers out to me. She's the size of a human, but wings, oh, definite wings, and she's wear-ing a gray uniform with an insignia. There's a ship shaped like a bird embroidered on her chest.

Angel? Angel-bird-creature-thing? What the hell am I look-ing at?

"Who are you? Where am I? Don't touch me!"

The owl is definitely trying to check my vitals, but hell no, I'm doing it myself. If you're a person who's professionally sick, you get to be ridiculously expert in checking yourself for signs of death.

Maybe the poor owl's a human nurse and I'm a raving feral thing. It's not my fault if I am. Morphine? But morphine means bad things. If I'm on a morphine drip in a hospital, they're making it hurt less. Which means I'm dying painfully.

Which means—

Rewind. Back to the ambulance. Back to the dark. Back to the silence and the snow falling down over the world.

Jason, Eli, my dad, my mom, my oh my god, I—

I *died*.

What. The. Hell.

Aza, *what the hell?*

Where am I?

I lose it.

"Where're my mom and dad?" I manage to ask the owl. "Where's Jason? How am I not dead?"

The owl clucks. "No need for such fear and fuss, nestling. You're on a ship. Welcome aboard *Amina Pennarum*."

I realize that everything she's saying is in a language I understand, but it's not English. I don't know how I understand it. When I try to focus, I can't. I look up at her through tears.

The owl's head rotates all the way around, and then back again like the world globe in my history class, a dented sphere from the 1970s, its face pocked with pencil marks. She has black spots in white hair. She has freckles all over her face, and her skin is pale and kind of silver.

Her fingers are yellow, and scaly, and the nails are black.

There are gold rings on all of them, all connected to one another. The rings are connected to something else, under her clothes. I can see chains running up her arms.

Some kind of harness? Is she a prisoner?

Am *I* a prisoner?

In what country? In heaven? Wait, what heaven? I don't believe in heaven!

"HELP!" I shout again.

"Hush," she says, her tone warm but impatient. "May the Breath take you, if you keep shrieking that way. You're not a newborn, nestling. You're much too shrill. You hurt my ears. Hush now."

My chest rattles. From inside it—inside my lung—comes one high note. I have an image of the bird in my room. The yellow bird. The one I swallowed.

Four sunrises, the bird in my chest says, in a voice totally normal, except that it is COMING FROM MY LUNG. *Four sunrises you slept.*

I gasp and brace myself to choke on feathers.

But I'm not choking. I can breathe. I test. I breathe in all the way slowly, and then out all the way, even more slowly. I've never been able to do that before.

I stop crying for a second and listen. None of the normal hospital desperation sounds and smells, no people dealing badly with their kid's upcoming expiration over crap coffee in the waiting room.

My screaming didn't seem to scare the owl, who is now just looking at me calmly and taking my pulse. I try questions.

If this is a hallucination, she'll answer like a nurse. If this is heaven—

"Are you an angel?" I ask.

She laughs. "So you *can* speak politely. We weren't sure you could. All you've done since you got onboard five days ago is shriek, tell everyone you're dead and that this isn't how dead is supposed to be, and then pass out again."

I might be hyperventilating slightly. I get questions out between gasps, but I'm still not coughing. I should be coughing.

"Where am I? What happened? What the hell is this? Who the hell are you? *IS THIS HELL?* Why are you a bird? Is that a costume? Do you exist? Are you a nurse? Is this a hospital? Am I on a ship?"

The owl looks at me, tilting her head with an expression that looks as though maybe I've already had this conversation with her. She tugs at my covers and straightens them. I notice I'm naked.

I have a vision of a morgue. Am I in a morgue? Am I frozen in a drawer? I don't feel dead. I feel crazily alive.

"Nestling. You were brought aboard in considerable distress, by a Breath summoned in emergency when I and the rest of *Amina Pennarum*'s Rostrae couldn't convince you to come peacefully. You would have died down there, trapped inside that skin, had Milekt not found you.

"This isn't hell, but the sky," she continues, "and I'm not hell either, but Wedda. Greetings, it's nice to meet you too. I am no bird. I'm *Rostrae*. And of course this isn't a costume. These are my feathers."

Right, that explains everything.

This is some kind of meltdown. My brain floods with things I've read, Milton, William Blake, and *Moby-Dick*, plus Disney movies viewed unwillingly in children's hospitals plus

Christmas specials, plus New-Agey yoga moves that put your brain into some kind of cosmic release state, and I. Do. Not. Know. What. To. Think.

Settle, instructs the bird in my chest. *Nest. Feed.*

"She hungers, it's true," Wedda says, talking casually to my rib cage. "It's not natural to sleep so long."

She leans over and starts trying to feed me something with a spoon, spilling food on my face. I fail to open my mouth, but she smashes the spoon against my lips, and I finally give in and take a bite of something sort of oatmeal-esque.

I can feel wind coming in from somewhere. Like, ocean breeze. The sounds I first vaguely thought were the beeping of machines are not beeping at all. They're birds. Birds singing and screeching and peeping.

"Why are you here?" I ask the owl.

"I'm your steward," she says. "The officers aboard *Amina Pennarum* all have stewards from the feathered class. You don't know anything, little one, and you have a lot to learn. You've been gone a long time."

Disregard the words "gone a long time."

"What ocean is this? Is this the Pacific? Are we on a cruise ship? A hospital ship?"

She laughs again. "When you came aboard, you were a nestling fallen off the mast and too young to fly. But now, I think you're recovering. Questions and questions. Let's get you into uniform. You've been in bed long enough. You're in need of fresh air, and exercise."

"I'm fine," I say, uneasy and lying. "I can dress myself. I can feed myself too. I don't need a steward."

Wedda sighs. "By the very Breath! I don't need a nestling to dress either, but you and I aren't in charge of that, so I suggest you make it easier on us both and let me do it. Then we can go about our business."

She reminds me so much of a nurse; matter-of-fact, and intolerant of smack. I have a pang of good memory, a nurse laughing in the middle of the night, hearing it down the hallway outside my hospital room. Oh god, where am I? What happened to me?

Wedda gives me a tight blue jacket and trousers, a shirt and underwear made of something soft. Then she tugs at me until I'm dressed. So much for being a functional person who can do everything for herself. I feel so weak that I barely understand buttons, and these buttons are more along the lines of hooks.

"But," I say hopelessly. "What's *Rostrae?*"

"You were taken when you were very small. You remember nothing at all, do you?"

"Taken."

She nods, as though Taken isn't a thing. But it *is*.

"A Rostra, little one, is what the people below would call a bird. Except that Rostrae are birds who aren't always birds," she says. "My kind travels in drowner skies, and up here too. Not all birds you see below are like us. Only a few."

I think about birds: crows, magpies, sparrows. I imagine a whole flock of geese shape-shifting into creatures like Wedda, but on the surface of a lake. There are fairy tales with that sort of thing in them. And ancient myths.

I think about all the birds on my lawn that day, whenever *that day* was. It's a firm piece of memory—all those many kinds of birds, staring at me, and ropes flying through the window—

Also, *Drowner?* What's a drowner?

She pushes my feet into boots made of gray leather. "These, for example, are made of dove skin," she informs me. "Not Rostrae."

Right. I feel their fluttering silenced hearts through their dead skin.

Nope. No, that's impossible. I shake my head.

"Are you prepared, nestling?" Wedda asks, fluffing her feathers back into place.

"For what?"

"It's time for you to meet the ship."

"But I'm—"

"Captain!" Wedda shouts. "Aza Ray Quel is awake!"

Outside the cabin, birds screech, and with a big whoosh of weird I realize the noise I've been hearing is language, birds arguing about who gets to see me first.

The door bangs open, and a rush of not-people enter. Wings of all colors, and beneath the wings are faces. I take a queasy step backward, and Wedda keeps me stable.

Oh god, Aza. What's happening?

Bright blue feathers on a girl with an indigo mohawk. Red-feathered breast on a man with a long, skinny face and dark hair.

Rostrae. All in uniform.

They bow. I don't know why.

Then there are the others, just a few of them, uniformed as well, wearing medals and insignia. These are tall, thin people who at first look human, but have dark blue lips and blue skin. Delicate bones, pale, cloudy patterns on throats. If I saw them against the blue sky, I might not see them at all. They're *like* humans, enough like humans that—

What are we talking about here, Aza? What, exactly, are we talking about?

Humans?! *LIKE* humans?!

You don't believe in this. This is UFOs and tinfoil hats and hoax-central, Jason Kerwin–style. This is—

Beautiful, interrupts my brain, at which point the rest of my senses notice the tall blue person standing directly in front of me. His skin is no color that exists. Bluer than mine has ever been. He has black hair and eyes so dark I can't see the pupils. He's staring at me so intensely that it's not a certainty I won't become a crumpled-up pile of knees and elbows. I make an embarrassing snorting sound, which is me choking on nothing.

The boy looks me up and down, and I feel myself blushing crazily. I glance down quickly, because I feel as though I might be naked again, but I'm totally covered. Good thing Wedda was in charge of buttons.

"Aza Ray Quel is skin and bones," barks the boy, and looks accusingly toward Wedda. "She's supposed to be fit for duty. Can she even walk? Can she sing? She's half what she should be. By the Breath, I thought she was supposed to be the one."

He puts out his hand and pokes my shoulder, hard, which mobilizes me.

"Excuse me?" I manage. "Who are you?"

Everyone's staring at me, diagramming me, bird people and blue people alike. They're making little sounds of displeasure. "Can someone please tell me why I'm here?"

"This can't be right," one of the blue people says to Wedda. "This pitiful nestling cannot be the one we've been hunting all this time, Aza the Kidnapped. She's nothing."

"She's damaged by her time among the drowners," someone else says.

"And by the Breath that brought her aboard. That probably damaged her too. It *carried* her," says another, in a tone of revulsion and horror. "I heard it cut her from the skin she was in. Unspeakable."

The room shudders.

"It's shocking she lives at all, after that," says the first blue person.

I feel seasick now. One of the blue people touches my chest with sharp knuckles, prodding, and I hear the bird inside my lung trilling, raspy and muffled.

"Her canwr's nested in her lung," Wedda says. "He'd never nest in another. That's proof enough for the captain, and it's proof enough for me."

There's a sudden jostling, a murmuring. Whispers and sounds of discomfort. Everyone seems paralyzed, and then everyone's standing at attention.

Someone's come in. A woman tall enough to brush the ceiling.

"Captain," says one of my visitors. "We've been assessing the new addition to *Amina Pennarum*—"

The woman snarls at the rest of the people in the room. "You presume to discuss her condition without me? You presume to debate whether she is who and what I say she is?"

She's right in front of me then, bending over me. The woman has coils of black hair twisted into complicated knots, oil-field-slick eyes atop navy blue. Slanted cheekbones. Sharp nose, eyebrows like slashes of ink, arms ribboned with tattoos, spirals, feathers, and clouds made of words.

I recognize her. I know her face. I know her tattoos.

I've been dreaming about her for years. The two of us. A flock of birds. An anchor. A cloud.

The woman reaches out a trembling hand and touches my face.

"*Ah . . . zah*," she whispers, the voice not coming from her mouth, but from her throat.

The way she says my name is almost the way Jason and I say it when we're leaving room for the &. Nobody else says it that way. Her voice grinds. It's not the same as the other blue-person voices in the room, which are smooth. There's something different about it. It's harsher, stranger, a wounded whisper.

"I'm Aza," I squeak, in the most normal voice I can manage.

She turns to Wedda.

"She's healthy? Her fever's down?"

"It is," says Wedda. "She's regaining her strength."

"Explanations?" I try to say, but my voice is dying in my throat. I look down at my blue hands. They are *extremely* blue.

The woman (the captain?) touches my face again, with cold, pointed fingers. I want my family very hard. I want my mom, and I want my dad, and I want Eli and I want Jason.

"So, where's my mother?" I say. I try to be casual about it. I do not make any of the whimper-y sounds I want to make.

"Here," the captain says.

"No. Where's my *mom*?" I say more urgently, in a shameful little-kid way. I want to hide my face in my mom's sweater, and I want her hugging me.

Her voice floats to me through my memory. *You can go if you have to go, Aza—*

Oh god, my poor mom thinks I'm dead. She'd be here

otherwise. That's the only way this could have happened.

Wings all around me, and faces pressing in closer, blue faces, feathered faces with beaks.

Wedda fluffs herself, a mother hen instead of an owl.

"Stand back," she says, loud and intimidating. "Let the little nestling breathe. She has no notion of who you are, nor of what happened to her." They shuffle back, but only slightly.

I touch my chest, looking for the comfort of the crooked center bone in my rib cage. It's there. But it feels—suddenly— like a wishbone.

I want a stethoscope. I want my doctor. I want her knocking at my chest, hunting for intruders, because this is INTRUDER CENTRAL. This is hallucinatus maximus.

There are all these familiar things, these déjà vu things, from the planks on the wall to the way the captain's face moves, inches from mine. The way it looks, the way *she* looks.

She has a strange necklace, and it hangs over me as she bends, almost hitting me. A tiny little nub of something—coral or bone?—embedded in clear resin at the bottom.

The earth tilts. I feel like I'm not in my body.

"Milekt found you," the captain says. "We reeled you up from the drowners, just in time. You were almost gone."

She covers her mouth and pauses a moment. Her eyes are filled with emotion. "But you're finally home."

In my heart, in this crooked, half-crushed heart I've always had, there's a dizzy, weird thing.

"I don't even know you," I whisper.

"Of course you don't remember how it was before you were taken, when we were on *Amina Pennarum* together. You were so small. You were only a baby. But even then you were extraordinary."

A tear glitters down the captain's cheek, dark as ink from an exploding fountain pen. She presses her hand against my face, in the same place my mom would, and I stay still this time, overtaken by this strange sense of:

H O M E
O   M
M   O
E M O H

"I'm Captain Zal Quel," she says. "You're aboard the ship *Amina Pennarum*."

I blink. She's still here. She's still looking at me expectantly. I'm still here. I'm still looking at her.

"You're the Captain's Daughter, Aza."

And when I continue to stare, speechless, she finishes her sentence with the words I somehow knew she was going to say.

"I'm your mother. And this is Magonia."

CHAPTER 10

{AZA}

No.

I shove hard out the door, through feathered people, blue arms, gray uniforms, and I'm running, running, running through a corridor lined with hammocks.

"*Magonia*," Jason said. But we were talking about fairy tales, not reality. He was talking about history and hallucinations. It was crazy! I was sick!

I push past the crowd, the bird inside my lung screaming at me. *Respect your station! Zal's the captain! Salute her!*

I slingshot myself up the ladder to the upper deck, push open the hatch, and sprint out into the light.

I'm expecting to breathe in the fresh air and cough, to touch the hospital gown embroidered with my name, and to feel frozen on my back where the thing gaps, but I stumble out into the cold air, and there's no parking lot. No *EARTH*.

No.

There's only a sky. A huge sky.

And it's full of ships.

All directions, at all distances, all kinds—small sailing

vessels, big ships similar to this one. Ships veiled by their own weather.

A bank of vessels moves together, bringing a larger storm with them. Little boats, catamarans, yachts, freighters—all moving through the sky.

All flying. The ships are flying, yes, yes, that's exactly what's happening, and they don't have wings. They're just . . . floating along in the middle of nothing.

And I'm standing on the deck of a huge ship too. Sails and rigging. Planks. We rock gently in the breeze.

In a moment, Zal's behind me, holding me up, because I'm swaying like I don't even have legs, a jellyfish.

"Aza Ray Quel, this is your country," she announces, her voice booming over the deck. "These are your country's ships. *Amina Pennarum* is first among them. There is no better and no braver than she."

A crew of blue people clusters around us.

"These are her officers."

"Captain's Daughter," they say in unison, these uniformed blues with their impossible whistling voices. They raise their hands to their brows. They salute me in the same way everyone saluted the captain.

Throwing up is the only rational option.

I lean abruptly over the rail and look into the tossing clouds there, stomach spinning.

Something enormous looks back at me. Sleek silver skin with a slight pattern on it, tiny eyes. It blinks, opens its feathery fins, and scatters drops of rain. It fountains a gust of wind and rain out of its . . . blowhole?

It swims sideways through a cloud, and as it swims, it sings.

Sea of stars, it trills—in words, kind of, but not. *Greetings*, it sings in a beautiful voice. *Sea of rains and snow*.

Legions of therapists have tried to make me understand the supposed healing powers of tears. I've never understood them until now.

"Don't cry, Captain's Daughter. It's only a squallwhale," says a feathered crew member from behind me.

Indigo mohawk. The blue jay girl, I realize.

Only a squallwhale. I glance over at the giant creature—it's not below us now, but above the level of the deck rail.

"One of our pod," says Zal. "They make storms to hide us from drowner eyes. They're part of our camouflage."

I stare at the shifting vaporous edges of these creatures, half whale, half climate.

"Not all the clouds you've spent your life looking at are squallwhales, but some are."

More of that, then. "Not all, but some."

I look down, past all the ships in the sky, past the cloudy, misty whales, and suddenly below me, there is a checkerboard of green fields and roads and buildings. Earth. I'm paralyzed with wanting, but I'm not allowed to keep looking down.

"This is *Amina Pennarum*'s mainsail," Zal says, pointing up the mast.

The mainsail looks down at me and makes a high sound of recognition, a cry of song.

Flyer, it says. *Welcome, firefly*.

The mainsail is a giant bat.

Giant, as in the size of a living room. A tremendous white-silver bat, its body chained to the mast, its fingerlike bones splayed, stretched out, wings wide open for the wind. It looks down at me, its teeth slightly apart, tasting the air. *Girl*, it says, and whirrs a high whirr.

A crew member flies up to bat-face level and offers the bat something fluttering from a bucket. A moth, I realize. Albeit one the size of my head.

The bat snaps it up and moves its wings, and I feel us sailing faster.

I notice a nose-prickling smell of oil and fire. The crew's scrubbing the deck. Black marks. A hole in a rail.

Déjà vu pulls my gaze up again to the bat. There's a burn on its silken wing, healing, but bad. Something about that, something about a crash—

But it's gone. I can't remember.

"Is it hurt?" I ask.

"Don't bother yourself. Batsails are only animals," Zal says. "Ours is well cared for. They don't understand pain."

I spin slowly around to look at the rest of the deck. There's a wheel to steer by. There's a very solid-looking metal crane, dangling over the side of the vessel, huge and covered with chains and pulleys.

And at the top of the mast, there's a little house filled with yellow birds. They're the same kind as the one that flew into my mouth. The one that flew into my *lung*.

"The canwr," Zal says. "Our cote of lungsingers. Milekt's kind."

I touch the spot on my chest where I feel fluttering, and there's a severe shriek from the bird in there. *Milekt*, says the bird in my lung. *Milekt*.

It's only when one of the little golden birds above me takes flight that I notice the tethers. It flies out to test the wind, screals, and returns to its perch, tied there by a thin cord. For a moment it looks down at me, black beady eye, but it has nothing to say. It doesn't shift into anything human-ish.

"This is my ship. Your ship now. This is my crew. And these are the rest of the feathered class," Zal says. She claps her hands. "Rostrae!" she shouts.

Birds start dropping out of the sky, landing on deck, ropes in their talons. Many of the same birds that came to my backyard, I realize with a jolt. They carry a tangle of ropes, small ones, large ones, some gossamer fine, some heavy as chains, all attached to the masts and deck. Three more owls. Hawks. Crows. Birds I've never seen before, tiny and covered in candy wrappers of feathers, bright red and blue and green, pink and silver. It's as though a piñata has broken.

A golden eagle sails down and looks at me, its eyes the color of caramel, but made of fury. Nothing kind in that gaze. It looks like what it is, a hunter. Its wings must span eight feet. It has talons as long as my fingers.

My knees are shaking, and my head is spinning, but I stay upright. Zal's hands are on my shoulders.

A hummingbird the size of a bee buzzes up to me and hovers, turned sideways, considering me with one eye at a time. Next to my face, a robin, but not an American robin, a European one. Even here I know things from Jason. Such as, European robins are smaller than ours, and much fiercer. This one looks at me, with a black, gleaming eye, and makes a judgmental chirp.

Then all the birds shift.

They stretch their wings and their bones crackle and groan

as they expand, gaining height and weight. Their beaks open and open until faces appear around them, heads bowed with feathers. They ruffle up their plumes and then, with a shiver, a new thing where the bird was standing.

All of the birds have shifted into people.

There's a tiny, beautiful man where the hummingbird was, his nose a beak, his fingers fluttering, a giant woman where the eagle was, her hair golden feathers, her arms muscular. The robin morphs in ways I can't even remotely describe into a man with orange-red tattoos on his chest and dark eyes lined in white.

All these imaginary things look at me. All of them salute me, a fantasy made up by some little kid—like the little kid I was, the girl who read every book of Audubon, the girl who cut ships out of paper and got harassed by the classroom canary.

"Captain's Daughter," the bird people shout, all in one voice. Twenty-five different songs, but they agree on who I am. There seems to be no doubt.

Everyone feels certain of my identity but me. They stare, waiting.

I look at the captain.

"I want to go *home*," I say as politely as I can. This feels like my last chance at something I've already lost. "Something's confused, okay? I'm not actually your daughter. I was born in a hospital on earth. My dad made the whole staff margaritas in a blender he'd brought in the car. He had four hundred limes. There are pictures of me being born, bloody ones. I'm not adopted. I'm not who you think I am. I want to go home. My parents are going to think I died. Please, let me go."

Another memory surfaces—Jason, oh god, Jason, holding

my hand, telling me he'd find me. How can he find me if I'm *here*?

The blue-skinned boy from my cabin, the beautiful, rude one, is suddenly right in front of me, and he looks at me directly.

"Permission to speak?"

Zal nods. "Granted."

"As predicted, she wishes to return to her situation. Perhaps we should listen when she says she doesn't belong here. We can't afford to waste any more time."

Zal turns me around to face her. "The drowners didn't know you needed Magonian air. They didn't know you needed your ship, your canwr, your *song*, because they know nothing about how we live. There, you were dying. Here, you thrive. This is your country, Aza Ray. We've brought you home."

"But," I say. "I'm not who you think I am."

"Look at yourself," she says, and smiles, holding out a little mirror. "See who you are."

My reflection's blurred at the edges, dark and tangled, and for a moment all I can focus on is the hair that moves and twists as though it's made of snakes. It whips around and everywhere, and then it moves away from my eyes and—

I see my face, kind of, the face I've always had, angular and weird, huge eyes but—

But this girl has wide, full indigo lips instead of my skinny, grimacing ones. And—my eyes—I recognize them as my own, but there used to be a dark blue over the colors I see now—gold and reddish, like fish deep underwater.

This girl has high cheekbones, and when I open my mouth, her teeth are sharper than mine.

I'm looking at her skin, at her hair, at the echo of my face, then the forever bone-thin-weakling-no-boobs Aza body I've always hated, and my body, too, is converted into something else entirely.

I don't know what to say I don't know

what

to

do.

I want the old me. I want her pale skin and gaspy voice, I want her skinny arms.

I don't even notice that I've dropped the mirror until glass splinters all over the deck.

I look up at the captain, my jaw slack. Zal doesn't flinch. She regards me steadily.

"You are my daughter, Aza," she says, and her voice softens. "Your life here is better than it could ever have been below. The undersky is a shadowland, and the drowners are a shadow people. You were kidnapped and placed below as a punishment for my sins, not for your own. None of this was your fault. It was mine."

Another black tear on her face.

"It's been sixteen years since you were born to me, and fifteen since you were taken. You do not know the pain of it, Aza. You do not know the effects it's had on Magonia."

She straightens up and smiles, shaking her shoulders.

"But tonight, as is fitting, we celebrate. The time for mourning is done. Tonight we glory in your birth and your return. Dai—"

She turns to the black-haired boy, who still looks at me, grudgingly, judgingly.

"—the drowners will be celebrating her birthday with a burial."

I jolt.

"We'll do something finer. You'll give Aza a taste of Magonian song, the first she's heard in fifteen years. The one she'll join in for the deliverance of her people."

He hesitates, but nods, and then closes his eyes for a moment. The skies have gotten much emptier than before. I can't see any other ships around us now. This ship is moving very quickly, and I feel the wind kick up as, in his chest, he starts singing a complex song full of beats and trills.

Then his throat starts to sing along with the melody already begun.

I feel a rattling inside my ribs. This boy—Dai—has a bird in his chest, just as I do.

They sing together in gorgeous harmony. The sound is so beautiful, I'm blown away.

In my chest, Milekt trills out, *Sing with him. It's what you're meant to do.*

"No," I say, irritated with Milekt's insistence, and my own strange desire to do his bidding.

There is something massively important about song here. I suspect—no, I know—that it can do things.

It makes me feel nervous and too excited just thinking about trying. It's a feeling like—

The thought surges into my head. *Jason.*

Dai's looking down at me with a twisted expression on his face. I hear a fussy trill from his chest too.

"No," Dai barks, and thumps his chest with his fist. "It isn't time. She's not ready." His bird shuts up. He spins himself high into the rigging, twisting his arms in rope. The crew stands at attention, and Dai sings another note. As if he's summoned them, stars wink on all over the sky.

A few are brighter than the rest, flaming extra hard against the blackness that surrounds them.

I count. Sixteen of them. So bright that they could be candles.

Up at the top of the mast, the other birds join in the song, and then my own bird starts, too, from inside my chest. He fills in the gaps in Dai's song with his own notes.

I suddenly know that I should be singing too. I almost can't keep from doing it, but why?

Seriously? I'm not a singer.

Finally something starts to emerge. This song, it causes the air to wobble around us, around Dai and me.

Who is he?

I don't know, but my heart is pounding, and then, arcing across the sky, the Northern Lights appear, rippling out in the dark.

Green
blue and
     r
       o
         s
           e
         and
        R
      E
    D
   and

t
a
n
g
e
r
i
n
e
and
w
h
i
t
e
and
SILVER.

The colors drape over our ship, and I look at Dai, glowing under the lights.

He throws his head back and sings a note into the stars, and I feel my chest shake in response. My bird trills again, and another color, pale blue, rushes out from the edge of the Northern Lights.

Dai climbs halfway up one of the masts—scaling it as though it's nothing. A soft violet dust falls from the sky.

I'm jaw-dropped. Zal's face is gentle as she lays her hand on my chest again.

"Happy birthday, Aza," proclaims Dai from up on the mast. He bows his head to me.

"Happy birthday, Aza," says the rest of the crew, in unison, and they bow too.

"Happy birthday, Aza," says Zal, and she smiles at me.

This is the birthday I wasn't supposed to live to. I'm supposed to be dead, but I'm not. I'm supposed to be on earth, but I'm not. I make a noise I don't know I'm going to make, a long wail of unmistakable despair, and from somewhere deep in the ship, there's a faint answering wail. The crew rustles nervously, looking around, but I clamp my mouth shut.

I'm supposed to be polite, and respectful, and grateful. But I'm on a ship in the sky and I've been kidnapped from my family, and apparently everyone I love thinks I'm dead.

I do a quick pass through my memory, and determine that I don't remember anything I'm sure is real past chocolate éclairs in my kitchen, footage of a silvery giant squid circling up from the bottom of the ocean, and Jason and I, almost—

And bang, there it is. The dividing line between fact and fiction. I spin to look at the captain.

"You said they'd bury me on my birthday. Who's my family burying if I'm here?" I shout.

"Enough!" Zal shouts back at me, right into my face, but I'm losing it completely.

"No! Take me home!"

"I said this would happen," Dai says, descending from the mast. "She's broken."

Zal goes rigid. "She isn't. Aza's strong enough that no Breath could injure her." She squares her shoulders, looking carefully at me.

Then she laughs the kind of loud, booming laugh you'd hate in a movie theater.

"You are my own daughter, for all that you were raised by drowners," she says. "I wouldn't believe what I was told either, not without making sure. Not from strangers. Not even from friends. I will show you, daughter. And then you'll believe. You'll know who you're fated to be."

And that's how we end up flying over my funeral.

CHAPTER 11

"When you die in Magonia," Zal informs me, "you'll be given a hero's farewell, quite unlike this one."

She's handed me a wood and brass spyglass, and I'm looking through it, down at my high school's parking lot. I lift my head when she says that.

"It sounds like my funeral here's already planned."

"Living's a risk, Aza," she says sharply. "Heroes die young. Would you choose to be less than a hero? Here, the sky will light with fire for you. Our funerals are their sunsets."

I see. How comforting. (How insane.)

Below us, on the ground, people start to come out of my high school, dressed in black. I'm breathing fast, but I'm finefinefine, completely and totally fine—

—until the moment the crowd parts for the tall guy in the alligator suit.

Then I'm not fine anymore. I say his name once, quietly, then louder. "Jason."

I can see, even from this far away, that Jason Kerwin's faking fine. The alligator head's in his hand, and I can see his chapped lips through the spyglass. Chewed. I can see his eyes, red rimmed. He looks like something attacked him and won. Again that sound, that pitiful wail, from somewhere deep in the ship. I look up at Zal, but she's not reacting to it. No one else is either.

"You see?" Dai mutters, suddenly next to the captain. "It's the drowner she cried for when she came aboard. Maybe he's her ethologidion, not—"

"He's only a drowner," the captain says, and snorts. "She can have no bond to that. He's below even the feathered class."

I don't know and I don't care. I'm watching my funeral procession.

Jason's car leads the students and teachers out of the parking lot. They're honking their horns in rhythm. He has them honking a message. I catch some of it. Not all, but enough.

Dai's still muttering, judging the tears on my face as weakness, but everybody else—except for that wailing bird—has the good sense to shut the hell up.

At the cemetery my parents get out of the car, looking ten years older than the last time I saw them, and I feel a horrible surge inside my heart. The captain has my arm. All I can do is watch.

Eli stumbles out of the car behind them. Her hair's not in its usual straight line. She's given herself more than a trim. She's cut her hair off, and the bottom is insanely ragged.

On purpose. It must be. There's no other explanation.

I finally get why people are scared of dying. I finally get why no one wants to talk about it. Santa Claus in Reverse is carrying everything about my life away in a big sack, and I'm supposed to be fine with it.

My dad's carrying a wooden box, the size of a shoe box.

I accidentally whimper.

"Is that me? In that box?" I ask the captain. My chest feels too tight, but it's not because I'm dying anymore. It's because I'm missing them. I can see my mom's sweater cuff, unraveling. I can see my dad limping, because stress makes his back go out.

"Of course not," Zal says, impatient. "You're here beside me. They have only the ashes—from the skin," she says, like we're talking basics.

"The skin?"

"The Breath left it when they brought you up here. Surely you recall your liberation? From the report, it was an unpleasant thing, and close, but you were dying. I'd never have let one of them near you had we not been out of time."

Again, *the Breath*. I keep hearing that term, in that creepy tone.

But down there, my family's left a gap where I'm supposed to be. I'm a {   } in the middle of the people who love me, an emptiness in their sentence.

I feel sobs tsunami-ing. I can't move. I can barely see, because now I'm watching black tears drop from my cheeks. I'm feeling my mouth contorting around terrible sounds and the muffled bird below, whatever it is, echoes me. Zal's head snaps up, and she listens, but says nothing.

My mom trips, and my dad catches her. Jason's between them now, holding them up. How can this be what we're doing? How can I be dead to them—and alive up here?

"I want to go home," I hear my mouth saying, and apparently I don't care that at home I'm in a box, that at home, my family is carrying me toward a hole in the ground. "Please let me go home."

No one on the ship has anything to say to that. Home is where they think I am.

"Home," I whisper, but no one cares.

Jason's passing out balloons and people are attaching envelopes to the strings. Jason's the last to let go of his, a big green one. He lifts his head as he does it and for the first time I get a real look at his face.

He clearly doesn't see anything, no ship, no sails, no me. He lets go.

The green balloon is rising, closer, up, up, and I run toward it, stretch for it. I can't get it.

"Enough," says Zal, as though anything could be enough. "This is the proof. Now it's time to begin again. You have much to learn, Aza Ray Quel, and little time."

She motions to Dai, who takes the wheel.

"Rise," she says.

"JASON!" I scream. I hurl the spyglass over the rail with all my strength. "JASON, I'M UP HERE!"

The ship explodes with shrieks and cursing and feathers; Dai's spinning the wheel hard.

"LET ME OFF THIS SHIP!" I scream again, trying to get my voice down to Jason. "I'M NOT LEAVING THEM! LET ME GO!"

"Retreat!" Zal shouts. She wrenches me off the rail and tackles me to the ground. I bash my head on the way down with a sickly crack, but she doesn't seem to notice. The ship pushes up, away from earth and home.

All the Rostrae whoosh and shift back into birds, grabbing ropes and hauling us higher. The batsail's wings are wide and beating.

My head feels like it's detaching from my body.

My heart feels like it's still down *there*. I can't scream, but I'm sobbing, gasping, and the bird belowdecks is screaming for me, an eerie siren call.

"May the Breath take you and tear you with their teeth and claws! May the Breath consume you!" Dai shouts. He's taken Zal's place holding me down while she's back at the wheel. "You think the drowners love you, but you're wrong. They'd kill you if they knew what you are."

I feel painkillered, drugged, numb. Maybe concussed. I don't know anything.

I keep seeing Jason in his alligator suit. I keep thinking about him in the ambulance, telling me he'd find me, that he wouldn't let me die.

But he did. He let me go. And I'm up here, and he's down there.

"Jason," I whisper. Dai's watching my face.

"You're bonded to that drowner filth. I knew it."

He drags me to my feet and over to where Zal's working the wheel, moving the ship through heavy clouds, forcing it up into the storm. She shoots Dai a reproachful look, and pins me with her stare.

"You *will* learn to follow orders, Aza Ray. You just risked your ship and everyone on it. We're forced to report the loss of the spyglass to the capital, or risk sanctions. That means that Maganwetar will have official eyes on us. We didn't need their attention."

But I'm elsewhere.

Jason saw me. We've spent our lives seeing each other. He must have seen me.

"This ship searched for you for years," the captain says. "Do you want to be taken again? Do you want to be seized?"

I feel nauseous, blurry-edged, grief-stricken.

"But I love them," I say quietly.

Zal whispers, her voice raw. Her fingers pinch into my arm, holding me upright. "I don't care who you love. You *will* understand what you mean to Magonia."

She grits her teeth.

"I've given up nearly everything to reclaim you. You may think this is nothing, but you're everything to me, Aza Ray, more than the sky and its stars, more than this ship we sail on. You're loved here, you're needed here, and even if you don't respect that, your time below is over.

"Look around, Aza. Look at your crew. Their survival is up to you. Would you see them perish? Because you refuse to claim your home, your power?"

Zal's fingernails have broken the skin on my upper arm now, and I'm wincing. I try to pull away, but she's staring into my eyes with such intensity I don't know how to get loose. I have no idea what she's talking about, but this is the farthest I've ever felt from home.

I cry out. The bird below shrieks.

"What's that?" I ask Zal, because I see her face change at the sound. "Is someone hurt?"

"No," she says, and that's all. But I see her eyes well up with black tears, and I wonder about them.

I jolt awake to the sounds of a tortured song, my heart racing, tangled in my hammock. At first, I think the voice is part of a nightmare, but then I hear it again. The same voice I heard before.

Blood bone tear take hurt bite beast, someone screams.

A long, wailing shrill, high and horrible, ear-bending. A bird of prey of some sort, the kind of call you might hear when something's hunting, but much worse, because it has words.

Broken torn kill kill kill me, screams the bird.

Wedda comes into the cabin as I'm trying to get loose from the hammock to help . . . whatever it is.

Her presence is oddly calming.

"What is that?" I ask. "What's happening?"

She looks at me for a moment with an unreadable expression. Sadness, I think.

"It's nothing," she says. "This ship is haunted with the ghost of a canwr. He's the captain's business."

I blink. "A *ghost*?"

"Dead long ago. He lives only in echo," she says, and sighs. "By the Breath, I would that ghost were softer. He's been rattling the ship since you came aboard. We're all on edge about it, but there's nothing to be done. Leave it alone."

Yeah, except that it feels like the bird is calling *to me*—the same way this ship did, the first time I saw it in the clouds. Zal says this ship is mine. Does the ghost belong to me too?

"You'll get used to him," Wedda says.

"What's happening to him? We need to help—"

"That's just how the ghost sings, nestling. It will stop. Caru never sings longer than a few minutes at a time. Old sorrows. It isn't your business to calm a spirit. Let's get you washed and dressed."

The sound hurts my ears and my heart, but after a few minutes, the bird stops. I don't hear anyone running around the ship. No one seems upset by the cries but me. Maybe Wedda's right. Maybe it's better to ignore it.

Wedda pushes my arms through my jacket sleeves, tugging them into place. She washes my face for me, because apparently I'm five years old. No. I take the cloth from her.

"I'm fifteen. I can wash my own face."

"Sixteen," Wedda says, and I inhale. Sixteen. She's right.

"I don't believe in ghosts," I say. Then, "What if *I'm* a ghost?"

Wedda clucks. "Nestling, ships have their secrets. Magonia has its secrets too. You'll learn what you need to learn soon enough. For now, your only duties are dressing, eating, and reporting for duty."

Wedda fastens my buttons before I get a chance to do it myself. Today she yanks my hair into braids, twisting it in her finger-talons.

"No," I protest feebly. "I can—"

She shows me myself in a mirror. I'm not used to my new

looks. I don't make eye contact with my reflection, but my hair's an intricate, beautiful mass of braids that resemble some kind of sailor's knot.

"Can you?" Wedda asks, laughing. "This is the captain's knot. Do you know it, then, ground-dweller? Have you studied the styles of the sky?"

"Not so much," I mumble. "I didn't know the sky had styles."

"We have no time to waste on teaching you basic Magonian grooming," she says. "The captain's made that clear. You're here to serve a higher purpose. But there are procedures," she says. "There are rules. Hair remains braided so that it's less accessible should the ship be boarded by pirates."

I stare at her. "Pirates?"

She snorts. "Of course."

She tugs my braids into position and whirrs in satisfaction, or at least, in some sort of pleasantry.

I pull at my uniform, straightening it.

Is this the deal with the rest of my life, then? Seafarer? Captain's Daughter? At least no one's lacing me into a corset, or fitting me for a tiara, or making me take elocution lessons.

I was never princess material. When I think about it, this ship, fairy tale or not, is tailor-made for the likes of Aza Ray Boyle.

Here, I look the same as everyone else, and I'm dressed the same way everyone else is, with the exception of the insignia on my uniform. I look down at it, studying. A little crest showing a bird with an open beak, singing to a storm cloud.

It matches the captain's.

I lace my boots and look at Wedda, like, yeah, Aza Ray can lace her own boots, Aza Ray has total skills.

Aza Ray Quel, not Boyle, I remind myself.

Wedda laughs an owl laugh, which is more cough than laugh.

"Report for duty," Wedda tells me. "You belong to the first mate, lucky thing as you are."

I haven't learned to read her yet. I barely know her. But it's not as though I don't recognize sarcasm when I hear it. I was made of sarcasm for fifteen years.

"Belong?" I ask.

"So he'll make you think," she answers, and huffs. "Though you're not his property. Remember that, nestling."

Definite sarcasm. Okay then.

I climb out onto the upper deck and see why. The first mate is Dai, the black-haired boy who sang stars for me, and officially, already, does not like me.

I feel instantly stupid. This, it occurs to me, is the first time I haven't already done the reading. I've never not been ahead of everyone else. I'm sitting at the bottom of the class, clueless.

Dai's looking pressed, polished, and preemptively pissed off. For someone who can't be much older than me, he has the attitude of a fifty-year-old general.

It's a shame because, for a blue person, he's hot.

I mean, maybe if I just admit it, it'll lose its power.

There are stabby black metal earrings hanging from one of his ears. Fishhooks.

A little voice, not that of Milekt, but of my own idiot self, echoes through my head. *Stop staring at him, Aza, you're staring.*

"You slept long enough," Dai says. My cheeks flush.

The sky is pale orange and pink. The sun hasn't even broken the horizon. "But it's early," I say.

"It's been two days. Do you always sleep for years at a time? Now that you're my charge, you'll get used to seeing the dawn. You've wasted enough of our training time already."

"Training?" I question. He doesn't answer.

Instead, he leans in and jabs his finger into my insignia, right in the crooked place in the center of my chest, where my lung tilts over onto its side. Dai's looking unhappy. I notice that his crest is just the basic, the ship shaped like a bird.

"Don't think you're special because of this, no matter what the captain says. I'm the first mate on this ship. You don't even have status, Captain's Daughter. You're an ordinary skyman and you're late."

I look down at my chest, wincing at a sudden sharpness. The skin over my left lung is exposed by my uniform's neckline. It's blue and smooth one second, and in the next there are outlines of a circle, deep, in indigo, darker than my skin.

It's almost a tattoo. Except that then the circle—it pushes out. It tilts.

And it opens.

Opens. No blood. No pain.

There's a door in my chest.

A little yellow bird trills from his perch atop the mainmast.

I know the bird already. They've called him Milekt. Gold wings. Black beak. Black eyes, flashing at me. He coughs, a delicate sound of feathers and hollow bones. He stretches his wings.

The bird swoops down and into the air. He hovers, trilling

wordlessly before me, and then flits into the cavity exposed by the opening. The door closes behind him, painlessly, like he was never there.

I'm frozen.

I knew he was there—the bird. I've felt him before. But this? This is too much to—

Sing with him, says my chest, so hard that I actually choke. Milekt rustles around and kicks inside my lung.

"Where are we going?" I ask Dai. "This ship? Are we on a voyage?"

He looks at me in a way that says I'm very, very dumb.

"A *voyage*?" he says, making the word "voyage" sound idiotic. My mind flashes to Jason, who'd never look at me that way. I feel weak and lost, and then, no. No more thoughts in that category. I can't afford them.

Dai stretches his arms for all the world like he's a jock on the football field, showing his ease in his authority.

"By the Breath, you act as though no one ever taught you how to speak. The ship is *foraging*, and *patrolling*. Your duties are following my orders and learning to sing, neither of which require commentary."

I glance around, looking for the captain. Zal's standing just a few feet away with the blue jay girl, who is holding a chart out for her perusal.

The chart looks like something I'd drool over at a museum— yellowed, decaying at the edges. Half star map, half monsters in the water. In one corner, I glimpse a giant mouth with pointed teeth rising up out of the sky, and in another, a city in the clouds.

I angle my eyeballs to get a better look, but I hear Dai behind me.

"Ordinary Skyman Quel," he says. "You take orders from me, not the captain."

Zal looks up at me, and nods. "You're assigned to the first mate."

Salute her, shrieks Milekt. I salute as best I can.

Zal smiles slightly. "Daughter, you're doing that with the wrong hand."

I'm medium-embarrassed, but it's not as though I grew up on a ship. I have a history of hosp—

"Where's that?" I say, pointing at the chart. There's a cluster of buildings. All around the city, there are whirling lines. "Are there cities here? What are those?" I point at the lines.

"That's Maganwetar, our capital, and those are its defenses. The capital is surrounded by winds."

The name of the city cues a memory in me. Old High German? That's what it is. Maganwetar—the word for whirlwind.

Jason. I wince.

"Aboard *Amina Pennarum*, we prefer the open sky to cities," Zal says. "The residents of Maganwetar live in buildings tethered to one another, their whirlwinds and tempestarii keeping everything but provisions out. It's a city of sleepers and storm magicians, but the residents of Maganwetar are lazy as drowners."

"Drowners like me?" I ask.

"You, Aza, were never a drowner," says Zal. "We're in the skies to defend Magonia, even if there are those in Maganwetar who think they need no defenses, no strategies, no battle plan."

Her lip curls.

"Things are changing, Aza Ray, and you're part of the change. Now, I expect you to learn your duties."

Dai tugs me away to another part of the deck.

I'm exploding with questions.

"Are we going to Maganwetar?" I ask. "Where is it?"

Dai looks grudging. "It moves. And we're not going there. You're not welcome in the capital, nor are you safe."

"What do you mean, not safe?"

"You're not an official crew member of *Amina Pennarum*," says Dai, hesitating only a moment.

"How am I not official? Didn't the captain send someone to get me? A Breath—"

Dai jerks, looking around. "Don't mention them," he says. He holds my eyes, deadly serious. "Trust me. They're nothing you want to call to this ship, not without a good reason, and not without funds to hire them."

"But what are they?"

He doesn't answer. "You were reason enough for the captain to summon one, but I cannot think of another. If we come into proximity with an official ship, you are to disappear into the holds below and the rest of us are to deny that you're here. These are the captain's orders."

I glance toward Zal, who isn't looking at us. I watch her take the wheel, this giant thing, big spokes and handles around it, which I'm only really noticing now. It's made in the shape of the sun, so the handles are the rays, and the ship is steered by rotating.

"But where are we going?" I ask again.

"Your duty is to watch, not talk," Dai says, sneering a little.

For a moment, I'm not sure exactly what I am supposed to be looking at. Then one of the Magonians sings with his canwr, and operates the crane by crooning into its gears.

Another Magonian's song lights a fire in a little bowl, and

makes a meal of toasted grain. He shares it with his bird.

Let me out, howls Milekt from inside my chest. I feel his grumpy fluttering and battering around in my lung. *I'm a canwr, not an ordinary. I'm not meant for this. I'm for singing, not standing around, mute.*

I have no time for this complaining bird, but I wouldn't mind lighting fires with my voice.

"Do I have to let him out?" I ask Dai, and Dai smirks.

"No. But you might want to. He'll scratch."

And he does, his little-bird toes climbing inside my lung.

The thought makes me queasy, but I swallow the rising bile down. "How can there be cities in the sky?" I ask Dai, trying to distract myself from the scrabbles of Milekt. "What do they float on?"

Dai sighs.

"Do you know everything about the undersky, then? Why their heavens are blue, and how their rooms are lit in the dark? Do drowners know how their airplanes move through the sky? Can you tell me how they fly?"

I'm both sucked in and harrumphed by Dai's simple questions. Yeah, I DO know those things. Maybe we have things to tell each other. I feel a duel coming on.

I'll tell you how airplanes fly if you'll show me what you know about this place.

I'm just opening my mouth to tell him so when he snorts and laughs at me.

"I could talk for a hundred years, Aza Ray Quel, and not tell you everything about Magonia. There was a time when we and the drowners consorted. Then, even the worst of our cities, the ones where everyone starves, were seen as heavens by the people below. And we were angels or, sometimes, gods."

He pauses. "Have you ever swabbed a deck before?"

"There really weren't a lot of boats around my house, since you know, no ocean. And, I was sick. So, swabbing . . . um, no."

Dai holds out a mop and a bucket. I'm about to take them when he lets out a note, and I can hear the bird inside him join the song.

The mop levitates, then whips around, so that it actually scrubs the deck.

He stops. The mop falls to the floor, and is still.

"Sing this deck clean."

I look into the bucket. There's a scrubbing brush floating in soapy scum.

"Um," I say.

"Stop wasting my time. Last night, I threw supernovas into the sky. Surely you can manipulate a mop."

Milekt perks up and stamps his feet inside my chest. He's ready. I'm at a loss.

"I'm not—I can't just start singing," I tell Dai. Why doesn't he understand? I barely had enough air to speak before, let alone sing.

"And you're not willing to learn, apparently," he says. "So you can scrub the drowner way until you change your mind."

I sigh. It's only a matter of time before I get assigned to clean the heads. I'm probably lucky right now, dealing with decks instead of toilets, and so I roll up my uniform sleeves and get down on my knees. In my chest, Milekt shrieks.

Release me! I sing, not *scrub.*

"Sing then," I tell Milekt, and it's totally fine that I'm talking to a bird inside my chest.

I work, but it isn't easy to clean when all around me are miracles, just casually happening.

I watch a Rostrae deckhand spread his green wings and take flight, with a net made of what seem to be very strong spiderwebs. He slings it out into the sky and brings it back full of moths, which then get fed to the hungry batsail.

I watch a Magonian crew member sing one of the other sails into an unfurling, and the sail shakes itself as though it's an animal, getting rid of water in its coat.

The Rostrae crew practices rope tricks, lassoing and twisting, but with a crazy kind of grace. *What would they lasso up here?* I wonder, but I have no idea.

It's sunny above me, but there's a pod of squallwhales swimming alongside the ship, making a light rain below. I watch them out of the corner of my eye as I scrub. The calves play together, butting up against the mothers. The babies sing, too, not complicated songs, but long, dazzled ones, mostly made of happiness.

Sun, they sing. *Sun. Bright. Drink the light.*

The mother's blowhole rainstorms, and the calves whip back and forth, swimming through the fountain like kids in a sprinkler.

They have mothers they trust, and a sky they understand.

I envy them.

CHAPTER 13

{JASON}

Air-traffic-control research. I'm hunched over my desk, hacked into some major things. I could just be listening to controllers talking, hoping to run across something in all the sound, the way the people looked for the giant squid for years: basically, stick a mic down there and hope.

But, luckily things have gotten better, search-wise.

So, I'm using an app (not officially sanctioned, and not mine) to keyword search through everything air traffic control has said, in a variety of city and rural airports, for the past three weeks.

Carol shows up at my bedroom door and looks at me from the doorway for a full three minutes while I scroll.

They take effort, social graces, but the moms will kill me if I abandon them completely in favor of a person they think is a ghost. So I say, "Hi."

"You have to go to school, kiddo."

"I *am* going to school," I say.

It's not a lie. Periodically I show up and pass tests. I'm still part of a grief exemption. And I saved my sick days in case. So I have a couple of weeks' worth for the year, before anything too truant happens. People are probably relieved to not have to see me anyway.

"You have to actually *go* to school."

"Independent study."

She rolls her eyes.

"The history of human innovation is independent study," I tell her. "We can fly because of people who didn't go to high school."

"Those people weren't my kid," she says.

Eve joins her, stepping into the room. Without making a big thing of it I put a few papers on top of something on my desk.

Carol takes her usual unhappy gaze around at my stuff. She doesn't know about the storage units, and she doesn't need to. Some things have to be bought in bulk.

I don't know where Aza is. I don't know what she's doing. All I know is where she was three weeks ago, when she died holding my hand. And then a few days later, when I heard her voice coming out of the sky.

She's alive. Aza's alive.

I know it like I know my own name.

I just need to figure out where. I checked wind currents and mapped the possibilities, at first in a pretty primitive way, and then in a more functional one.

Unusual storm patterns moving east across the country. Reports from weather balloons and satellites.

As far as I can tell, those patterns are moving in an unusually coherent clump, and they're still over land. I have a master chart at this point, and a program that runs it on a variety of axes. This isn't just my own obsessive doing. I *wish* I was a full-on programmer, wish I was a full-on anything other than this, but I know people.

And this is one of the uses for the money earned by my hotel-bed-making devices and instant dry-cleaning sprays.

There's not anything really concrete to go on and I don't even exactly know what I'll be going on to do. But there are plenty of scraps out there, things about ships in the sky, things about weather and weirdness. Then there are other things, dug up out of places I'm *really* not supposed to be looking.

Official places. Government places.

"You need to say good-bye to Aza," Carol says, and takes Eve's hand.

"It's important, baby," Eve says.

Their front is worryingly unified.

"I DON'T have to," I tell them, though we've been through this already, too many times to count. I was prepared for dead, as prepared as you can be. I wasn't prepared for *this*.

Ship. In. The. Sky.

I'm not a fool. I haven't told my moms anything about the ship. They would look at me for about three seconds, and then put me into the car, and take me directly to the children's hospital (an insult, but it's where you go until you're eighteen) where we'd have a speedy meeting with the psychiatric unit. So, no, I don't tell Carol and Eve about the ship.

In fact, I tell them nothing, beyond: I'm working on a project. My moms have the look of people who might be getting ready to take me offline. The Great Unplug has happened only once before, when I was nine and in the obsessed throes of memorizing a chunk of the OED. The moms did not approve.

Memorizing took up the extra places in my brain that were otherwise occupied with counting down the seconds of Aza's life until age ten, when the doctors had, at that point, decided she was going to die. It was about this time my moms discerned that meds were required.

"So," Eve says. "Do we need to take you offline?"

"I'm not even on right now," I say, lying.

She looks at me and raises an eyebrow.

Yeah, Eve has a bandwidth monitor. I find this hilarious. They got the monitor to keep me from looking at porn, I assume. They were definitely convinced that's what I was doing when I was working on the OED project. Carol burst into the room all, AHA! And found me midway through *L*.

Maybe I've looked at *some* things on the internet in the category of naked. Who hasn't, I ask you? But there are a million categories I care to look at, and most of them aren't porn.

Categories like historic UFOs. Categories like history of flight. Categories like peculiar weather patterns since the eighth century. I'm compiling said categories into one larger thing in my computer. Because, reasons.

"I'd actually not be that unhappy if you *were* looking at porn," Eve says, reading my mind, and sighs. "At least you'd be human."

I look up.

"You wouldn't be happy," I tell her.

"I would be reassured that you were normal," she says.

"Yeah, but I'm not," I say.

"Go outside," says Carol.

"It's cold outside."

"See a friend?"

"In case you missed it," I say, playing the illegal card, "my only friend died."

"She wasn't your only friend," Eve says, impervious to my attempt.

"Name another," I say.

She can't.

I do have other friends. Those Who Live Online, in Other Time Zones. Mind you, I'm not nine anymore. If I ended up unplugged again, I'd get around it.

"School tomorrow," says Carol. "We love you, and we understand what you're going through, but it's either school, or doctor."

Understand what I'm going through? They do not. I'm going through the history of civilization, basically. Not a big deal. Only minor work there.

I wait for them to leave my room, and then I'm back. There've been several sightings since the funeral. One person saw weird lights. Another saw a bright thing near the horizon. Another actually saw something he said was a rope.

Sir, you have my attention. But then he recanted and said some stupid stuff about downed power lines. Whatever.

There were other sightings of the same kind earlier this year— one above Chile, one in the air over Alaska, one over Sicily—but none of them helped me. People, alas, don't document things with any kind of precision. They fill Twitter with blurry photos.

Now, however, we live in the epoch of the app. The official ones, and these, the nonofficial. Forget jailbreaking your phone, I'm talking about the ones that require you to break that phone out of Alcatraz.

There are a few hundred of us who develop them (See: Friends in Other Time Zones), mainly because someone else on-list dared us. I'm a midlevel amateur at this point, but they magnanimously let me on the message boards, and even allow me to throw down the odd gauntlet to the real players.

Hence: I now have a sky-anomaly app. You just aim your phone at wherever you saw the strange thing—cloud formations, weird lights, storms out of nowhere—and the app plots coordinates and checks with satellite info to gauge air displacement, mass, humidity, condensation of whatever you're looking at, cross-referenced with similar reports.

The world is sometimes amazing.

Most of the sightings I'm researching are clearly fake, but three have been real, or as real as I can figure. I think they're from the same clump of impossible sky out of which I heard Aza's voice.

I'm done with being cautious now. I'm just going to call it what I think it is.

So, henceforth, we will be referring to that piece of sky as Aza's ship.

Aza's ship is heading northeast, slowly, spending a lot of time over farming areas. Those areas have been plagued by hailstorms, windstorms, lightning. Tiny tornadoes have scattered and flattened several fields. No crop circles. Just unforeseen, chaotic weather patterns, destroying harvests.

What Aza said she saw—what Aza *saw*—is part of a long tradition of things seen in the sky since the sixth century. In 1896, for example, there was something called the Mystery Airship scandal. People all over the western US saw skyships, brightly lit, flying fast. People in Illinois saw some kind of airship on the ground, and watched it take flight. After it was gone, they discovered footprints all around the place it had been. And the thing they said, my favorite quote?

"Something has happened above the clouds that man has not yet accounted for."

Yeah. So that's where I'm working right now. Something above the clouds.

I interviewed some farmers (I claimed I was reporting for small newspapers that actually exist, in case they checked) and they talked about it like, "Well, the world is ending and all I can do is try to harvest when I can." When I asked about the whereabouts of the damaged crops, they kind of didn't have an answer.

"Well, they're ruined, son, that means they can't be sold."

Most of us don't notice waste, so if all the corn blows off the cobs, or gets trampled, what we notice is that it's no longer edible, not that, hey, a lot of it is straight up *gone*.

There's a pattern. The events, the sightings of the odd lights, the weird white clouds, they're all moving in a straight line.

There's a destination. I just need to find out where it is. I stare and plot the course. I stab virtual pins into a virtual map.

CHAPTER 14

Amina Pennarum is a fishing boat, I decide, except not, because we're fishing not in an ocean, but on earth.

A launch loaded down with apples waves a flag to ask us if we want to trade. The robins in its crew lift the boat to our level, and Zal comes out on deck to offer them a sack of dry corn from our hold in exchange for the fruit. We trade for a pig from a small tug. Our Rostrae haul it aboard and it totters past me, heavy and determined. I feel vegetarian just looking at it.

We fly over a field, and a swarm of bees appears over the rail. The cook tromps up from pig butchery, wiping blood from his knife, and barters with them for honey. (Yeah, *with them.* The bees themselves. They speak to the Rostrae. I don't know how that works, but it's a kind of humming whirr from both parties.)

Midafternoon, *Amina Pennarum* goes low, in a hailstorm created by our squallwhales. The blue jay girl does some of that twitchy lasso work along with a couple of other Rostrae, and the ropes swing out of a little cloud, slipping around something down below, which gives a disgruntled moo.

I stare. Are they pulling up . . . a cow? Our rustlers attach the ropes to the big crane jutting over the edge of our back deck. Its engine runs and we haul the creature up. You've never seen surprise until you've looked into the eyes of an ascending bovine.

So. Those legends about UFOs stealing cattle? Right, apparently the cause was not UFOs, but Magonian ships.

Mostly it seems we just milk the cows and let them go. The poor girls sit around in a pressurized hold, until they get grumpy for lack of grass. Which is more quickly than you might imagine.

It's like we're on a floating farm. Except we don't grow anything. We just take it. We've got corn and wheat, animals that rotate in and out, and animals that end up meals for the Magonian crew.

For a week, the sun rises and sets. I'm put to work, I'm put to bed. Every morning I wake up expecting my room, my comforter, the life I knew.

Every morning, instead, I'm greeted by Wedda's clucking, scouring, dressing and braiding. And then Dai's stern face as he lectures me about finding my voice—and gives me something new to scrub until I do.

I feel like I'm in a book written by George Orwell.

Except that this is nicer than Orwell. This is *Animal Farm* plus *Peter Pan*, plus . . . squallwhales and bird people. And, somehow—somehow it's real. I have to keep reminding myself it's real.

I know it is, because I've attempted to determine my aliveness or deadness in several ways. *Be she alive or be she dead, I'll grind her bones to make my bread, fee, fie, foe, fum,* and no, that doesn't help me, but it's what I mutter when I'm at a loss these days, even though I didn't climb a beanstalk to get up here. Most of my tests have involved infliction of medium amounts of pain. Vital signs, modified. Each of my experiments yields the same result: alive. Alive and presumably sane, yet completely and utterly messed up.

Because Logical Aza, Rational Aza keeps wanting to wake up—to shake someone by the shoulders and scream, *Ships can't fly! You can't sing something into happening!*

Except that they can. Except that Magonians do.

I'm trying hard to stay calm and deal with all of this. All things considered, I'm doing reasonably well. Practice gained from years of dying. Credit due.

This morning, I'm in a harness, trying not to look down at earth while I'm carefully washing the figurehead on the ship's bow: a patchwork bird carved and painted. One crow's wing, one thrush's, half of its head an owl's, half a parrot's. One heron's leg and one flamingo's, and a bird of paradise's tail. Apparently the mascot of *Amina Pennarum* is a messy hybrid creature, which makes me feel sympathetic toward it, given that's exactly how I feel.

"I've heard we're embarking on a special mission," Dai says. He's agitated, as usual.

I stare at him, awaiting the further explanation that I know is coming. Dai loves nothing so much as the sound of his own voice. It's the only reason I know anything about this place.

"Before we got you, we were on field duty, sending Rostrae down to net crops. It was dull. Feed the capital. Send our forage off to them. This new mission, on the other hand, is what Zal's trained this crew to do."

I lean forward, but he shuts up, because the golden eagle

Rostrae lands on the deck rail, and with a shrieking stretch transforms into a shining woman, her hair to her waist, her eyes yellow.

Another Rostrae lands with her, the girl I keep noticing, the blue jay girl with the electric-blue mohawk. She considers me for a moment, her black eyes with white streaks beneath them, and a yellow stripe on each of her cheekbones. She's more beautiful than anyone I've ever seen, though she also makes no sense with her combination of human features and beak.

She could *be my age,* I think, *or near it.*

"Nice scrubbing," says the blue jay, and grins. She looks at me for a moment in a way that might be friendly.

I'm shocked to discover a smile spreading across my face. I've had plenty of attention since finding myself here, but no one's been actually friendly.

Do I want a friend? I've only ever had Jason.

I look around for Dai, but he's wandered off, nowhere to be seen. Not surprising. He doesn't relish fraternizing with those beneath his rank.

"I'm Aza," I say.

"Thus revealing an impressive grasp of information we both already possess," she says, and tilts her head.

Is she . . . joking with me?

"I just thought—I want to ask—do you think you might be able to answer some questions for me?"

She shrugs elegantly and her shoulder feathers ruffle. The trim on her uniform is as bright as her plumage.

"Possibly," she says. "I don't know how helpful I'll be. I'm only a sailor."

"I'm only a skyman," I tell her, and she laughs.

"An ordinary skyman with more power than all the other officers on this ship combined," she says, pointing at my insignia. "Captain's Daughter. Savior of Magonia."

Savior?

She's mocking me, clearly.

"It's Aza," I insist.

She nods. "I'm Jik. I was born aboard this ship, and I've been part of the effort to locate you—ever since I can remember."

"So I guess, thank you?" I say weakly.

She smiles. "You look like anyone else, Aza Ray Quel. It's hard to believe you'd be capable of so much."

"What does that mean?" I ask. But Jik turns toward some piece of business and, despite her human form, I see that she has a long, blue-feathered tail. It's weirdly glamorous—tails on a tuxedo.

I'm entranced.

The Rostrae she's with don't correct my scrubbing and washing. The Rostrae seem too busy with their own crew assignments to stop and stare at me.

And soon, it seems they're sharing a meal.

"Birdseed," one of them says, looking dismissively at a cake of some kind in his hand.

"We'd be better feeding below, where there IS food," says Jik. She's quickly shushed by an older crew member, a robin.

"Do you wish to make trouble? This is our ship, and we are lucky for it. Not all of us have access the way you do. Your place is assured, but what will become of us when she's through? Have you thought of that?"

The robin glances suspiciously at me and then walks away, leaving me scrubbing.

"What was that?" I ask Jik.

Jik shrugs.

"Magonians can't go to ground to bring up wheat. They need us to pull the ships, to net their harvest, and to be their help shipboard. I'm a part of the *Annapenny* as much as the rigging and the sail are. And I'm as easily replaced."

"That can't be true," I argue. "You just said you were born aboard."

She nods. "Yes, and I've done every job on this ship—from knotting nets to braiding hair." She pauses. "Captain's Daughter, I don't know if you know this, but you don't inspire confidence. You're pretty unskilled."

She smirks and looks pointedly at a streak of grime I've been unable to buff out of the figurehead.

I laugh. It comes out a giant, sarcastic bark. "I don't know how to do anything . . . except talk. I'm not great, am I?"

"Perhaps." Jik regards me a moment. "But you're not the worst." She nods to where Dai is striding back into view. Then she flies up to the top of the batsail, grabs a rope, and tugs it until the bat's wing is straightened out.

"What's this new mission?" I ask Dai when he's at my side, keeping my voice low.

"We're hunting," Dai says casually.

"Something alive?"

"It's classified. Ordinary skymen don't have that information," he says smugly.

Superior show-off. I'd give him an ostentatious eye roll if it wouldn't turn into a *thing*. I've already had to endure about a million too many of Dai's lectures on proper protocol and duty.

He observes the streak of dirt Jik pointed out moments ago.

With a "tsk" he takes the brush from my hand and swings like some kind of acrobat out onto the figurehead. Securing himself in place with his feet, he makes quick work of the grime while rattling on about technique. A tuck and a backflip, and he's returned to the deck again. I have small struggles about my gaping jaw. No, thou shalt not gape.

I distract myself from his gymnastics routine by scrubbing the figurehead until its every tiny painted pore is clean. All the while, I try to put things here in perspective by thinking of them in terms of my old life.

This boy, Dai, he's nothing to me. He's essentially one of the kids from school, tramping down the hallway, not super interesting.

But um, except not really at all. And I can feel Magonia sidling up around the edges of my brain.

I should be grateful, it says. *I'm walking around. I can breathe. I'm not the dead girl I was always going to be.*

I'm something else. Something important. What? No clue.

It's different here. YOU are different here. Better?

But no.

Even if I'm in this place for the rest of my life. Even if I never see my family and Jason again, I can't forget them. I won't. Because, what if I forget myself along with them? Who will I be then?

I scrub until my fingers bleed blue, and as I scrub, I chant.

"Jason, Eli, Greta, and Henry. Jason Eli Greta Henry. Jasoneligretahenry. And Aza."

When I look up, Zal's standing above me, a disappointed look on her face.

She kneels, and extends her hand to help me back on deck.

"I started out at the lowest rank on this ship and made my way up to captain, faster than anyone imagined," she tells me. "These were the years when everything went wrong. Magonian ships couldn't harvest enough to sustain even our own sailors. Our squallwhales sickened. Our people began to know hunger.

"Our problems are worse now than they were before. The world's overtaken with drowner poisons. Magonians suffer and die. We're at their mercy.

"You'll soon understand, Aza, what it means to be in charge of the future of your people. Some of us are born to crew ships, and some are born to captain them. This ship was my salvation, as it will be yours. And as you will be to your people."

Zal puts her hand on my back, and it feels strangely good. Is it because she's my mother? Or is it because of her power aboard the ship? Is it because part of me likes being in favor, being special?

"*Amina Pennarum* sails for treasure, Aza," Zal whispers. "You'll be the one who raises it from the deep."

"Treasure?" I ask. "What do you mean?"

"Learn to sing for us," she says. "And you'll see. You must see."

My brain whirrs. Is there actually still treasure in the world? The notion is exciting. I think about curses and pirates. Skeletons guarding booby-trapped hideaways.

I think about the bird I keep hearing—the one who sings along with my emotions, my pain—the one Wedda called a ghost.

I mean, obviously it's not really a ghost. But what do I know about Magonia? There could easily be ghosts all over this sky. I wouldn't know. I'm a stranger here.

Zal takes the ship's wheel, her charts open to some highly cartographed territory. I can see monsters drawn in the margins.

Below us, for a moment, I see a flash of earth, but then a squallwhale comes between us and the ground, stirring the air until there's only cloud, and we're only a thing hidden inside it.

Jason (stop it, Aza, just stop thinking about him, just stop) would love it here. He'd be prowling around with his hands out, asking question after question after question. And people would answer him, because he never met an expert who wouldn't tell him anything he wanted to know.

He never met a fact he didn't want to add to his secret fact-hoard either.

There were things Jason didn't know, of course, but in the realm of the memorizable, not that much as far as I could tell.

What did he *not* know? How to be a normal person? Neither did I. But apparently I have a better excuse.

God. Jason, my best friend and the most annoying thing, who'd rattle off a thirty-minute monologue of his mind's flotsam and jetsam and then cackle when I didn't have the same levels of geekitude at my disposal.

Jason, who once forced me to dance in front of all the curators at a museum because I lost a bet.

Jason, who once in a while, when I'd be coughing, wouldn't even be there at all. He'd be standing right next to me, yes, but inside he'd just be a frantic calculating machine, tallying oxygen percentages and dust quotients, pollens and amounts of time between wherever we were and the hospital.

Which I hated, because it reminded me that I was sick.

Some days he'd be muttering to himself, diagramming things he wouldn't show me, thinking things he wouldn't discuss.

So he wasn't perfect, Aza. He wasn't. It's just that your brain keeps trying to revise him into something he never was. Never mind that the moment you saw him, your first memory of him in the alligator suit, you thought, *Oh god, finally, someone like me.*

He's not like me.

He's human.

Right, then.

Shut up, Aza's brain. Shut up.

I hear, from far off inside our ship, the awful cry of that invisible bird again.

No, he sings. *Leave me or kill me.*

He shifts into wordless screaming, which chills my whole body. The ghost bird—Caru, I remember his name now—sings again, an anguished wail. Everyone pretends it's not happening. Everyone ignores him.

I try to block out the sound, but then, from nowhere, I get flashes of something I can't quite—

Someone leaning over me in a crib.

For a moment I see my own tiny hand held in a black-gloved one.

And that's all I have, a gasp of a memory.

Kill me, the ghost bird screams. *Broken heart. Broken string.*

I'm jolted again by Dai shaking my shoulder.

"Move, if you're not working," he says. "You're in the way of the nets."

"Do you hear that?"

"Hear what?"

"The bird?"

He tilts his head. "No," he says. But he does.

What am I remembering?

I tug Dai's sleeve. "Magonian babies. What are they like?"

"*They?*" he says. "*We.* We hatch. A lot smarter than drowner babies when we do." He struts a little. "I can remember my own hatching."

I don't give him the satisfaction of seeming impressed.

"The screaming bird?"

"The *ghost*," Dai says tersely.

"Is it a canwr?"

"That's two questions," he says grumpily. "Or four, depending how you count."

"Dai, please."

"Just—" he hisses, glances around, then pulls me away from the nearest crew members. "Just let it go, Aza. The ghost's been agitated since you came aboard."

I pause, thinking. "But, if it IS a ghost, it WAS something else. What was it?"

Dai sighs, impatient with my ignorance. "A *heartbird.*"

"What's a heartbird?"

All he says, after a minute, is, "Heartbirds are special, but this one was broken long ago. He can't hurt you. He's gone but for his sorrow. I assume that's why he lingers here."

"Are you sure he's—"

"I've never seen him, Aza, and I would have if he were real. He's nothing. Old sadness with a loud voice. Broken bonds are serious things. Sometimes death doesn't close them. Feed the sail."

He hands me a small net, and points me toward the fat moths batting about the ship's lights.

When I bring it its wriggling meal, the batsail looks at me and I look back at it. Its obsidian eyes are weary, and . . . kind?

It sings softly so only I can hear.

Find him, the bat trills. *Heartbird.*

That night, I sleep badly in my strange hammock; I dream of being kidnapped, of being lost, and of losing everything, and all night, the heartbird's song haunts my sleep.

CHAPTER 15

{AZA}

Dai and I are out on deck at twilight, sharing watch, peering off into the sky. There's nothing in view, just a darkening not-much, a shiplessness.

I think about the crew's tall tales—the ones I've overheard or, lately, asked about. They're reluctant to share with me; they peek around corners, drop their voices to a whisper. Still, I'm learning.

They talk about airkraken, and about ghost ships in the skylanes. They whisper about fields of Magonian epiphytes, these magic plants that can grow in the air. These plants were once so common, they'd halt Magonian ships. Fields of them all over the sky, and their roots would tangle in the batsails' wings until the Rostrae grew weary, and they fell from their flight.

Some of this must be pure legend, of course. But some of it seems worryingly plausible. So it's not crazy that I'm constantly looking over my shoulder, off the deck rail. If the crew's to be believed, there's plenty to be afraid of.

"What am I doing?" I mutter to myself after I've been staring into the dark for a while. "Nothing's out there."

"*Everything's* out there," Dai says.

He's pacing, and I'm dithering starboard. Despite the cold, he's shirtless, possibly just to stress me out. His canwr, Svilken, is in and out of his chest, singing and chattering to the birds above us in the cote.

Against my will, Dai's biceps keep appearing in my peripheral as he climbs around in the rigging and circles the deck. Magonians are casual about nudity, and seem not to feel cold.

Well, unless they're me. Apparently my ability to regulate my core temperature was ruined by years in the milder climate of the undersky. I have no likelihood of shedding my shirt out here.

Also, I'm still Aza from earth, so shirt-shedding? Never, never, no, and no.

I've been on *Amina Pennarum* almost four weeks, or at least, that's what I can count. I've started understanding things, started remembering that I do, in fact, have a brain, even if I'm new to this world. And I may not be singing the way Dai desperately wants me to, but I can listen.

Periodically another ship comes alongside us, unloads our holds, and takes our harvests to Maganwetar—the Magonian capital. So there's plenty of food around, but as far as ship's rations go, the crew—the Rostrae—live on what seem to be cakes of birdseed.

There are no plants in Magonia, of course. So our foraging from earth, our storm creation, is necessary.

Up here, all the weird things people see from below and wonder about make sense: the freak snowstorms, the rains from sunny skies, the way a wind can kick up out of nowhere and blast half a city block. Super tornadoes. Hurricanes. Giant thunderstorm cells?

Magonia, all of it.

Apparently, once, in the 1600s, Magonia harvested a bunch of fields of blooming tulips from Holland, because Magonians assumed the tulips were food. They weren't. Disgusted Magonian ships ended up dropping tulips from the sky, and the poor people of Amsterdam must have been utterly bewildered. It was like a rain of frogs, but flowers instead, and it made a mess of the economy.

(I would've loved to have seen that.)

The Rostrae do most of the hard work—both onboard and during harvest. When they visit earth, and drop below a certain height, they transform from the human-bird hybrids on deck up here, into normal-looking birds.

The Rostrae know basically everything about all things sky-related, so I make conversation where I can.

The golden eagle told me a story about the extinction of passenger pigeons.

"The horizon used to be full of silver ships crewed by them," the eagle said. "To hear my ancestors tell it, they'd stretch to the edges of the sky. But they were all gone by the time I was born. An entire race exterminated. The drowners shot into the sky and ate them."

She shuddered then, understandably. Because, genocide.

"The drowners tried to kill my own tribe too. Eagles' eggs went soft and broken, because our nesting areas were destroyed. But we survived. We'll survive Magonia too. Perhaps you'll be the one who helps us, Captain's Daughter."

Before I can ask how, or what she means, she takes flight, and around her talons her chains glint. When she flies, she tugs *Amina Pennarum* higher.

No one here seems to question their duties, or their station. The whole ship sings the same tune.

The ghost—the heartbird, Caru—is the only thing that disobeys, the only creature that dares to be dissonant.

He screams no matter what Zal says. The bird's voice is so agonized, so painful, so lonely, that I feel tears starting every time I hear it.

He's singing now, in the growing dark.

A few of the squallwhales come closer to the ship, pinging at Milekt, who informs them snarkily that I'm *only sad. Not hurt.*

Will she cry a storm? one of the calves asks, and I can feel its pleasure in my tears. All it has to compare them to is the squallwhale storms. It can hardly be expected to understand human sadness.

"I'm not even crying," I protest. "I'm fine."

The mother squallwhale looks at me with first one eye, then the other, buffeting bits of gray storm about with her feathery fins.

Sing, she recommends, like I'm her calf.

I frown. It's not as though I need yet another mother.

I scrub my face with my sleeve.

Magonia functions in other ways I have yet to understand. Earlier tonight, another ship sent us a message by shooting a glowing arrow with a letter attached to it onto our deck.

"Among the drowners, I've heard they call that a shooting star," Jik told me out the side of her mouth. I imagined the astronomers below us watching this light arc across the dark, charting it. "Here, it's a letter from captain to captain."

Zal pored over the message.

"Stay on course," she muttered at last to Dai. "They acknowledge the loss of the spyglass and demand a fine. They've employed a Breath to fetch it and clean up any repercussions. They don't know about Aza."

"Better than expected," said Dai, and he nodded.

"What do you mean, clean up repercussions? What do you mean, don't know about me?" I asked, relying on her lack of focus. Also, the word "Breath"—I keep hearing people use it, and I still don't know what it means.

"The capital knows I brought a harvest up from below, and that in doing so, I lost the spyglass. Maganwetar tracks everything. The loss of the glass wouldn't have escaped their attention. Artifacts from Magonia have fallen amongst the drowners before, and created undue interest from below. Those who dropped them were punished."

"Why couldn't you say you were recovering your daughter?" I asked her. "Are you ashamed of me?"

She looked at me in a way that said I'd missed every memo ever sent.

"Far from it, Aza. You are the answer to everything. And, simply, I could not," she said.

So—onward, into mystery.

Sometimes the air around us is warm, and other times there's ice in my hair, and Milekt complains and roosts in my chest, irritated. Milekt is a grumpy teacher. In between irritations, he drills me in Magonian alphabets, which are sung rather than spoken. I spend my time singing ABCs. I've reversed course and become three years old again. How am I supposed to learn a whole language in just a few weeks? How am I supposed to know everything everyone else knows?

I catch Dai staring at me, concentration in every line of his insanely beautiful face, but he looks away fast, like he got busted leaning sideways to get a look at my homework.

I sing Magonian ABCs silently in my head, and gaze out into the mist—there, a dotted line coming in from the horizon, above the clouds, up where the highest insects float. Bats. A whole colony of them.

They angle toward the boat and part in two when they meet the prow. Then they soar further up into the sky. One of the bats brushes against my cheek.

They remind me of hotel maids, these creatures. Industrious, rolling the evening into alignment, straightening it with small pulls, high voices chattering in a song that now I hear and a little bit understand.

Hunter, this bat informs me, its voice high, and I say it back as well as I can, proud that I'm starting to learn how to speak its language.

The little bat looks out into the night, at something I can't see. *Hunter*, it says again, looking at me. The batsail looks down at us. *Hunter*, it echoes. The ghost bird cries out from below.

I peer off into the bluish dark. We're drifting into a cloud of smoke. Not clouds—no, actual, thick acrid smoke.

There's something over there, something kind of roiling, something full of bright spots. A flash of lightning resolves into a long streak of white.

A creature.

Something with a lot of teeth and then it's gone.

I'm sprinting to Dai.

"What's that?" I ask, stabbing my finger urgently in the direction of the chaos.

He squints at the thing happening not that far from us. Not that far at all. He looks worried. Seeing his expression makes me feel I should be worried too.

"Stormsharks," he says, and he adjusts the knife in his belt.

Did he just say *stormsharks*? My inner nerd is elated. Can anything I will ever hear from now until the end of time sound cooler than stormsharks?

Dai steps protectively between me and the ship's rail.

"Um, do I need to freak out?"

"As long as they already have something, they're not coming for us," he says. He squints at the twisting mass of white dappled dark. There's something in the center of it, something I can't quite see. Our bearing takes us closer. Twenty feet, now fifteen.

A mast. Sails. A ship. And white flames all around it.

A high, high call from the ship's batsail. *Comrades*, it cries. *Distress! DISTRESS!*

A flash of lightning and I see things better suddenly. A pointed mouth, open wide, and a stormshark leaps up out of the sky and over the mast of the other ship. More distress calls.

"By the Breath!" Dai curses. "We have to intervene!" He takes off running. "Captain!"

Our batsail opens its wings and our Rostrae surge up, tugging lines, throwing hooks and ropes overboard and flying at the fray. Zal's on deck, shouting. She sees me and barks an order. "Belowdecks! You're not here!"

Then she's running too.

"Stations!" she shouts. "Squallwhales!" Through some sort

of amplifier, she screams out over the storm, into the space where the sharks are feeding and the smaller ship is being overwhelmed.

"SQUALLWHALES!"

Our whales come surging fast, storming harder than I knew they could, and suddenly there's a rush of rain over the little ship. It pours out of the clouds, and the whales sing ferociously.

"THIS IS CAPTAIN ZAL QUEL! PREPARE TO EVACUATE YOUR SHIP!"

There's a thud, a reverberating hard bash like a pileup on the freeway during rush hour—and then planks and ropes snake out from our crew and onto the deck of the injured ship.

Ignoring Zal, I peer over the railing. There's a captain there, but with a sudden weirdness, I realize that the captain is tied to her mast. There are bodies all over the deck below, and bags of grain, slit open and spilled.

What?

The fire I thought was on the ship itself suddenly looks to be off to the side, on a little boat, and contained. A moment of confusion on *Amina Pennarum*, and then—

"PIRATES!" Dai screams.

WHAM. A surge of Rostrae and Magonians up from below-decks of the little ship, all armed, all screaming.

A pirate Rostrae drops down in front of me, black mohawk, red streaks in his hair, and comes at me with a sword. I have only my mop handle in my hand, and I swing it hard.

I'm fighting like someone who knows how to fight, like this is what I was born to do. A surge of weird exuberance.

I've never been Aza the sick, only Aza the warrior.

I hit him in the side of the head, and there's a sickening crack and maybe I killed him, but then he's up again, and shrieking, transforming into a magpie, running and leaping off the edge of the ship into the air.

Screaming and screaling, my crew and theirs. The smell of fire and feathers. Our batsail is shrieking in fury and I look quickly up and see the pirate ship's sail clawing at ours, the two sails crossing, their wings scrabbling, the masts bending.

I hear myself shouting *"AMINA PENNARUM!"*

My crew shouts with me. I don't see Zal anywhere now. Only smoke and swords lashing through ropes, the contorted faces of my crew shifting into bird form, Rostrae rising up, talons out.

Dai's swinging an ax. Everywhere people are notching arrows into their bows, drawing knives.

I swing for the head of a tall figure who's appeared in front of me, a blurry-panicky-shaky swing.

It's Dai.

"Get down, Aza!" Dai shouts. "That's a mop! Idiot, get below!"

He swings at a pirate, and their blades whack together.

I'm paralyzed momentarily, and it's enough time to find myself face-to-face with another invader. He raises his dagger, but Jik grabs me by the hair and tugs me away just in time. The pirate's blade meets only air and before he can recover, there's a swoop and a screech.

Wedda. She leaps onto his shoulders, her beak tearing at him.

I retreat toward the hold, but the battle, the smoke, and the sounds of fighting, and killing and dying are too much. I hit the boat rail and scream as my feet fly out from beneath me. I catch the bar, panting. And I see them. The stormsharks, dead-eyed and made of power. Sizzling light. I swing my mop handle at one of them, crazily. It surges back at me and I find myself engaged with a crashing, slicing whiteness, the teeth so close, and each one of them gleaming and electric.

"Down below, Aza, now! Where it's safe!" Jik grabs me and hurls me back on deck. There's a flood of Magonians, a spray of red. A Rostrae cabin boy, oh god, his uniform slashed and burned at the edges of the cut, his bones showing and one of his wings hanging by a tendon.

"Fire!" I hear Zal shout, and from the bowels of *Amina Pennarum*, there's a boom. The ship shakes and the pirates scream in fury. All around us I see lightning, and our ship lurches again, and begins to tip.

I lose hold of the ladder and start to skid across the deck. I'm clawing at the boards, trying to get my fingers on something, but it's slippery with blood.

No one notices me, because this is a ship full of people who can fly, and half of them aren't touching the deck.

For a moment, I'm in the ambulance again. There's flashing light and a terrible sense of inevitability as *Amina Pennarum* tilts up on end.

I slip from the deck of the ship,

O

    F

      F

        A

          N

           D

D
O
W
N

into open sky.
I'm the dying girl again.

I'm dropping back to Icarus and his wings, back to me and Jason on the roof.

I'm dropping back to the grave I never occupied.

Air and storm, rain pouring, and me, arms out like a sky-diver, falling faster than I thought anyone could fall.

The air is slick, clouds are in my throat, and hail in my hair. I can't hear my own voice, and I can't hear Milekt, either, because he's not with me. He was with the rest of the canwr when we heard the distress calls.

No one knows where I am for the first time in a life of being watched, a life of buddy systems and care.

I'm alone.

I'm alone in the (how many?) minutes before I smash into the ground. I'm going to die now, and no one will know.

A flick of sharp dark fins circle suddenly below me.

Red eyes, hooked beak, long neck covered in rough pink scales, hungry and joyful. Its wings beat slowly, up and down, their tips peeking from the top of the clouds, and it starts to sing out, calling to others. It grabs my clothes in its talons, and my falling slows.

Dead thing, I hear, a whistle croak. *Dead thing falling.*

Vultures. Not sharks.

Another flaps into me, bumping my side with its beak, wings cutting at my skin. The first vulture drops me. *Dead animal*, the new one whistles, *dead, dead, sweet new dead blood, dead.*

There's a clattering cackle, birds surrounding me, looking into my eyes.

Dead thing! they shout, all their voices colliding with me. They're huge, and starving.

Then I hear a scream from above, a precise song with beats of silence and rattling percussion, tiny clacking beak closing and opening, guttural whistling of rage and relief.

Milekt. I turn my head and see him diving, a golden beacon.

SING! he screams, and I tap my chest, opening it for the first time without help. Milekt is in.

I open my mouth and because this is it, I give in.

I feel a surge up from my lungs into my vocal cords and instantly—harmony.

Millekt and I are singing together. With one voice, we chant this single two-pronged note. It's a howl of holding, it's a screamed lullaby, no sound I could ever make alone.

With the song, something changes. The air feels . . . denser.

I'm hanging from the wind now, like I'm floating in a swimming pool. There's tension in the air beneath me, the feeling of it supporting me—

I stop falling. My heart slows. Between my feet I see the earth still far below and I—I *hover.*

A rope with a hook attached comes spinning from above me. There's a violent snap as I'm grabbed by my jacket. Then they're reeling me in, yanking me up through the sky, jolting and tugging.

I'm heaved into a launch boat. It's Dai, sweating, swearing, bleeding.

"Oh my god," I say, gasping. That's all I've got. "Oh my god."

Dai grabs me and holds me tight, and I'm uncertain. I think for a moment I'm still singing, but I'm not. I'm crying and panicked, my heart pounding hard.

"I saw you fall," he says. "I wouldn't have gotten to you in time if you and Milekt hadn't sung. I thought you were gone."

I'm shaking and shaken. So's he. His arms wrap around me, and mine around him, and—

Rostrae all around us—the birds from my ship, led by Jik, some of them mid-transformation, their arms half feathered.

The spotted wings of the sparrow, the golden brown feathers of the eagle-woman. The hummingbird a buzzing dart.

My crew. They're saving me.

Dai takes my hand.

"You're pretty good with the mop handle," he says, and for a second, I'm laughing, and I don't know why. I'm shaking with adrenaline, wobbling and surging and I want to sing and fly and battle some more.

The Rostrae lift our launch boat up, through the fog and white again, through clouds scented with lightning, and into the shadow of the ship.

I look down at the deck of the *Amina Pennarum* as we rise up to its level. I look at Dai.

His face goes ashen. All over the deck, there are dead bodies, and when I look around, in disbelief, I see our crew has lost.

Blood and feathers and gore, and the pirates—now that I finally get a look at them, are all over the place—a group of ragged Magonians and Rostrae. They hurl ropes around us the moment our launch is in reach, and yank us down, and we don't have time to do anything. I'm grabbed by a big pirate, my arms wrenched behind my back, and Dai is too.

Zal's tied up, bloody-faced. I see her see me and take in a gasping breath of relief. Wedda's near her, and half the crew, many of them wounded.

"A trap," Zal spits at the pirate captain, whose back is to me. "It's against the laws of the sky to tempt a ship toward false rescue. You killed that captain and crew to summon me under their signal, and no doubt they were innocent. I'd expect as much from you."

The pirate turns toward Zal. She has long gray hair, twisted into ropes of knots, nothing like Zal's pattern. These are a whole other kind of complicated.

What would normally be the whites of her eyes are dark blue. The sides of her cheeks draw up as though there're strings attached to them, and maybe someone's trying to make her smile, but she's baring her teeth instead. She's thin in a way that looks hungry, not purposeful. Her face is sunken. She's wearing a tight uniform, but it's got tears and bare spots all over it.

"Where are you heading, Zal Quel? We heard rumors you brought something you'd lost up from below. You don't sail as invisibly as you imagine. We knew which quadrant you flew in, and the sky? It whispers. I heard a rumor among the corsairs that you'd brought a girl aboard," she says. "Where is she?"

Dai makes the mistake of glancing at me.

The pirate captain's head whips around. A blade is suddenly at my throat. I feel its edge. I'm holding my breath, panicking.

"Identify yourself," the captain of the pirates bellows into my face.

"DON'T," says Zal, nearly levitating with rage, and with something else too. Fear? "You owe her nothing. Keep silent, *Amina Pennarum* crew. If we plank-walk, we do it without words."

The pirate captain looks closely at me, examining me, and I feel like prey. Dizzy, tiny, skinny, unmuscled, and powerless.

She pokes me in the chin with her sword, and it doesn't tickle. It hurts.

"Who was that singing, girl? Was it you? This boy leapt off the ship midbattle to bring you up, and *Amina Pennarum*'s Rostrae saved you. You are not what you seem. No, I think you're much more."

I see Zal signaling with her eyes, willing me not to tell them anything.

"It was me singing," says Dai, and steps forward. The pirate captain looks at him dismissively.

"No male could sing so powerfully," she says.

One of our masts is broken. The batsail looks wild-eyed and furious, though it's uninjured, and it shrills at me without words. I hear an echoing wail up from belowdecks as well, the ghostly bird screaming. This ship, and everyone on it, is in danger.

I still don't even have a sword.

I swallow. Milekt rattles inside my chest, angry and still feeling the song we sang, just as I am. I take a step forward. I inhale, and I feel Milekt opening his beak too—

Dai jabs me in the ribs with his elbow.

"Yes. You're right. I'm the Captain's Daughter," I blurt, instead of singing. I see Zal struggling against her bonds.

The pirate looks at me. I can't get a read on every emotion that flits across her face, but there's relief. Sorrow. Anger. Guilt.

"Of course you are. Aza Ray, daughter of Zal," she says simply. "So the rumors were true. You're why we're here."

The pirate captain seems weirdly more familiar the more I look at her, and I shudder.

"Captain Ley Fol. I left you among the drowners, long ago."

Zal shouts from across the deck, "Stay away from her, murderer! Betrayer!"

"Betrayer? I turned my back on your insanity," says the pirate.

"You turned me in," Zal spits. She's frenzied, and there's still a sword to my throat. I can't sing, though Milekt is battering me from the inside, raging. What the hell is going on?

"I've no more love for Maganwetar than you do, but you'd have brought disaster on us all."

Zal manages to loosen her bonds, slightly, glowering with fury. The pirates around her step forward in warning, but Ley nods to them. "Let her speak."

Not that they're going to keep her silent.

"You stole my child!" Zal screams at her.

"I *saved* your child. I was ordered to kill her, Zal. Do you think anyone else would have spared her? The capital knew what your plans were. And they knew her power—"

Kill *me*? And "my power," again, "my power." Everyone talks about my power. WHAT power?!

Ley continues. "—but I wasn't going to murder a baby. I kept her safe. Whatever they say about Captain Ley Fol, I never murdered a child. Which other captains can say that? Can *you*?"

Zal steps forward again. Ley's pirates grab her arms.

"You hid my daughter from me for fifteen years!" Zal shouts. Her eyes are full. Even as she's shouting, she's weeping too.

Ley Fol turns to me.

"If Maganwetar had known you were alive, they'd have ended you. I paid a Breath to put you in a skin and substitute you for one of the drowners they were bringing up. I thought to bring you back to Magonia when things were calm, but the capital's memory is long." She looks harder at me. "If you are what you were, I gave my career for a reason. If not? The fates are cruel."

She turns back to Zal.

"And so you've found her. I trust this isn't merely a sentimental recovery for you."

"I love my daughter," Zal cries, indignant. "I've never stopped loving her."

Ley nods at the pirates, and one of them gags my mother. She struggles, still shouting into the gag.

Ley looks at me and sighs.

"You should be dead, Aza Ray. How is it you live? How did the drowners keep you from collapsing?"

"I don't know," I say. And it's true, I don't know anything.

"That song. The one that saved you just now. You sang that same song on this ship when you were small, and it gave your mother ideas. It made her think you were the one to deliver us from all our hardship. Sing it again, little one. Show us what your mother wishes to do with you." The expression on her face is hungry, searching.

"I don't really sing," I say. "I don't know how. I don't know what you're looking for, but it's not on this ship."

"You do," Dai whispers from behind me. "Sing the way you were singing when I caught you."

I feel Milekt inside my lung, rattling, scrabbling. He wants to sing too. Everything feels slow motion.

Caru echoes from belowdecks. The notes of the ghost bird echo through my head, looping around me, raging against this ship, this life. I feel that song almost like I'm the one singing it. There's a hum in my ears.

One of the pirates is at our batsail, tracing its wings with a sword. It makes a horrible high-pitched noise of pain.

I feel a jolt. That's *my* sail. I realize, suddenly, that's my *friend*. And no matter what Zal told me before, it feels pain. It's being hurt.

I squeak out a single pitiful note of Magonian song.

Ley looks at me, her head tilted, her face tense.

"Perhaps your song isn't what it was. Perhaps I might have left you with your mother after all."

I make another peep, and she starts to turn away.

"Her time among the drowners has changed her, or we were wrong in the first place. She's not the same kind of singer Zal was. Take *Amina Pennarum*'s grain," she orders her crew, her voice strangely sad. "Take their stores. And sink them. Put Zal in the brig."

Does she think I'm weak? Does she think I really can't do anything?

Are they going to kill me? Will they kill us all?

One of the pirates grabs me by the arm. I throw myself backward hard, but I'm not strong enough. He marches me toward the stern. Milekt shrills inside me and the ghost bird calls out. The sky below me, and my toes, one, two, three up the deck rails, lurching, struggling, hanging over open sky, and I'm thinking, like this? After all this? After I saved myself, after Dai saved me?

NO.

This time it actually comes out of my mouth, a raw screal, a loud whistling note. Milekt joins in with me, high and furious as I feel.

Something changes, fast, a whipping energy coming out of my mouth and into the sky.

The horizon goes from blue to black and the air feels dense. There are raindrops over the pirate's ship, for a moment, before the raindrops become something else. I see Ley look up, her strange eyes flashing.

The sound coming out of me is nothing like a cough, nothing even in the category of a song, but some kind of bird-of-prey roar, shredding my throat, pulsating my fingers, and Milekt beneath it, singing inside my voice, amplifying me, and making me stronger.

The sky roils black, and full of fast wind, lightning sparking out of every raindrop. There's a weight in everything.

People have started to cover their heads and their faces.

Sand starts to pour from the sky, from the clouds that surround their ship, wrapping around the pirates, making them stagger. A rain of pebbles. Then larger rocks, and people are screaming and dodging.

The air gets muddy between me and Ley, who's yelling orders at her crew. I see the enemy ship tilt, lurching up onto one end.

Zal is staring at me with a kind of eager joy.

There's something I learned from Jason last year. *Sous rature.* If you need a certain word to communicate something, but that word happens to have years of baggage, and you want to get rid of the baggage it comes with, you cross it out, but use it anyway. Some people do it like this: ~~love~~.

With this song, I write over the place where the old Aza was. I'm not that person. I'm ~~Aza~~. I scream a song, punk rock without a microphone, the kind that makes boulders fall from the heavens.

Transforming rain into rock.

Destroying everyone who can hear it.

I'm avalanching the sky.

And I have no idea how I'm doing it.

A rock the size of my head lands on our attackers' deck and splinters the boards.

I sing something that unbinds my crew's hands, something I don't even know. I move rope and chain. I'm not doing it on purpose. It's unfolding from the song. I don't know how it's happening, but everything's shifting, whirring, surging around me and Milekt.

Like I'm in a movie,

like I'm not me,

like I'm someone I never imagined—bigger, stronger, and fearless. I grab the pirate captain's sword and twist it to point at her chest.

Milekt trills in my lung, his own solo song of triumph. I

open my mouth and let loose a whoop.

I'm standing in the center of the deck, this time with a sword, not a mop.

I'm the Captain's Daughter. I'm everything they thought I was, and more.

"On your knees," I tell Ley. I nod at Jik and she ties the pirate's wrists. My crew moves quickly to disarm the rest of the pirates, and suddenly, *Amina Pennarum* has won.

Zal is free of her bonds, and laughing, looking completely exhilarated. Her shirt is torn. I can see a long scar running down the center of her chest. From what?

"Surrender, Ley!" she shouts in triumph. "This sky isn't yours to command."

But Ley doesn't surrender. She stands, bound, looking defiantly at Zal.

"Where were you heading, Zal? To the north? Breaking every vow you made? You and I both know you want a new world. Maganwetar won't forgive you twice. They'll take you for treason, and this time you'll *both* be executed—"

Zal looks sharply at Dai, and he moves quickly, gagging Ley with his scarf.

"Who else knows we have her?" Zal says, looking around at the other pirates. "From where did the rumor come? Who spoke to you?"

They just look at Ley. All the pirates are on our deck, bound.

"If you will not answer, you'll share her fate."

They remain silent. Zal nods at me.

"Sink that ship, and its pitiful cargo," Zal says.

"What do you mean?" I ask her.

"Sing it," she says. "Sing the sky into sand, Aza. Milekt knows the song."

Milekt sings a new note and I follow his lead. We sing rocks onto the chains fastening the other ship's bat to their mast. We can all see the links breaking until finally they're gone.

Their batsail stretches its wings, and for the first time I wonder how batsails end up tethered to these ships in the first place. The pirate sail spreads its wings and billows out and is gone, gliding out into the dark as the empty ship sags in the sky.

When I finally turn to look at Zal, I see her standing beside Ley, staring down at her, a hawk studying a rabbit. Except that they're *both* birds of prey.

Milekt and I sing heavy air into the pirate ship, and without its batsail, it drops. I sing sand until I can't see it anymore. Until all it can do is crash onto the world below.

At this height, there'll be little left when it lands. What will the humans call it? Asteroid? Meteorite? There's so much they don't know.

I stagger a little. My knees are majorly weak. I look around. Everyone's staring at me, the Rostrae and the Magonian crew alike, Zal and Dai and Jik, everyone.

"Take Ley to my cabin," Zal says, and two Rostrae carry the other captain down the ladder and into the belowdecks. She doesn't even struggle. She just looks at me evenly, and so does everyone else, my whole crew. The rest of the bound pirates go too, into the brig.

There's blood on the deck and holes in the ship and prisoners in the hold and I wonder if I've done something massively wrong, something that I can't—that no one can ever—take back.

And then I hear it. Streaks of bird voice, long trills and screams.

Jik's grinning and Dai's shouting in triumph, and with a great noise our own batsail spreads its wings and we push out hard, our squallwhales singing us a storm.

Cheers and shouting as the crew sets about making our ship whole again. And I'm glowing with what I just did, the craziness of it, the confusion, the ~~Aza~~ of it.

I'm dizzy, and so's Milekt. I can feel him inside my chest.

THIS, then.

This is what everyone meant when they said *sing*. This is what they meant about power. Dai's hand is in mine. I don't know how it got there, but it sends a pulse through me. Zal takes my other hand and raises it up. We stand there, on the deck of our ship, surrounded by our crew and I'm maybe someone who's finally been found. Dai looks at me.

"Together, Aza," he says.

"Together," Zal says.

"Together," I whisper, because this is nothing I've ever felt. The batsail sings out to me, and Milekt, in my chest, sings too. The Rostrae look at me, and the Magonian crew nods in approval.

I turn my head and look at Dai. I'm not sure what all this means, not even sure what I did.

"You did *everything*," he says, reading my mind. And he grins, and squeezes my hand hard.

For the first time in my entire life, I have power. More than power. I feel like I belong. Like this is my ship.

Like this is my country.

Like this is my destiny.

There's the cry of the ghost again, all around me. I glance at Zal, but she's already walking away. The ship is sailing noticeably faster, and I look up to see Rostrae joined with the batsail to pull us at a greater speed.

We fly.

CHAPTER 17

{JASON}

It took a lot of walking in small, frustrated circles after I heard Aza's voice at her funeral, after something fell out of the clouds, but I found it.

It's here in front of me right now. Under the papers. I'm waiting until the moms leave the house, and I can look at it again for the millionth time.

It's a spyglass.

It's old. As in, incredibly. It's made of dented brass and scarred wood. You can't see through it, because it has a lens cap or something, made of harder wood. It fell a long way. The cap is smashed in place over the glass, and I can't get it off.

It's scratched all over with strange characters, in a language I haven't been able to find any kind of translation of.

Yeah, you heard me. I can't get a translation. Not even a wildly erroneous one from someone lurking online.

So there's that.

In some of the illuminated medieval manuscript stuff, which I ended up wandering around on the Harvard Library's site, there are bird people, and other kinds of people too. Angels from that period, particularly the ones that deal with crops and weather tend to be human-looking, but feathery. And then there's is another section of angels from this period who are just . . . blue.

Not that this is any indication of Magonia, really. No one says "Magonia" in those margins.

But there are similarities.

The history of humans is 73 percent people talking about the weather in freaked-out ways. The discussion of Magonia is basically that: *Where did that storm come from? Oh my god, the clouds. The clouds are crazy.*

Jacob Grimm—not Mr. Grimm, my English teacher, but the fairy-tale guy—talks about a country where people sell the wind. Selected quotes (I'm being kind and not making you scroll through the thousands of pages of information available on the issue):

"The witches of Norway . . . tie up wind and foul weather in a bag and, at the proper moment, undo the knots, exclaiming 'wind, in the devil's name' and then a storm rushes out, lays waste to the land, and overturns ships at sea. . . .

"A violent thunderstorm lasted so long that a huntsman on the highway loaded his gun with a consecrated bullet and shot it off into the middle of the blackest cloud; out of it a naked female fell dead to the ground and the storm blew over in a moment. . . ."

And this is the kicker: "Sometimes the aim of sorcery is not so much to destroy the produce as to get possession of it, to carry it off the field, either to one's own garner, or that of a favorite."

So we're talking stealing crops. From the stories, the thing in common is that anyone floating around in skyships up there is hungry. That makes sense. I mean, what the hell would they be eating up there? Gnats?

The crop-destroying storms plotted by my app seem to stay in most places for several days, and then move on.

There was an enormous storm in Iowa a couple of weeks ago, and that storm was one of the few where people actually reported loss of crops. At the end of it, some farmer's cornfield was stripped, like locusts or crows had taken it down. Each cob bare. The farmer mentioned seeing an eagle that day, right before the storm came in.

The strange reports and stories continue to move along the trajectory I plotted for them with such accuracy that I can nearly predict where the next one will be. So what's across the sea, to the northeast of America? That's where it looks to me this thing is heading. No crops on water. The islands out there aren't fertile—just rock outcroppings in the middle of the ocean.

I'm not pretending this—my being right about everything— isn't causing me to have a pretty major existential crisis. I might be reading a few philosophers. I might be losing my way just slightly. Eve and Carol might have reasons to be worried about this whole situation.

I keep waiting for Aza to fall out of the sky and into my arms. I know I sound unbelievably sexist saying that, but I keep wrongfully imagining catching her like a fireman outside a window.

Just thinking this way makes me want to bang my head against the floor.

If she were here, listening to me, she'd be puking right now because I'm losing all my dignity.

But. I can't text her, can't email her. Can't call her.

This is sucking, Az.

~~I hate it. I'm scared that maybe I'm missing some kind of giant point, something everyone else knows, that I'm trying to hunt down a dead girl who doesn't even exist anymore, a dead girl who's alive only as a figment of my Vivid Imagination, like Aza always said she had. Me and Aza, Vivid Imaginers. Maybe I should just be taking myself to her grave, and sitting down beside it, and saying, for once and for all, good-bye.~~

But I don't think she's dead. I don't think I'm crazy.

I have something in front of me on my screen, a little scrap of video that some girl in Maine took with her phone.

It's about a second long, the important part. It's a ship. Just a part of a ship, with portholes and full rigging, sailing out of a cloud and then disappearing.

It checks out with my charts, the weather conditions. Other people saw something, and there was a jokey news story about illusions. Sky mirages and long winters. Newscasters made fun of the people in Maine, saying they were drinking too much. There was an essay in the *Onion* that spoofed the whole thing pretty accurately, a bunch of drunk people looking up at the sky and seeing ships. Exactly what people said in the 1890s.

I saw something out Aza's window, the day she died. I saw a mixed-up flock of birds on her lawn—majorly out of season. I heard something in the sky on the day of her funeral, and ~~I don't think I'm losing it~~ I'm not losing it.

After Aza's funeral, after her voice coming out of the sky, I remembered the helicopter. Of course.

I know what you're thinking. *Pretty stupid, Jason, to not think of it before,* right?

Yep, pretty dumb, because there's a black box.

That's a new thing for helicopters. Not all of them have them, but life flights get sent into insane weather.

Today, I got what I needed, through some of my more reliable and illegal back channels, I had it emailed to my most secret account.

I hit play on the helicopter audio. It's all communications with the hospital at first, talking about where exactly the life flight needs to go to pick us up. I can picture it in the most horrible way. All over again, us in the ambulance, Aza beside me.

The audio shifts to the medic in the ambulance itself, updating the copter on Aza's condition.

I have to move the cursor. I'm afraid I'm going to hear the rattling, terrified sound she made at the end, and I can't hear it again.

A second later, I'm listening to something else, the flight, the pilot, and the medic in the copter with him, talking about the storm.

"Whoa. This came out of nowhere," the pilot says.

"Global warming," says the medic. "We okay?"

"Yeah, it's good, we're fine," he says.

There's a moment.

"Wait. Did you see that?"

"What?"

"What the"—jumbled sounds—"is that a—"

"Ropes? Oh my god—"

And then there's a sound, a huge, screeching ripping of metal, smashing of glass, crush and tear and screaming from both of them, and what they say, what they try to say is—

Yeah, no, because I can't. I can't listen to their last words. It's too horrible.

A moment later, there's a huge explosion. Singing and shrieking. The sound of flapping wings.

Birds.

Someone says, in the faintest and most scratchy voice:

"What are you?"

That's all there is to the audio. I keep listening to it over and over again. Between the first talk about the storm and the crash, maybe two minutes.

I have to give that a moment. I have to sit with it, because. All of it. The sounds of people dying. The sounds of birds. Last things said before these poor people fell out of the sky, tumbling down, on fire.

The pilot and medic, their families don't have this. Only me, and the people I got it from. It wasn't just the two of them that died, but the medic from our ambulance too. He ran out trying to flag them down, and they never found his body.

I'm sitting at my desk, not crying, but—

Yeah, I am. I'm crying.

What are you?

That was the night Aza died. Five days later, I heard her voice coming out of the sky.

No, not paranoid, not looping, no. Not conspiracy, not obsessive, wrong notions in my head.

I'm sure, if this hit the internet, some people would say the pilot and medic were confused by the storm, air pressure, and lack of oxygen.

That "*ropes*" was not really what they said at all.

But if not "ropes," what?

Out my window there's suddenly a lot of wind and rain. I get up and shut it. Freezing.

What are you? What are you? The voice repeats and repeats in my head—when the doorbell rings.

Carol or Eve, forgetting keys. It's almost always Eve. Her brain gets snarled on things and then any hope of not forgetting is over. Not that I'm not exactly the same. Lots of not being picked up at school in my childhood. I spent afternoons at Aza's. Fine by me.

I close the tab with the black box audio, just in case, and make my way to the front door.

Someone rings again, and then bangs. Not Eve. If it was Eve, she'd be outside my window, tapping the glass and performing "face of the forgetful mother" for me.

I have a moment of nervousness. I'm doing the kind of hack stuff that if it gets traced back, causes you to be investigated, locked up, and/or sued into oblivion.

I peer out the side window, but I can't see a police cruiser. No flashing lights. Of course, if it was federal, there wouldn't be. I scan the trees across the street just in case. Lots of wind out there. Blowing.

I worry about myself for a second.

The person hits the door again, hard. All I can see is a shoulder in a blue coat, and a little bit of black hair in a ponytail.

Calm down, Jason. Maybe someone's trying to give the neighborhood religion.

Have you thought about hell lately?

Nope, I'll say. Everything else, yeah, but not hell. Or not exactly.

I unlock the door. I open it.

Aza Ray Boyle is standing on my front steps.

CHAPTER 18

{AZA}

Zal wakes me, shaking my hammock. "Daughter," she says.
"On deck."

It's not like I'm asleep. I've been thudding with exhaustion
since the pirates and the song—but then I started thinking
about what got said on deck. And how many gaps there were to
fill in between the words Ley and Zal spoke and what I know.

You and I both know you want a new world.

I trust this is not merely a sentimental recovery for you.

The one to deliver us from all our hardship.

What? My brain won't let it go.

Zal takes me to the wheel, and we look out across a star-
filled sky.

"You must be wondering what happened today," she says,
understatement of the year.

"I know what happened," I say. "I defended the ship from
pirates who wanted to kill me. What I don't know is why."

Zal looks at me, and smiles unexpectedly.

"In good time, Aza, you and I will have no secrets. The
pirate Ley Fol was a surprise, and not a good one. Her presence
in these skies means that knowledge of you has gotten out into

Magonia. The Breath I brought aboard to bring you up from below, perhaps. I thought he could be bribed, but one can't wholly trust them. They're monsters."

I take a moment, imagining what the hell a monster might be to Zal. To Magonia. Visions of tentacles and Godzilla, visions of teeth. Those stormsharks were monsters to me. The Breath are something different. And, seemingly, more feared.

"But *what* are they?"

"They can walk among the drowners. They can be paid for their services, but they're nothing good."

Have I ever seen her look frightened before? It makes me nervous.

"There are things here that needn't be called by name. This is a new world for you, and for us, with you in it. You're the center. You're something Magonia needs."

Some*thing*. Not someone.

"So what am *I*?" I ask Zal.

She grins, showing her sharp teeth, her hair boiling up around her collar.

"You, Aza, are my daughter. You were born to sing the elements into submission. You inherited that song from me. Though my voice was taken, we have yours."

She hesitates, then: "There was a time I could sing the way you can."

She opens the neckline of her jacket and shows me the dark, ugly scar down the center of her chest. It's not just a scar. It's worse than that. The place where her canwr would go has been welded shut. It's a harsh dark line of indigo skin, twisted and gnarled.

"I was punished for trying to change Magonia with my song,

to shift us from dependence on the drowners. The officials of Maganwetar broke my bond to my canwr to stop me. That won't happen to you and Milekt. We're stronger now, all of us."

For the first time I really hear what isn't there. I can't believe I didn't before. Her voice is so raw because it's solo. She has no canwr. Her bond's broken.

That's why Caru screams. It must be. Caru is Zal's heartbird.

"Is he—was he—"

Zal glances sideways. "You've heard him singing," she says, reading my mind.

"The crew says the ship is haunted by him," I say. "They say he's dead."

"He sings nonetheless," says Zal, but something in her face, something in her movements makes me wonder.

"When they broke your bond, did it make him insane?" I ask. "Or was he already that way?"

"You've heard the remnant of our song," she says, her face grief-stricken. "I thought I could heal him, but I could not." She shakes herself. "Nothing can be done about that now. All we can do is move forward.

"Ley and I, when we were young as you, read the stories of an old Magonia, free from our relationship with drowners. Those stories are not fantasy, but history. I believed in them. I thought she did too. She lied."

Something occurs to me.

"So," I say, "why? Why'd they punish you? What was your crime?"

The look in her eyes startles me. I feel something, and for a second, I don't know what it is. Sympathy? Belief?

"Telling the truth," she says.

"About what?"

Dai appears from belowdecks, swinging himself around aft.

Zal nods in his direction. "Dai was hatched on a Magonian ship settlement largely forgotten by the authorities. Once they'd had plenty of food, grain from below, their own small ships for forage, but when the drowner world began to dry up and they needed assistance, Maganwetar denied their rations. His people's ships degraded into splinters. Their batsails died of old age. There were no squallwhale where he came from. There was no rain at all. His people starved slowly, as below them, drowners starved too. They could see drowner cities burning beneath them, and the green going to brown.

"Their Rostrae fled, taking flight for better forage, nesting in the rigging of official vessels. Dai's father went on a mission, elected by the ship settlement council. Dai was seven. He was with his father in the launch when they becalmed. They drifted, hungry and parched, desperate for water.

"Dai's father died trying to let himself down from the launch and into an oasis. His body fell into the desert, his bones picked clean by vultures."

Dai works nearby, and I notice his arm. A long scar runs its length, something I'd seen but not understood. Everyone in Magonia seems to have scars.

"Vultures. Similar to the ones that tried to get you." Zal grins halfheartedly. "Dai was thin, and he mostly escaped predators, but when he returned home, his world was broken into pieces, everyone skin and bones, everyone dying. His mother. His brother. His sister. Starved by the drowners, who'd broken their own land and scorched their own earth. And forgotten by a capital who cared nothing for them."

I take another look, longer this time, at the Magonian boy—my commander, my taskmaster since boarding *Amina Pennarum*. Suddenly, he seems like only that to me—a boy. Maybe not as strong or sure as he pretends he is.

"I found him," Zal says, following my gaze. "This ship was hunting for *you*, Aza, searching the skies of the world, when we happened through Dai's section. It hadn't occurred to me that you might have been dropped undersky. I sailed through his drifting ship settlement, and docked my own ship, traveling by jolly boat through the empty skyways.

"Dai saw *Amina Pennarum* and stowed away on her. Days later, I found him in our hold, eating a handful of corn. My heart aches at the pain Dai has known. No creature—human, Rostrae, or Magonian—should have to suffer that way.

"I taught Dai how to sing," Zal continues. "And I spent years reading the history of Magonia in eggshells, hatchlings that perished before they could fly, abandoned ships, skypictures and squallwhale song—"

This gives me an image of Zal I wasn't expecting. A Zal kind of in the same category as me, in the library, reading and reading.

"I voyaged through the parts of the sky that went bad first. I watched the heavens toss with winds we'd never seen before, whipping storms we had nothing to do with creating. Below us, the seas flooded over drowner coastlines, and crops died.

"They willfully destroy the earth they live on, and in doing so, they destroy us," says Zal.

They.

What she means is all of humanity.

I try to think of Magonia as I would've when I lived as a

human. A parasitic kingdom feeding off of earth's crops?

But then I imagine Dai, tiny, hungry, in a boat all alone.

I think of my family in their car, driving from place to place, spitting toxic things up into the sky and spilling them down into the ground.

Down there, cities glow out of the dark, red and green and white. The whole planet's made of cars trying to get somewhere.

I feel like I was blind when I was down there, and now?

"What do you want from me?" I ask.

"Look," Zal says.

I follow her finger, pointing into the dark. A mass of clouds that, as we draw near, resolve into something else. Zal stands beside me, her wiry weight against my shoulder. She points to a place darker than the rest.

Our pod of squallwhales, I realize suddenly, isn't with us. "Where are—"

"They won't come here," Dai says, approaching us and once again breaking into my thoughts. "They await us on the other side. Look, Aza. Look what the drowners did with their poisons."

Dai aims a light at the mass, and then I see it. It moves a fluke, and then another. A small eye, rolling in the giant squall-whale's head. There's a wound on its skin, dripping from its tear duct to its jaw. There are wounds all over the squallwhale, not the wounds of weapons, but of something else. Burns. Bleeding.

It tries to sing, but it can't. I watch as from its blowhole comes something red. I watch it fall, and I know exactly what this rain is called on earth.

The squallwhale keens and rolls in agony. It blows a storm from its blowhole, toxic red and black, shifting to clear with an oily shimmer. I've never seen a squallwhale storm-sing with anything but joy before. The sight makes me feel sick. I have to swallow bile.

"There are many of these, all over Magonia. New ones are born daily, making storms of poison," Zal says.

I look into the squallwhale's eye, and want to cry. *Sing*, it says, looking at me. *Nightsong. Deathsong.* As I watch, several more wounded whales appear and swim past us, their bodies glowing with wrongness.

They can't even talk to one another. Most of the noise they make is just jumble and screaming.

Milekt starts up a song from inside my chest, and what comes with that song is fury. It shakes me.

As Milekt's song swells, my momentary thoughts of all the good people on earth, of Eli and my parents and Jason, get tangled up with a rage that makes me clench my fists. I feel Dai beside me, vibrating, too, and in his chest, Svilken sings.

"What are we really doing?" I ask Zal at last. "Where are we going?"

She looks hard at me, staring into my eyes. "The drowners are destroying us, and so are the policies of Maganwetar." She pauses before continuing. "The capital's position is that Magonia has no choice but to live hidden from those below us. Maganwetar is not the same as most of Magonia. It's a hungering mass of citizens, scavenging the crops below it wherever it moves. It takes its tithe from whichever ships acquire the best forage. There's more food in Maganwetar than its citizens need, but the capital demands the best of everything, and its leavings are the bruised and the moldering, the shriveled and the withered. Drowners starve and poison even their own people. Yet Maganwetar remains locked in the past when it comes to our policy."

"It's no longer possible to follow the official position," Dai says. "The drowners destroy our skies, our people, and our air."

Humans don't know about Magonia. They don't know what they're doing, a part of me wants to shout. But I'm looking at this giant animal singing acid rain. Humas know about acid rain but do nothing to prevent it.

"The capital believes we need drowner crops," Zal says. "But it's a myth. There is another way."

I can't imagine a miracle that will fix all the burnt, broken places on the face of the earth.

"How?" I ask.

"We need you to retrieve something," Zal says. "The drowners put it beneath rocks, in a place they thought it would be safe. We need you to turn those rocks to water. You and Dai. Together you'll be strong enough. Then, we'll bring it up into the sky."

"What is it?"

"Aza," she says. "If the drowners starve themselves, we starve with them. If they destroy our skies, we die with them. We must take back what belongs to us. You'll help us steal something that was stolen from us, long ago." Zal smiles and it pulls me in. "The drowners have our plants underground, in a hidden vault in the North."

The crew's been cautious with me, I realize now. But there are a lot of stories about the Magonian epiphytes, because apparently they were magic food, enough for all of the skydwellers. Did some kind of bad bargain with earth take them away?

"Why doesn't Magonia just negotiate with Earth?" I say, and Dai looks at me and laughs.

I imagine a delegation of Magonians landing on the lawn of

the White House, asking to talk to the president about trade. It's pretty obvious that said delegation would get shot out of the sky before it even landed.

Okay, yeah. I get that.

"There can be no more wishing for our people, no more relying on others to do the right things. Do you see what you can do? For me? For us?" Zal taps her chest, right over her scar.

I look up at Zal. "A plant," I say.

She nods. "A plant, yes. And much more. You, Aza, will save your people."

Even though a small part of my brain is muttering about how no deal is ever simple, the angry song Milekt sang is still rattling around in there, and it drowns everything else.

"Yes," I say to Zal.

"Do you swear to it?" she says, and puts out her hand, blue and callused.

I offer my own hand, but I'm not prepared when she slashes my palm with a tiny silver knife. Inky blood, and pain, a searing sense of flood. I stagger back, but she presses her own palm to mine, her own cut.

"We already share blood, daughter," she says. "But this is ritual. We're vowed to our mission now. Swear it."

Our blood drips onto the deck as the pod of injured squall-whales swim slowly past us.

"I swear," I say, watching them go, listening to their broken, breathless song. Dai stands beside me, his hand on my back. Somewhere deep in the ship I hear Caru call, just once, a long wail in the dark.

"Daughter," Zal says, and kisses my forehead.

I close my eyes and for just a moment, I'm on earth again.

My mom putting me to bed, keeping me safe, keeping me alive every night.

Then I open my eyes and it's cold wind all around me, and the fading song of the sick squallwhales as we sail away from them and into the night.

I'm at Dai's cabin the next morning, pounding on the door.
He opens it, looking like I woke him up.

Does he ever wear a shirt? He stretches his arms. I try not to
be taken in by the look of him, but it's useless.

This guy jumped off the boat to save me from vultures and
pirates.

Um, you were already in the process of saving yourself,
my brain points out, but I'm not in the mood for logic.

Dai cared. I can trust him. I want to trust *someone*.

"So, I'm not just a normal Magonian singer. My song is different, right?"

"What do you think?" he says, and grins.

"And according to Zal, according to Wedda, according to
everyone, you're supposed to sing with me," I tell him, trying
to keep my voice under control. "That's supposedly part of your
official job description."

"It is," he says.

"How come you never do?"

"Because you weren't ready."

"How do you know that?"

"Because you never did what you did yesterday," he says, fairly reasonably.

His eyebrow goes up in a way that reminds me of—

I imagine Jenny Green ringing Jason's doorbell, looking at him with sympathy in the wake of my death, and him answering the door muttering pi.

No. Jason wouldn't actually want Jenny Green.

(He might.)

He wouldn't.

Dai must see the messed-up look on my face.

"Are you okay?" he asks, and he puts his hand on my shoulder. The warmth of it makes its way through my jacket, and it apparently doesn't matter that I just got derailed by sad; I feel my heart pounding as though I'm singing all over again.

I'm standing here with a boy who lost his own family, in a totally different way than I lost mine. Who am I to be sad? My family on earth is still alive. His isn't.

"Fine," I say, even though I have to grab my own fingers and hold my own hand to keep from touching him. It's such a want that it's almost not a want at all, but a need, like the need for water or food.

I try in vain to swallow down the guilt and the weirdness and the want and every single thought except about what's in front of me. Dai shrugs on his shirt and jacket, giving me so much view of his back, his shoulders, his profile, I have to actually shut my eyes.

"You're shy," he says, reappearing beside me, and he laughs.

"You weren't wearing enough," I say.

"Drowner," he says, but for the first time, it's in a teasing voice.

"Exhibitionist," I say.

"What's that?"

"Someone who has a compulsive need to show other people his attractiveness," I say. Primly.

Then I curse internally.

I'm awkward because of exhaustion. Because of the insanity of yesterday coupled with the captain's ghost bird calling me in my sleep—calling for the sky, calling for freedom.

But it's dead, I remind myself. A dead thing is already free.

Something else kept me awake as well. I felt the power of my song and there was no doubt it could go further. That it could be stronger. There was MORE to it.

Whatever more there is, I want it.

"You're the first mate," I say. "You're supposed to be professional."

"And you're beautiful, Aza Ray Quel, Daughter of Zal, singer of sky into stone," he says. "Even if you do need singing lessons. And lessons in everything else too."

Then he's past me, out of his cabin and up the ladder before I can say anything at all.

I climb behind him. The inside of my skin's too hot, and my brain's too small. My ears burn, and my heart pounds. Beautiful?

I hoist myself up on deck, and distract by looking at an airplane, far down, underneath our squallwhales. *Aza Ray,* I think. *Aza Ray, your life is so gigantically not what you thought it was going to be.* Your life is awesome, in the old sense. As in, full of awe. Though, um, the old word for "awesome" was actually . . . "awful." A factoid from a certain person creeps in. I shake my head fast to rid myself of things I can't think about.

"You have to play by the rules," Dai tells me, sitting down

on the deck beside me. "This isn't about you. This is about Magonia. You're just a piece of it."

"Then what are the rules?"

"We're bonded to sing together. I'm your ethologidion."

"You know I don't know what that word means," I say,
because he uses it with a tone meant, I swear, to drive me crazy.

"Your partner. You have your skills and I have mine, and
they're compatible. I've never heard of anyone singing the way
you can, except for Zal, and that was before I knew her. She
trained me to complement your strengths."

I can't decide if this is creepy or cool.

"I don't need a partner. Zal doesn't sing with one," I say.

He snorts, like I'm completely clueless.

"Zal can't sing at all anymore," he says. "But I'm here and
alive only because of her. If she breaks Maganwetar's laws, I'll
break them with her. We're on the same mission. Are you?"

"Yes," I say, my voice wobbling for reasons I can't quite figure out.

"Then we have to learn how to sing together. I think we're
halfway there." He runs his fingertip down my cheek, and I turn
away. "Tell me you don't want to sing with me, Aza Ray."

"What if I said no?" I ask, just to check.

"Things aren't disposable here the way they are undersky.
There, they throw things away. Here, we keep them forever."

I consider him for a moment and think—

{Forever.}

Then—

~~(I { } you more than {{{{{{ }}}}}}.)~~

I stare out at the sky, the way I made it hold me up yesterday. I wasn't flying. I was floating.

"I conquered an invading ship," I say.

"You did," he says. "But were you sure you could? I wasn't. You need to learn how to control it. I'm a focus for you. A magnifying glass in front of the sun. My song will make yours stronger."

"So in this analogy I'm the sun?" I say.

He doesn't smile.

"Yes," he says. He takes my chin in his fingers and looks at me. I look back.

His eyes are long-lashed and very, very dark. He leans in and I want to laugh because it's so ridiculous, it's so *stupid*.

(The last time I was this close to a boy's face I—I don't think about that. Nope. I don't.)

"Like this," Dai says, and sings a note into my mouth, very quietly, more of a breath than a note.

I pause for a second, shaky, and then sing a note back. We're both without our birds, so it's not official.

It is, however, totally enough. I sing my note in Magonian, the note that means "*rise*." Dai joins in with a low note, this undercurrent, which is part "rise" and part "more."

I feel my heart start pounding again, and I can see his pulse in the side of his neck, beating nearly in time with mine.

His note gets louder, and mine does too. We increase our volume together, and as we do, I notice that my hand is on his chest, where his heart is, near where Svilken should be, but isn't.

I yank my hand back, feeling scalded.

I'm blushing severely. I don't know how that looks on Magonian skin. Dai smiles at me, and hums a different note. He puts out his fist, and knocks once on my breastbone. My chest opens for Milekt, which startles me totally. It feels intensely intimate, Dai initiating this. Milekt flies down and in.

I rap as coolly as I can on Dai's chest, and it, too, opens like a window. His canwr flies down from her perch, too, and into his lung.

He's as awkward as I am, suddenly.

"We're in this together," Dai says. "Zal's plan. There'll be consequences if we fail."

"Would totally help if I knew the entirety of Zal's plan," I tell him. "So, if you feel inclined to tell me, now would be an excellent time."

"When you were a baby, you sang something that pulled an entire lake up from undersky, turned it into ice, and dropped it back down again," Dai informs me. "It's pretty legendary. Also illegal. It got a lot of attention from the drowners, and then a lot of attention from Maganwetar. If you could do that, what else could you do?"

The deck sways beneath us. I look up into the rigging, where Jik is perched, sitting on a sail-supporting rope. The expression on her face is both curious and suspicious.

When I make eye contact with her, she turns away.

Dai stares at me intently, and after a moment, he puts out his hand and touches my fingertips.

"I'll sing a storm cloud now," Dai says. "And then we'll sing a raindrop."

He makes a high-pitched noise that flattens my ears to the sides of my head, and a miniature cloud mists into being. Svilken sings with him, and between us, in the frozen air, a raindrop appears. I open my mouth, and blow the rain away, like I'm blowing out birthday candl—

A flash of memory, a chocolate éclair.

"What should I wish for?" I hear myself asking Dai, and he looks at me, but he has no idea what I'm talking about.

My wind's still blowing, gusting between us invisibly. Without his prompting, I turn the raindrops to ice—each one a prism containing a tiny rainbow.

"You have to learn how to do this." He frowns. "These songs have been sung since the beginning of Magonia. You can't just make up new ones."

Milekt agrees with Dai. He sings briefly with Svilken.

Obedience, sing Milekt and Svilken from our chests, *duty*.

I inhale, reach out, and take Dai's other hand, and the four of us sing together.

All of us, a single song, four voices bonded into one, and the sky around us blazes up insanely bright. My whole body shakes. Dai's in front of me, his eyes on mine. The song is sweet, but deep in my chest, it's hard as hell.

Something's about to happen. I feel like we're holding each other up as our voices twine.

I watch as a coil of rope on the deck rises up of its own volition, called by our song, as planks start to loosen, and the crew starts to rise even as they stand on deck, not flying, *rising*, because we're singing them up.

I feel something starting to detach somewhere else, far below us, and I look over the deck rail to the ocean. A wave is rising, a curve of water so huge I can't see its edge. The water stretches toward us.

Dai leans toward me and I lean toward him, and we sing into each other's lungs. All over my body every cell calls out. The notes shimmer, and I feel as though we're ascending, but not in a safe way. We're rising toward a fall.

I can tell he feels the same way. We're singing a tsunami until I come to my senses and pull back, gasping.

"Stop!" I manage, even as my whole body wants to keep going, even as I want to keep singing. If this is what singing is, I want to stay this way forever, but I can't. He looks as ragged as I do.

"Oh," he says. I've never seen him look surprised before. "Oh." He staggers.

The wave folds with a distant crash back into the ocean. My heart slows.

I think about what a tsunami can do. I think about the fact that I created that wave from nothing—from air—from breath.

The ability everyone was talking about. My power. I know it now. And *our* power. I know that too.

It feels terrifying.

It feels amazing.

Dai gives me half a smile, and I try to give him one back, still reeling.

CHAPTER 20

{JASON}

"I'm back," Aza says. She's standing on my doorstep. "I came home."

I held her hand as I rode with her to the hospital.

I held her hand as she died.

I held her hand until they told me I couldn't hold her hand anymore.

I read the coroner's report.

There was a body. HER body.

I'm hyperventilating.

I'm passing out? I'm breathing too fast? Am I starting to scream?

"What are you looking at?" she asks me, stopping me from all that, in a classic Aza tone.

A mirage. I'm staggering through the Sahara. I'm a dying man looking at the bouncing of sunlight, but no, because sunlight just rang my doorbell and pounded on my front door. Sunlight is staring at me and pursing her lips.

"Aza," I say. That's all I can say. I can't even get close to letting anything else out of my mouth.

"Jason Kerwin," she says. "It's nice to see you too."

She holds out her hands. Not blue.

She comes in for a—

I don't, I—

She presses her mouth to mine, very quickly, not the way someone who is dead would, not the way a ghost would, and before I can even tell what's happening, she's leaned back again and she's looking at me.

I might fall over or run away, or—

Super-fast calculation of probabilities that I can't compute, of time travel that I can't do, of doppelgängers that I can't imagine, of secret twin sisters, of Hitchcock movies, of *Vertigo*.

Vertigo, that's where I am. Pi wants to take over, but I don't let it. Looping wants to occur, but I remain sentient, and I don't do any of the various forms of out-freaking I want to do.

In one and a half seconds flat, I compare my in-brain Aza to the girl in front of me.

She looks healthy. Strangely so. I can't see any veins under the surface of her skin, the way I've always seen them. I've made a career of watching her blood running through her body, but now it's invisible. Her mouth is not only *not* blue, she's wearing lipstick. Her cheeks are pink. I've never seen the clothes she's wearing. I don't think I've ever seen her hair brushed before.

The last time I saw her, her strange ocean-depths eyes were shut. I was the one who shut them. Now, she's—

Aza holds out her arms in exasperation.

"Aren't you happy to see me at ALL?" she asks, and her voice is Aza's voice, a little snarky, a little hurt. But not breathless. I can't even process that.

"I thought you'd be happy. I can't believe you haven't even hugged me yet. I *kissed* you."

My heart's pounding so hard it should be rattling the window glass, and then I pick her up off the steps and hold her as tightly as I can, and she's not gasping, not coughing. She's in my arms. She's in my—

The last time I saw her, she was dead. I hold her out from me and stare.

"Did I dream it?"

"No," she says. "You didn't dream it."

"Am I crazy?"

"Maybe," she says. "Tell me what you've been doing the past four weeks and I'll tell you if you're crazy."

"Seriously?"

"I'm really here."

"*Aza Ray Was Her*," I say. She looks at me curiously.

"Aza Ray is me." She smiles.

Which, as always, takes me down. Her smile is like no one else's. Even though it's weird to see her normally dark-purple mouth painted pink.

She drops out of my arms and walks past me into the house. I stand for a second looking out at my street, which seems to have become a street in heaven, and then I follow her into my living room.

"Where are your parents?" she asks.

"They went to the grocery store," I say, oddly formal. I want to tell her everything. I want her to tell me everything.

She patrols the edges of the room, looks at every detail closely, then goes into the kitchen, looking at the cupboards, into the fridge. Normally she'd just get whatever she wanted.

"Are you hungry?"

"No," she says. "I ate."

She perches weirdly on the edge of a chair. (Not-a-Ghost verification: the chair is dented by her weight.)

"Am I dreaming?" I ask again.

"You're not dreaming," she says. "You're part of a secret. Can you keep a secret, Jason Kerwin? I need your help."

Why does she keep saying my name that way?

What happened to her? Would I be strange, too, if I died or didn't die, if I god-knows-what-ed? Yes. Obviously, I would.

I reach out and take her hand. Her skin's warm. She's never had warm skin before. There are calluses on her palm, new ones. Or at least, the last time I held her hand her skin was smooth. Now her hand feels as though she's been doing work. Like, heavy labor, in coming back from the dead.

And wow, I'm focusing in too much on the details. The world's shrinking down and all the things that should matter disappear into a blur when I'm this way. I try to breathe.

Is this shock? I think I'm in shock.

"Where've you been, Az?" I ask her in a pretty calm voice. Like it's no big deal that she died. Like I haven't been losing my mind. Like I am not losing my mind right now.

She's looking around the room, her head moving oddly, tilting and then tilting again. She looks scared, the way she's moving, but her face doesn't show "scared," and then it occurs to me she's looking for something. It's a movement I've seen in birds hunting insects. She zeroes in on something, looking out the window. She smiles, and for just a second *I'm* scared.

Jason Kerwin: crazy.

I hold her hand tighter. I don't need to be counting her freckles and comparing them to a tally in my brain.

I'm not scared of Aza.

I've only ever been scared of losing Aza.

She looks straight at me, and again I'm hit with adrenaline. I want to bolt out of the room. Why? What the hell?

"Where've you been?" I try it again.

"What do you know?" she asks. "I'll tell you everything, but tell me what you know first."

I'm about to start, but then again that movement of her head, tilting quickly, turning quickly.

I don't know anything.

She moves closer, leans in, puts one of her hands on my knee, which is so unlike Aza that I'm completely at a loss. I look down at my knee, paralyzed.

"Okay. Basic things, Az. Do you happen to be dead?"

"Of course not," she says. "Look at me. I'm alive." She leans in again. Her hand moves on my leg. I'm not even close to being able to deal with that. I grab her fingers and keep them from moving.

"But you died, Az," I say. "You did. I was there. I saw it happen."

I'm cursing myself even as these words are coming out of my mouth, because she's more alive than she was when she was alive. She was always on the verge of suffocation, and now that's not what's happening.

When I hugged her I felt muscles in her back and arms. She has a . . . a *density* she never had before. Aza's body was always made of glass, and her brain was made of sharpened steel. Now her hair smells of salt and ozone.

Her skin smells like the ocean, which—we're inland. But there's stormy weather outside. Maybe something's blowing in from somewhere. Maybe she has new perfume?

Aza hasn't ever worn perfume before. She can't wear it because it makes her choke, and no one anywhere near her can wear it either.

I know this. She knows this. Why aren't we talking about this?

"Come on, Jason Kerwin. You didn't really think I died," she says. "You've been hunting for me. You've been tracking things in the sky, haven't you? Weather patterns? What did you find?"

My confusion must show on my face.

"You promised you'd always find me," she says. "So that's what you've been doing, right?"

I take a moment.

"Yeah," I say.

"I heard a rumor," she says.

"From who? Where've you been that you've been listening to rumors? Where have you been that there were people to whisper rumors to you? And if you WERE listening to rumors, why'd you let me think you were dead?"

I guess I sound a little overwrought.

Her eyes widen. She seems less sure suddenly. More lost.

"I promise I'll tell you everything. But we can figure it out together. I need you to help me until we understand."

Once, Aza Ray got bronchitis and passed out in my car. When she woke up in the hospital and learned that I'd carried her through the doors, she was mortified.

Even in the ambulance, right before she died, when she found out that I'd given her mouth-to-mouth, I could see the horror on her face.

We all knew how she felt about invalid blankets. I had a hospital hoodie custom-made for her, with a million pockets, zippable sleeves to let the phlebotomists in, and IV cord portals, so she wouldn't have to be wrapped in a blanket to stay warm.

But she's never asked me to help her before.

"All right then, tell me how to figure this out, Aza Ray."

Am I playing games now? Maybe she has some sort of brain injury. How can I even assess it?

The coroner's report—I have a PDF, scanned from a hard copy stolen by janitorial staff—was clear. Her body degraded quickly. The coroner was both surprised and dismayed. The report wasn't fun reading.

Adolescent female, aged fifteen years. *And 360 days*, I added, in my head, to the world.

There was no reason for him to do a full autopsy. We knew what happened. He didn't have the skills to do the kind of analysis someone with a disease like hers needed anyway. Same way no one here had the skills to keep her alive.

Her lungs went to a lab dealing with rare disorders. The rest of her got cremated. I haven't seen any of those reports yet. It's only been four weeks. There's probably tissue still in a freezer somewhere. I can't really think about that.

Aza sighs, and then stretches, arching her back, yogic, a new kind of fluidity to her movements, a new kind of grace. I'm reminded of a bird again, unfurling its wings. Aza pulls something out of her jeans pocket. She hands me a fat sheaf of folded papers, and I start shaking, because I wrote them. I attached them to the balloon I sent up on the day of her funeral.

"I acquired your apology list. It was really long."

Acquired? She digs in another pocket.

A much smaller piece of paper. She hands it to me.

I open it. And it's the note I gave her for her birthday.

Creased and rumpled and refolded and stained. In the corner of it there's a bite mark, and I know where it came from. Aza, nervous, fidgeting.

The bite mark wasn't there the last time I saw it, because the last time I saw this piece of paper, I put it in her hand. I knew I wasn't getting any more chances. I curled her fingers around the note so she'd have it where she was going. There are all those parentheses. All those brackets.

My body floods with some nameless emotion.

"Okay," I say. I can feel the crying I didn't do in the past four weeks rising up in me, and now that I maybe should be done crying, it rushes out of my eyes and runs down my face. "Okay, Aza," I manage between sobs. "Okay."

It's like she's never seen anyone cry before. I try to mop myself up using my own T-shirt.

I go into the kitchen, put my face under the cold water tap, and try to get myself under control.

"Have you been home?" I say from underneath running water. "You have, right?"

"Not yet," she says. I turn quickly and she's right behind me. I didn't even hear her come in.

She runs her fingers under the water, flicks it out from the sink, and laughs. Then she looks at me, tilting her head.

"Why not?" I ask.

"You can't tell my parents I'm here. Or yours."

"But, your dad," I say. "Your mom. They think you're dead."

I have my phone out of my pocket, and I'm showing her the number, but she takes it and puts it on the table, a little hard, a little bit point-making.

"Do you trust me?" she says. "Then listen to me. I need you

to tell me what you found while you were looking for me. I need you to tell me everything. It's important. Objects, data. Whatever you found. Did you find something, Jason Kerwin?"

"I—"

"Did something fall out of the sky?" she asks, and smiles sweetly at me. "On the day of my funeral? Tell me what you know," she says.

She leans in again. I'm backed up against the sink.

"What if I said I was on a ship in the sky, Jason Kerwin? What would you say?"

I'm quiet for a second.

"I'd say Magonia," I tell her.

I hear a car in the driveway. My moms. I turn to look out the window, and they're getting out with grocery bags.

I look back, and Aza's gone.

No. She's under the table. Curled into a ball. She looks up at me, her eyes huge.

I get down on my knees beside her.

"It's just Eve and Carol," I say. "It's okay."

"Who?"

"My moms," I tell her. "Who else? My moms."

She shakes her head violently.

"No one will believe me but you. They can't know I'm here."

I hand her my car keys. She looks at them, confused for a second, and then nods at them ferociously.

"The Camaro," she says. She says it carefully, and weirdly. Ka-marr-O.

"Uh-huh. Meet me in the car, back door," I say, and then I haul ass to the front to meet my moms. I spill a grocery sack to buy her some time.

I walk back into the kitchen and there's no evidence she was ever here.

I look sideways out the window. It's stormy still. I can see the trees leaning over, and there's that kind of slushy rain and I look up at the clouds and see nothing in them. No ships. No lightning. Just a smooth gray layer of nothing overhead.

And Aza slouching in the front seat of my car, fiddling with knobs. I mutter about something left at school, and the moms are pleasantly surprised to imagine that I've changed my ways, listened to them, and am going back without resistance.

"I told you it would be okay," Eve says to Carol. Eve looks at me for a moment, a questioning look.

I let the moment pass. I grab my computer and my bag, and I'm out the door. I knock on the driver's side, and Aza gazes blankly at me. Then, as if she's remembered something, she waves at the passenger seat.

Aza never drives. I'm—

I walk around the back of the car, and open the passenger door.

"We're going to your parents' house," I say.

"I'm not ready yet," she says. "They can't know anything. Unless they already do?"

She turns and looks at me. "Do they know about Magonia, Jason? What did you tell them?"

"I haven't talked to anyone about Magonia since you and I watched the squid footage. They know you *died*," I say. "Can we at least drive by? Just to see if they're home."

She sighs. "The ship will be looking for me. They're probably looking right now."

I can't get used to the sound of nothing in her lungs.

She starts the car and flicks on the windshield wipers. I watch her turn the wheel, not struggling at all, even though it sticks. Her biceps flex.

She pulls out of my driveway.

"Left," I say, when she hesitates. She turns left.

"Now right," I say.

She turns right without stopping at the stop sign, taking the corner too tight.

"I love you, Jason."

I look at her. "You love me?"

"Of course," she says after a moment. "Don't you love me?"

I look at her some more.

She's driving faster than the speed limit, and she's not paying any attention to the road. She's just staring at me.

"Left here," I say.

We approach Aza's house.

Eli's walking out the front door. I wait for Aza to slow down, but she doesn't. Eli sees my car, raises one hand halfway into the air and waves.

Aza doesn't stop, doesn't look to the left, doesn't do anything but drive.

Her hair is still neat in its ponytail.

"Where are we going?" she asks.

"This left," I say. "And now this one."

We pass through some fancy gates, up a long hill.

"Here."

We pull into the lot at the graveyard. It's empty of the living, because of the rain and the weekday, but it's full of the dead. It's out a ways from town, and on top of a pretty good cliff, looking out over the view.

It's one of those places made by pioneers. Closer to God, maybe, if you make it higher and more precarious. I always think about people trying to pack coffins up here in the days before cars. It must have been a horrible job. I thought about it the day we put Aza here.

"A graveyard?" she says as she gets out. "Really? Look at me, stupid. I'm with you."

Maybe I flinch. Maybe I don't.

"I thought you might want to see where we buried you," I say.

"Not really," she says. "It's not safe for me to be exposed this way." She looks up into the clouds. Her expression is one part expectant, one part certain.

"I want you to see your grave," I say. Of course I do. I need her to read the headstone.

She's beautiful, in profile, her head tilted up, looking at the clouds, but she's always been beautiful.

"I don't want to," she says slowly. "You need to tell me about the spyglass. And where you sent it. I know you have it. We're running out of time."

We're at her grave. There's no grass on it yet. The stone is there, though.

It says this:

AZA RAY
trust your heart
if the seas catch fire
(and live by love
though the stars walk backward)

She says nothing. The rain's all over her. Her hair's wet, and her T-shirt sticks to her.

"So, E.E. Cummings," I say. "You're the one who taught it to me."

She doesn't move. I look at her. "It's the one about not caring about how the world is, not caring about the villains and the heroes."

"Sounds stupid," she says.

"It's the one that ends with 'you are my sun, my moon, and all my stars,'" I say, because it needs saying. I didn't put that on her stone. I'd never.

"It's a love poem," she says. "Seriously?"

"It's a love poem written by someone who understood that love gets hit by death all the time," I say. "It's a love poem by someone who lived through war." I don't say anything about forever, but forever's implied.

She nods slowly and rubs her forehead. Something about her cracks open for a moment. She laughs, in a kind of mortified, despairing way.

"Do you ever wonder what your life would be if one thing hadn't happened? If that one thing made it so that you weren't you? What if I could remember this poem? I'd be more like you want me to be, then. Wouldn't I?"

She looks at me for a second, and then walks away, kicking at the dirt around the graves, looking up at the sky.

I'm down on my knees in front of Aza's grave. I'm looking up at the sky too. I'm thinking about the path of the ship, the way it's been taking on provisions, the way it's been traveling northeast, and I'm remembering something. An article Aza and I read together.

I think about what Magonians have been doing for centuries, all those almanacs and stolen harvests in the books I read, in the scraps of information I've been digging up. Magonians are hungry. They're looking for food. I know where they're going.

It was a photo essay, just a few months ago, a seed grown in India, held in the hand of a woman in a sari. Sealed in a plastic bag. Ready for transfer. Rows of fluorescent lights in a frozen place, long aisles, refrigeration cases.

The Global Seed Vault. In Norway. An underground repository where there are seeds for every plant on earth. Nice and cold, nice and deep, nice and un-tectonic, a safe complex where they keep lychee nuts, raspberries, long almost-lost fruits and vegetables, in case a disaster or rising sea levels take everything. In case humans mess it all up.

I'm shaking my head, muttering, considering. Looping in my revelation. Yeah. It's right. I'm right.

She's behind me out of nowhere. Right behind me. I can feel her breathing. She puts her hand over my shoulder and traces her name on the gravestone.

"Who have you been talking to? Who knows about Magonia? Who knows about this?" she asks.

I look at the gravestone. I feel Aza's hands on my back. I feel her bending. I feel her chin against my skull. I feel her arms, strong around my shoulders. I have a jolt of mortifying lust and a jolt of something else.

"I'm the only one who knows anything," I say.

"Give me the spyglass," she says, and I hand it over my shoulder. I watch her do something to the lens cap, twist it in a pattern, and then take it off. She looks through it, up into the sky, and exhales.

"Yes," she says. "That's useful, Jason Kerwin. What else do you have to share?"

I feel a rough sharpness against the side of my throat.

"Nothing," I say. Then I launch myself into her, as hard as I can. I slam backward and send her flying. The spyglass is knocked loose and I snatch it, forcing her to the ground. I pin her down beside Aza's grave and stare at her.

"Who are you," I say, and my voice is not my voice. "What have you done with Aza?"

CHAPTER 21

{JASON}

She's stunned. But it only takes a second for her to regain herself. She stares at me, warily, her eyes bright and the left, suddenly, the wrong color. She was wearing contacts. One of them slipped when she was looking into the rain, and now she has one pale, sky-blue eye, the color of Eli's eyes, and one dark blue one. She's got a knife in her hands. That knife was the thing I felt on my neck.

I'm shaking with fury. I've been controlling it for a while.

"Aza doesn't know how to drive a manual transmission. When she does drive, she stops at all stop signs and all lights, because she doesn't actually have a driver's license. Aza doesn't wear jeans. Aza wouldn't drive past her house, and past Eli. Aza knows all the collected poems of E.E. Cummings.

"And Aza Ray Boyle would never, never, not in a million years, tell me she loved me.

"So who the hell are you?"

I already know part of it. This is someone from *up there*.

I didn't want to believe it.

I wanted her back.

But now I know.

"I didn't do anything with her," the fake Aza says. "Her mother's ship picked her up."

Her mother's ship.

"Which ship? Where?"

"There are ships everywhere, Jason Kerwin," she says, and smiles. "There's a sky full. I guess you can't see them, can you? I guess you're not one of the lucky ones. But then, almost no one from here is lucky enough to live in Magonia."

"Who are you?"

"Are you going to kill me, Jason Kerwin?" she asks, tilting her head, looking at the sky at the same time. "I don't think you are."

She ducks forward and gets me around the waist. I'm fighting, twisting. She's fast and strong and tiny.

She flips backward, lands on her feet, and stares at me from ten feet away.

"You're not bad," she says, "for a drowner."

Drowner. I think about that for a moment. What it means to someone from the sky.

That legend of a person drowning in thin air after he tried to climb down an anchor chain.

"*You're* a drowner," I say.

"How dare you," she hisses. "I'm *Breath*."

It's a normal word, but the tone she uses makes me shiver.

I'm circling, trying to keep my distance, but also steering her. She doesn't know this cemetery.

She knows how to lie, though. She knows how to trick someone into believing in everything. Before she takes it all away again.

Aza liked the Hawaiian traditions, death-wise. Cliff of the

dead, and you would leap from it as a ghost, and go where you wanted to go. She wanted to be close to the edge, in case her ghost couldn't walk.

I feint, figuring out where she'll go in response, and yes, she steps back, one final step, a bit too far. And I'm so full of hate right now, shaking with so much rage, I see the way she's going, and I don't stop moving.

The grass slips out from beneath her and she staggers, gasps, and windmills her arms. I'm seeing her drop and oh god, and I'm shouting and changing my mind, reaching out.

But time goes slow, and she smiles at me, this wide-open, devil-may-care, don't-give-a-damn smile, a look I've only ever seen on one other person's face.

She falls backward, off the edge of the cliff—

falls

falls

falls

—and then a rope twists out of the sky. She grabs it, clings to it, and climbs. She tugs herself up, up into the clouds.

I pick up the spyglass from the grass by the grave. Now that the lens cap is gone, I can see through it.

After a second, I put it down so I can breathe.

The sky is full of ships. She's climbing up to one.

My field of vision is all cracked and crisscrossed and busted, a film watched with a broken screen, but even askew and crazed, I can see them between the jags.

Clouds with giant steamers in them. Sails and small boats, junks, catamarans. It's an armada's worth. The ship that's inside the storm is huge and silver, the bottom of a tremendous vessel, something as big as a football field, or more. She's still climbing to it, up onto its rails. It's surrounded by dark shapes, by darting, shifting shadows.

Sharks, made of lightning and cloud.

I need to get onto Aza's ship. I know where it's going. I *think* I know, even though all I really know, all I've really known since I was five, is that Aza is my universe.

I send a quick text while I stare up, and then an email. I start booking myself out into the distance.

There's a crack of thunder. I look up to the ship the fake Aza got on, and as I look I see a streak of lightning. And then another. And another.

I dodge out from beneath the tree I'm under, running to my car.

You can survive a lightning storm that way—in a car, if the windows are up. But my car's too far away, down the hill—

How do you run away from the sky?

The lightning's all around me. Strikes are raining down like spears, clots of fire hitting the damp earth, and I rack my brain—

Metal in my hand. Get rid of it, NOW. I throw the spyglass as hard as I can, watch it bounce off the rocks with a glitter of glass and go over the cliff.

I run another few steps, but there's no shelter here, no place to hide—

The wind whips up on one side of me. Then the other side. Then behind me. In front of me. I'm surrounded by spinning air, dust, and stones.

I look up at the big dark cloud and see lightning zing out of it.

Oh god. Something flips through my brain, wilderness

survival. Crouch into a ball so it can't hit your head. Does that actually work?

Shit shit shit.

There's a tremendous boom, and a ball of white lightning comes down from the dark cloud, fast, faster—

You're thirty times more likely to die of a lightning strike than of a shark attack. I'm about to die of both.

I drop down, crouch, put my arms over my head.

And there's the loudest sound I've ever heard and the brightest white I've ever seen, and I'm made of it, I'm—

I'm made of light

I'm made of heat

And I'm flying

Moms?

Carol, Eve—

Aza—

I'm sorry

I wake up panicked the night after Dai and I sing the wave.

A dream—Jason was in it. I can't remember it at all, or not enough. The captain's ghost bird screams horribly. *Sky!* he shrieks. *Sea. Light. Zal.* He makes a choking sound. *Fall. Die. Night.*

The voice seems to be everywhere, all over the ship, all over the sky.

"By the Breath," I hear even the Magonians cursing, though not at full volume.

"May the Breath take that bird and break him to feathers and bones," whispers someone not far away from my cabin, and then I hear Wedda hush them.

I sit up. I think about that.

Not "ghost." *Bird.*

I think about how the captain's voice can sometimes be heard, early in the mornings, cooing to something.

To someone.

The bird. She was banned from singing with it.

Kill! Caru screams. *Smashed nests, broken song, kill me.*

I curl in my cabin, listening to him, my eyes full. If that bird is alive on this ship, how is keeping him here okay? How is listening to him suffer? How is any of it?

Wedda shifts in her berth and her chains jingle softly against each other.

Almost a wind chime, almost a song.

So many tied to this ship, I think. Would they all rather be free? Would they be better off that way? Or are they safer here from the famine that afflicts the cities? Is this ship their home?

The solution to starvation seems so simple. Just a matter of providing food to a bunch of hungry people. Jason's mom Eve once told me that if everyone shared the resources they had, there'd be enough. Instead, we have this—parts of the world that have too much, and other parts that have nothing.

Magonia has nothing.

I think about Dai's family. I think about Dai. I think about how I've never been hungry. I think about how I've never even really thought about hunger before.

Nothing is perfect here. Nothing is perfect down there either.

I spend the next few days privately trying to figure out where the captain's canwr is hidden, and publicly practicing the old Magonian songs Milekt and Dai have taught me. I sing the moisture in the air into sand, then the sand back into water. I sing quietly, a small piece of ice made of a drop of rain, a drop of rain made of a stone. I sing things into their opposites.

I'm not perfect yet. Sometimes a note makes the air crackle, and Milekt scolds me. Sometimes a note meant to turn water to stone turns it to fire instead, and Milekt shrills and pecks me inside the lung.

But not so secretly, I keep hold of the missed note. Because water into fire? Um, hell yes.

It keeps me from obsessing about the sad song of Caru, and the dark misery I feel rising up inside me when I listen to it.

I have to find him.

I roam the ship, looking in every passage, but nothing. I search the bottom of the ship, in the cells, but I see only blackness, not even Ley, our prisoner, nor any of the other pirate prisoners either, which makes me wonder what Zal's done with them. Could they be dead? Did she throw them overboard while I was sleeping?

And there's no real bird. No ghost bird.

Is there some part of *Amina Pennarum* I still haven't discovered?

In the mornings, we're over silver-gray ocean, and icebergs. We keep sailing. Tiny little ice islands dot the water below.

Out in the Magonian sky, I see planes passing each other by. Each one its own world full of passengers, entwined with one another, overlapping one another, unaware of the rest of the people flying past out there in the air.

Just as earth is unaware of Magonia.

It's freezing. Even Dai's wearing a winter uniform, and Wedda dresses me in multiple layers of woven feathers beneath my spider-silk jersey and jacket.

I'm sitting in the captain's chair now, at Zal's encouragement. She's teaching me how to steer, how to read charts that go in multiple directions, up and down, east, west, north, south.

One level of sky contains stormsharks and ship-tilting

winds, and another contains firefish and airkraken, and then there's the possibility of colliding with mountaintops, and the danger of flying too close to city borders with a ship that is too large.

Dai's over my other shoulder, pressing his warm hand into my back, and I can feel our bond, bone to bone, voice to voice. Milekt is calmer now that we've sung. He chirrups in the canwr cote, and nests in my lung while we practice. Our control is better and better. Water to stone, stone to water.

I lift the liquid from a cup held by Dai, turn it to ice in midair, with Dai singing alongside, delicately, perfectly monitoring my strength. He ends up with a faceful of water, which he wipes off and flicks at me, laughing.

There's still fun despite the seriousness of what we're planning, the thing we're moving toward.

"We'll change the world. We'll bring the plants back to life. The way they were before the smokestacks below made them wilt into dormancy," Zal says. "I don't remember them. But there are legends of a time when the skyfields were full of them. All Magonia could eat. We used drowners' crops only to supplement our long voyages back then, and didn't need them to survive. With the plants back, our dependence on the drowners will vanish."

I think about the past two hundred years of machinery on earth. I think about how the Industrial Revolution starved Magonia. Now it's starving parts of the earth too.

Zal gets reports from elsewhere, birds landing on *Amina Pennarum*'s deck with letters from other ships. Flaming arrows shot after sunset. She spends a lot of time staring out like she's a figurehead, her face unreadable, but one letter, delivered by a ragged sparrow Rostra, makes her stand up straight.

"Breath ship in range."

Everyone whips to panicky attention. I can smell the dread, and it's mine too. What does that mean? Are we in danger? Are they coming for us? Zal keeps reading.

"They may be employed by Maganwetar, or someone else. We're not pursued. Yet. I won't risk it. Bring up the dead."

Dai springs down the ladder with several big, muscled Rostrae, and returns with Ley, dragging her up from her unknown dungeon. She's struggling, twisting, and chained.

"This goes against all law of the sky," Ley shouts. "I am owed a trial!"

Zal uncoils a whip from her jacket and cracks it. It's something not quite metal, not quite rope. It uncoils and hovers in the air, a twisting cat's tail stripe, just in front of Ley's face, twitching there.

"You're owed nothing. You're a pirate, Ley Fol," Zal says. "*This* is your trial."

Ley watches the whip warily, her arms pinned by Dai and another guard.

"Maybe we should wait," I say nervously. "Until we can—"

"Do you remember the day she took you?" Zal asks me. "It was the worst day of my life, and that misery lasted fifteen years."

"But you can't *execute* her—" I say.

"She was the worst sort of betrayer. A friend turned enemy. That you survived her sabotage is a miracle. A life for a life."

"But I'm not dead," I protest.

Ley looks at me. She seems apathetic.

"Don't trust your mother," she says. "She wants more from

you than she admits. She's bent on vengeance, not on reason."

Zal flicks the whip, and it lashes Ley's face.

Ley recoils. The whip leaves a line in her skin, first white and then blue, glowing letters of ice, slipping into her body. I watch as the chill spreads through her, a snake of light slipping beneath her skin.

"To die with dark secrets is to die without a deathsong," Zal says. "Who told you what I was planning?"

Ley cringes, sags slightly, but her eyes stay open. Whatever else she is, she's brave.

"Wait," I say. "She saved me then. They would have killed me. Drop her in the sky near Maganwetar. Put her on a launch. Isn't there a jail there?"

Zal looks at Ley, and then at me.

"You're alive, Aza, because you're extraordinary, not because she was merciful. She didn't save you. She betrayed *me*. This is an execution. Not a conversation."

Ley looks steadily at her.

"Sail the skies, then, Zal. Take what's ours from the drowners, flood their strongholds, kill everything below, but know that there can be no balance without the people of the ground, and without balance, Magonia falls. You're not the first to think she had a solution to the problem of centuries. You're wrong, as they all were."

"ENOUGH!" Zal's eyes are lightning, and her skin's actually shaking.

"Now I sing my final song," Ley demands.

"Oh, I think not," Zal says. "Those who refuse me deserve no privilege. Because of your betrayal, my first mate's family starved, ignored by Maganwetar. Had you not betrayed me? This sky would be fed now, and full. You ruined a future that would have been joyful. I might have spent the last fifteen years in a different kind of country, my daughter beside me, my heartbird singing. Instead?"

Zal pauses, and we all hear Caru scream, a blood-chilling lament.

"This was your doing, and for it, you die without song," says Zal. She pauses. "As a sympathizer to Maganwetar's policies, you've betrayed your true people. A deathsong is for those who die with honor. Not for you."

There's a slight movement in the crew, people shifting. I look around. The crew's all on deck. Some of them are spreading their wings in excitement or anxiety. I can see teeth and fangs and beaks open.

"It was him who told me," Ley says.

Zal jolts.

"Who knew your heart but him? He didn't agree with your plans. Caru told me everything. Your canwr betrayed you."

Zal is rigid. She takes one painful breath.

"Liar," she says.

Ley stares steadily at her. Her face reveals nothing.

"The deathsong," says Ley.

"Denied."

There's a startled shuffling on the ship, all the Magonians and Rostrae murmuring in shock as Zal breaks her word.

Zal waves a hand toward Dai, who brings out a long cloth from behind his back. He ties it around Ley's mouth, stopping up her voice. This, I realize, was planned. This denial of death-song was on purpose.

Ley takes a small breath through her nostrils. Then she

shrugs in the manner—I know it well—of someone who knows her time is ending.

I look around for an executioner. Hood. Ax. Nothing.

Ley nods. She takes a step backward, then another. Zal's face is tight, her jaw working.

Milekt lands on my shoulder, beak to my ear. It's no comfort.

Shuffling along the plank, Ley meets my eyes. She's mute. She sings no deathsong. The blue-white chain of light Zal sent into her moves through her throat and down her arms. She glows with it.

Her hands shake, and so does her chest. She stands at the end of the plank.

She looks only at Zal.

She opens her chest and shows her canwr, a black-and-white magpie, old as she is. She holds him in her hands.

Zal takes a step forward, meets her enemies' eyes, stretches her elegant blue fingers, and smiles coldly, just before she pushes Ley off the plank.

Ley falls backward into the sky, tossing her bird up into the air as she goes.

Deathsong, sings the bird, alone, blistering, dissonant notes as he cries, *fall, break broken bright light fall, fall.*

I'm standing, limp, undone. Off the ship's side, a vulture rises up and looks at me.

Ley's canwr keeps singing.

Then a final sound from him, wordless, a bone-chilling wail of despair. Caru cries out, an echo from elsewhere.

The vulture takes Ley's canwr.

Dead thing, another vulture croaks, and dives. I run to the rail and try to see down into the cloudy mists that surround us.

Nothing at first. Then a shred of fabric drifting up. A bit of her uniform jacket.

And a mist of blood, swirling through the air, coloring the clouds for a moment before that, too, disappears.

My stomach churns.

Zal passes close beside me. "One day you'll be a captain. One day you'll have vengeance of your own. This is how it is done in the real Magonia."

But her eyes are darker than they should be, her face drawn. She holds one hand to her heart. She walks away, leaving me. I see Jik glance in my direction as she follows Zal belowdecks. Her eyes, too, are dark.

The sky is full of shreds of clothing, drifting like milkweed. I can hear vultures below us, and more than vultures. I look down and see a giant smoky tentacle of something, moving slowly, taking some part of Ley's body, and curling away into a dark cloud. It's so huge I can't see all of it, but a flickering mass of eight silvery limbs, large enough to tear this ship from the sky, before it pulses away again.

Dai passes me and touches my shoulder. I shriek and clench my fist. He wrestled Ley up onto the deck. He's unquestioningly loyal to Zal and the ship. What does that mean? What would he do if I was on the wrong side?

Dai frowns, then swings himself back up into the rigging, Svilken chattering away at him, telling him to get back to work or there'll be more work later. Milekt flits away to the top of a mast, where he roosts in a hunched ball of brightness.

I feel sick. I keep seeing Ley fall, again and again. Her words—about not trusting Zal, about Caru, echo through my mind.

There's a feeling—a dread that doesn't go away, but there's nothing to be done about it. Ley is left far behind us in the sky, buried in the clouds and circled and consumed by creatures. *Dead thing.*

I remember the story Jason told me, four Magonians showing up in a town on earth, getting put in the stocks. But they would've drowned if they'd really fallen.

Maybe they did drown. The story didn't say how long they were down there, nor did it say what ultimately happened to them.

Magonians—we—don't look enough like humans to pass. If I went overboard and didn't die, what would happen? What would they do to me on earth now?

Some part of me still hoped that maybe I could go home—

But no. There's no maybe. I can't.

Eli might be going to school now. She might be in algebra; learning enough math to calculate the size of the universe. She might be in English, learning words to describe the way her sister left her one night in the middle of a snowstorm.

I'm never going to know what Eli will turn out to be.

And she'll never know I'm up here training to—

What *am* I training to do?

I grit my teeth and climb up into the rigging a little way below Dai. I look out at the nothing and wait for him to speak, but he doesn't. He just stares out into the clouds, looking worried.

I can feel something changing. I'm not Dai, trained my whole life to obey orders.

I can feel uncertainty, but also ferocity, branching alongside everything.

Dai puts an arm out, and I cautiously lean into him. Once I'm there, against his body, there's that rightness when we touch. He looks out at the sky.

"That was the first execution I've seen," he says, and I feel him shaking.

"Yeah," I say. "Me too."

For a moment, I think about my dream, the interrupted dream, Jason walking through the dark air of the undersky. Holding up his hands to me. Then I forget him again, hard, and on purpose, letting him go forever. He was a dream from a place I used to know.

He was a drowner.

And I'm Magonia.

CHAPTER 23

{AZA}

Jik shows up in my cabin before dawn. My canwr's in the cote, sleeping with the rest of the birds, and I'm down here, supposedly sleeping too.

Did I miss a watch or something? That would be Dai after me, not Jik. Jik has no authority.

"You should know something," Jik whispers after a moment.

I sit up, eager to listen.

"I feed him," she says.

"Who?"

"The captain's bird. It's part of my duties."

"But Wedda—" I say.

Jik shows me her hand, each finger surrounded by a metal ring, and shakes it in the air.

"None of us can be trusted," she says. "Wedda? And Dai? Have they made you think there's nothing wrong in Magonia? Magonians are at war with one another, and we, the feathered classes, are at their mercy. Don't you ever wonder—"

"What?"

"Which of the Rostrae and canwr who serve you do it willingly? And which do it because they must?"

The implications of what she's saying fasten into my brain.

"Your Milekt is a lungbird, and loyal to the captain. The captain was granted a heartbird, and when she lost her bond to him, she was unwilling to let him go."

"What are you trying to say?" I ask. "Just say it."

"Caru betrayed Zal. Her *own canwr* refused to sing her song with her. Are you sure you understand your mother? Are you certain you trust her?"

A few things are falling into place in my head.

"I'm not asking you to free the Rostrae," Jik says. "There is a time for rebellion, and it is coming. Some of us work toward those ends. Some of us work from the inside."

She looks at me, her gaze a challenge.

"Aza. There are places on the ground that will be lost to us all if Zal has her way."

"She only wants the airplants," I say defensively, hearing myself and feeling suspicious of what I'm saying.

Jik looks at me.

"Did you see what she did tonight? She broke her word. Denial of deathsong? That's against all Magonian laws," Jik whispers in the harshest, sharpest tones. Like I'm a fool. Like I know nothing.

"Do you trust a woman who would deny a deathsong? Your mother, Aza Ray, is a criminal. She has no honor."

It's too much.

"Do you presume to question the captain's judgment, *Rostrae*?" I interrupt, and I hear it coming out of my mouth, this wrongness, this not fairness.

Jik bristles. Looks at me icily.

"Her canwr rose against her. Now he's mad and broken.

How will *you* fare if something goes wrong with her plan?"

A moment and I'm up and moving.

I shove a little knife into my boot. I wrap a rope around my arm. I put on my warm uniform. If Jik is right and Caru's alive, then what he's been calling for is saving. He's been calling for me.

If he betrayed Zal, she'll kill him. I can't let that happen.

Not after

~~Ley~~

I just can't.

Something moves in the doorway. I look up and see Wedda there, her eyes glowing.

"Nestling," she says. "Jik wants trouble. Don't listen to her."

Jik's shoulder feathers spike up as though she's wearing a motorcycle jacket. Her eyes are wider than they were a moment ago, and her blue crest stands up, too, sharp and brittle. She looks small next to Wedda, though, and like a kid.

Like me.

"I don't want trouble," Jik says. "I want justice. You've heard Caru screaming as long as I have."

"Caru is a *ghost*," Wedda says, her tone tense.

"We all know he's not," Jik retorts. "The captain says he is, and we follow her orders and call him dead, but that bird lives in torment."

Jik turns to me again.

"You can help the captain. Or you can help us. You're stronger than she ever was—"

Wedda grabs her by the wing and hisses into her ear.

"Enough! Leave her. Leave *now*."

Jik spins and goes.

When she's sure Jik is gone, Wedda looks at me. "Do not," she says. "Whatever you're considering, nestling. It won't end well for you, nor will it end well for that bird. The captain's canwr isn't sane."

"But it isn't dead either," I say. I'm completely dressed—prepared, for what reason I'm not totally willing to consider, to go out into the cold.

I march past her, and Wedda reaches out. She clenches my hair into her fingers.

"You can't stop me, I—"

I realize she's not trying. She's knotting my hair in a way that feels unfamiliar.

"What's that you're doing?" I ask. "It's not the captain's knot?"

"No. It's your own," she says.

When I look in the mirror, my hair's twisted up into tight plaits, close to my skull, twirling and swooping nautilus shells.

"This belongs to you," she says softly. "Just as your mind and your will do."

I stare at my reflection, and Wedda behind me. I hear what she's telling me. I start to give her my thanks, but she cuts me off before I can even begin.

"If anyone asks, you chose this yourself, nestling. I'm a steward, not a revolutionary."

And so I go hunting a ghost.

I sidle my way down the ladder and into the galley, where I steal a piece of bread and a small piece of salted meat left from the pig.

I listen hard for the sound of Milekt's tone. The cote up there has only bitter things to say.

Some of them are hatchlings, as yet untrained to sing with their Magonian hosts, and thus far unbonded to them. Milekt and Svilken are teaching them. The little birds resist. They strain against their chains. When Magonians die, the canwr that are bonded to them die as well, but not automatically. They're killed. They can't link with another Magonian. Once the bond is made, it's permanent.

Oh god, like a wife burned with her husband's body.

Restraint, trills Milekt. I hear him say it to the hatchlings, training them. He's a drill sergeant. The same way he trains me. I hear Zal on deck, too, giving orders to the ship's crew.

I wonder if she ever sleeps.

I hear a quiet whirring from Zal's quarters. Knowing Zal's above, I don't even hesitate. No one would dare come in here without permission. No one but me.

I push on Zal's door. Inside, a large bed with red-and-gold bedcovers, an ancient, worn-smooth wooden desk, and rolled-up maps on parchment. Tons of maps. But they're not what I'm here for.

In the corner is a screen, and behind it is a cage covered with a dark cloth. Inside it I can feel Caru moving, spinning, stretching his wings out.

I've never been in here before.

This is why.

This canwr is contraband. He should be dead.

Aza, the bird says. I jump at my name.

Kill me, he says, voice quieter than it was. He's talking only to me, to himself.

No, I say. *Feed*, I tell him, in the Magonian I can manage.

Feed, Caru repeats. There's a darkness in that voice, a

rawness. I take off the cage cover, gently, quietly.

I meet his dark, shining eye. He's a falcon.

Gleaming black on the top, each shining feather flecked with gold. His breast is creamy with dark markings all over it, and the undersides of his wings are fire red. Enormous. His body's as long as my arm.

He's what I've been searching for since I came aboard.

I'm not sure what you want, I say, no longer in Magonian, but in my own language. *Eat*, I say.

I put my hand through the bars. Caru shuffles forward. I don't let myself recoil, even though I can feel the despair and longing that are driving him insane. Even though it all makes my heart hurt. He takes the bread from my fingers. He tears loose a bite of meat.

His sleek head turns to me, and he stares at my chest, making a low and dangerous noise, but Milekt's not with me. The falcon rocks on his perch, his eyes wild and nervous.

I look around. The key is hanging on the wall (just in sight of the bird, torture). So I open the cage. I hold out my arm, bare, trusting him.

He steps onto my forearm. Talons touching. They dig into my flesh, but don't break my skin. They feel as though they sink into me, fit me. I feel his weight.

Broken string, Caru sings, looking at me. *Heart battered home burned. Bound, broken, knots undone. Ocean, island, talons, feathers, nests. Fall, fall from the stars.*

Caru's wings spread slowly, and then he beats them and starts to rise into the air, just enough to scare me. I step back.

He looks at my heart, like he wants to tear it out of my chest.

But when he stares, I stare back. I watch his eyes widen, clear bright gold, and totally insane.

Aza, the falcon whirrs, quietly.

His voice is different now, less scared, less rageful.

Sing, he whirrs, the sharpness of his beak close enough to savage me. He ruffles up his feathers and shakes himself. His talons are as long as my fingers.

Sky, Caru says. *Take me.*

He moves his head forward and uses his beak to pluck something from his ankle.

I look at it. It's a ring. A gold ring, similar to the rings I've seen on the Rostrae, but this one is without any chains.

Caru drops it into my hand, and then looks at me. I don't know what to do. I could throw it off the ship. Would that release him?

Sky, says Caru again.

I keep my arm extended. I take a roll of charts from the desk and push them into my belt.

Caru looks at me. I put my cloak over his head, and wrap him in it. I hold him in my arms, and we go up in the dark. Caru croons into my ear—

A terrifying soft song, the song I wish I could sing. It hurts my head, bruises my eardrums. I shake my head to clear it, and Caru moves against my chest.

Sky, he sings in the smallest voice.

I walk to the launches pretending I'm not doing what I'm about to do. I see Jik lingering on deck, and then walking toward Dai with purpose. He looks barely awake, and she's distracting him.

I'm casual. Slow. I consider one of the launches, big enough to be stable in high wind, big enough to not capsize if something comes up beneath us.

The batsail looks down at me and makes a soft sound, high and quiet. A squallwhale passes close to me singing a delicate light rain.

Caru is still in my arms, but I can feel his heart pounding; it shakes his entire body. I step into the launch, and put Caru down inside it. He's not chained to anything, not captive.

I unspool the rope that holds us to the ship. I unknot the knots. I don't even remotely know what I'm doing. Stealing the captain's canwr? The captain I swore an oath to?

An oath. Aza, who are you? What life is this in which you're swearing blood oaths?

And who are you swearing them to?

I look up at the sails, and at the ship, at the night all around us. The batsail flexes its wings, pushing *Amina Pennarum* away from us, and with Caru in my boat, I push off from the side, and into the sky.

I start to row.

After a moment, Caru shudders beneath my cloak, and shakes it off his head, an elegant pool of fabric slipping from his shining feathers.

He makes a low ruffling noise, deep in his chest, a hum. I push us out from the ship, out, out.

I look out at the scip steorra, and aim myself toward it. I can hardly see the navigation lights of *Amina Pennarum* now. We just need to get far enough away that they won't see him take flight.

Caru tilts his head and rattles out a little cry.

"What?" I ask.

Prison, Caru says. *Torn from rain and sky.*

Who took you? I ask. I notice that I'm singing, suddenly, notice that I'm not speaking any language but the one I share with Caru.

Magonia, says the falcon. *Thieves! Home*, he sings, more quietly now. *Home.*

The pitch of the bird's voice goes into my heart, and my heartbeat aligns to it. A beat, and the bird cries out, another, and the bird cries out again, a metronome.

Slavebirds. Songbirds. Songgirl.

Caru stares into my eyes and his head weaves.

He stops singing, and stares at the sky, opens his wings wide, and then folds them again.

A breeze, and I realize my cheeks are wet. Tears are streaming down my face. Caru yearns for home. For [({   })].

Maybe he, at least, can have it.

It's quiet out here. There's no one, no other ship, no Milekt. All I have is the roll of maps I took from Zal's cabin, and this huge, mad bird, who could kill me and everything around me, simply by screaming an alarm. I think about Zal's plans, the ones she's told me about. I'm only supposed to steal the plants. She swore it.

Do I trust her? I just watched her break her word.

How can I trust her?

Caru's talons and my arm are one now, and I row. Caru's wings open, and together we push into the night.

Caru sings a string of jangling syllables. In front of us, stars begin to blaze brighter, one by one. A trail. Very carefully, hesitantly, I add my voice to Caru's and I start seeing before us a gleaming silver path, straight into the night. A mist rises up around us, a storm of soft sand, and hides us from the moon. We move forward in darkness.

But I look down, off the boat, toward the world, and for a moment, I lose myself. I imagine Jason seeing my rowboat making its way across a dark and highly trafficked sky. I imagine how much he'd love it. Part of me is drawn to the earth's surface, while another part reaches through the night for Dai. I ache a little more with each push of my boat. *Partner.*

My chest is hollow without Milekt, but the song of Caru has made its way inside me too. I feel something rattling in my heart, not a living being, but a want. To sing with Caru. To meld my voice to his. His voice is so strong—

But no.

He gets a choice.

"Go," I tell him, before I let myself be too tempted. "You're free. Go. Fly!"

Caru rises from my arm.

Go, I sing. *You belong to yourself.*

Caru looks down at me, eyes wild, wings wide, the red undersides visible. There's nothing keeping him here. He hangs in the air for a moment, above my boat, and then he arcs up.

He flies, a black-and-red flash of movement and silence, covering stars as he departs.

I hear him sing a bright white note. And then he's gone. My eyes are full of tears, but I put my oars out and start to turn my launch boat back to my ship. Back to . . . I don't know what. I aim toward the distant lights of *Amina Pennarum*, grit my teeth, and start rowing against the wind.

There's a strange sound. My head jerks up. The slap of ropes on wood, and then a rush of bodies rappelling expertly down, the impact of boots in the bottom of my launch.

Six of them, all in black, all wearing helmets, all silent. They're standing in my boat. Too many of them to fight off, if I even knew how to fight them off.

Oh my god. Oh my god, oh my god. There's only one thing this could be. *Breath.*

OH NO. Aza, Aza, Aza, you have made a serious mistake.

I tilt myself toward the edge of the boat. One of them looks at me and slowly, slowly, shakes its head. Black suits. I can't see their faces. Huge and muscled. A silent, terrifying, totally covered group of monsters.

This is what everyone has been talking about since I came onboard. Bulbous, reflective eyes, faces a mass of tubes and tissue, all covered in dark, almost invisible against the sky. Monsters, insects with human bodies, nothing I've seen, nothing I've imagined.

shitshitshit

There's a voice in my ear, jumbled and garbled, rough, right against my face.

"Aza Ray Quel," says the voice, gurgling, a broken ocean, someone speaking from deep inside whitenoise.

One of the Breath has my arms, and another has my legs, as though I'm strong enough to really fight them. Maybe I am. I don't know how strong I am. I don't know what I'm fighting.

"Aza Ray," says the voice again, a voice that reminds me of something, but they're all over my little boat, these black-garbed things, pinning my arms and grabbing me. I scream as they push a gag into my mouth. Someone yanks a hood over my head, and I can't see anything after that.

I'm a prisoner.

I'm hauled out from my launch, hooked to ropes. I swing out across space.

CHAPTER 24

I'm not on Amina Pennarum. *I can feel, by lack of sway, the* tremendous space this ship is taking up in the sky. The smell's different, too, cold metal rather than feathers and twigs.

My heart's burning and so are my nostrils and lungs. My bones are sticks. It's like I'm back on earth. Maybe it's the gag. I test, inhaling. No. I take a tight breath.

My chest is an empty hold in the center of a ship. No Milekt, and no Caru, either. I can feel the cold metal of Caru's ring on my thumb, but I'm not sure how it got there. I don't remember putting it on.

Breath are walking around me, boots, circling, circling.

One of the monsters rips off my hood, yanking my neck back, tearing out my hair. I wince, but the gag's still in my mouth.

A hold with metal, rounded walls. It's bright in here. Bright and dark at once, the way fluorescent lights are. I haven't seen any for a long time. And looking up, I realize I'm not actually seeing them now. There's a weird cold, gray light cracking along the ceiling, trapped against the walls, but it moves the same way lightning does, a tendril of fire, and then dark again.

A submarine. That's how this feels. A metal room full of Breath. I inhale, and choke, my lungs tight, my throat closing. They're going to kill me. I know it. I know it like I've never known anything.

One of the Breath takes off its helmet and I realize that it's a diving helmet, a kind of diving helmet. I brace myself for what I see underneath—

And—

And—

She looks at me with unadulterated hatred.

Long twisted black hair. Smooth pale skin. Needle-bright eyes, pale blue, not indigo. Skinny body, but less skinny than mine. She's made of muscle.

AZA RAY.

IS STANDING.

IN FRONT OF ME.

She's me. Oh my god, she's me. The me I was. The me I'm not anymore.

I throw myself backward in the chair I'm tied to and someone catches it, forcing me back into place. I can't speak. There's a gag still in my mouth, but I'm biting it.

Is this Magonian magic? A mind game? Is she some kind of . . . mirror?

Then, I realize. No, I know what she is. I know exactly what she is.

I know WHO she is.

This is Heyward Boyle. The baby who was taken from my parents by the Breath. This is the girl whose life I was dropped into. This is the girl whose life I lived for fifteen years.

Oh my god.

She's got a tattoo on her wrist, a stylized whirlwind, and I've seen it somewhere before. Not all whirlwinds are bad. Some of them bring new seeds to fertile ground. Some of them move ships across the sky. But the Breath are the kind that kill you.

It all unfolds now, a rush of revelations, the things I've heard whispered. The Breath: assassins and special agents. The Breath: mercenaries.

The Breath: humans raised in Magonia.

"Aza Ray Quel," she says, her voice no longer muffled by oxygen equipment. She stretches her arms, flexes them, and takes a step toward me. I jerk in my chair. Other Breath are taking off their helmets, and they're dead-eyed, the same way the stormsharks are. Rippling with muscle, and tense as springs.

They're human, but they look evil to me now. I feel small and Magonian. I feel like—

I look down at my blue skin, my indigo body, feel my twisting hair.

I haven't felt this way since I was on earth.

Alien. I feel like an alien.

Heyward assesses me.

"The renegade. Where were you off to?" she hisses.

A redheaded man is in front of me suddenly, and I know him. Oh god, I definitely know him. The medic who took me in the ambulance, the guy who cut me open. He was Breath. He's the one Zal sent.

He's scarier without his helmet, his suit unzipped to the waist. I can see a tattoo on his chest, a hurricane wind, flattening a tree into the ocean. It's as though Breath wear extra insignia on their skin.

"Commander," he says, and Heyward turns to him.

She's the commander? We're the same age.

"Confirmation," she says. "This girl is the one you harvested from among the drowners, and brought onto Captain Quel's ship?"

"One and the same. I delivered her to *Amina Pennarum*. It is my assessment that Quel intends to use her daughter's song in direct opposition to Magonian command."

My gag gets ripped out, nearly taking my lips with it, and I sputter, spitting and choking, still unable to breathe.

Heyward picks me up from the chair with no effort at all, and shakes me hard enough that my bones rattle. She's unbelievably strong. I'm tiny compared to her.

"What is this?" I manage to choke out.

Her suit is covered in embroidered rank badges. I may have stolen her old life, but she clearly has a new one. My head swims, and my hands shake.

"The rumors about Captain Quel were accurate," the redheaded Breath says. "It seems she's returned to her former ambitions."

I can't do anything but cough. My breathing is so short that I'm possibly going to die in this hold.

"Has Captain Quel spoken of Spitsbergen?" she asks me.

I fall into a racking spell of coughing. I'm not telling her anything.

"Or seeds? Plants? She has, I see it on your face. The same scheme, then."

"It is our opinion, based on the charts aboard *Amina Pennarum*, that Captain Quel seeks to use Aza's song to open the vault," confirms the redheaded Breath.

"It was the conviction of the drowner as well, judging by

his notes on trajectory. More than that," says Heyward, "Captain Quel seeks to open the world."

I'm blacking out. I'm blurring around her words, staring at her face. MY face. I can feel my strength ebbing, slipping out of me, something unspooling.

"Take her up. She's suffocating."

The Breath half carry me through a sealed corridor, and out into the main ship.

I can breathe again once I'm above deck, and after a coughing spell, the relief is so great I can't believe I could have forgotten how it felt to not be able to take in air.

I inhale carefully, looking around as surreptitiously as I can. The ship is storm-cloud gray, and teeming with uniformed Breath, anonymous in their helmets. Heyward's has a transparent face. I can still see her.

The sails are made of hum and speed. No wonder I didn't hear them coming. One is all gigantic black moths, their wings slow and delicate, but thousands upon thousands of them. Another is wasps. Another black hummingbirds, working as an army to lift this ship into the sky. The batsail on *Amina Pennarum* is one entity, reliable. If it's killed, the ship goes down, but this sail could abandon the ship in a thousand directions. I look at the figurehead. An oarfish. There's a slanting, tilted name painted on one of the masts: *Regalecus*.

The Breath, in their helmets, their strange tubes helping them to breathe. That's what strikes fear into their enemies.

By the Breath, they swear. Everyone in Magonia is scared of them.

If you've spent your life hooked to various oxygen equipment, those tubes aren't quite as foreign to you. I eyeball the line coming out from the Breath's suits and snaking to something on their backs. Not normal oxygen tanks. Something very small, and portable.

Heyward's fingers dig into my neck.

"You will be of use, Aza Ray," she says. "You'll serve your people. We're here, on behalf of Maganwetar, to make sure you do."

My heart fills with Dai, with the image of his family, dead. With the image of him, a little kid, gorging on food from Zal's ship's hold.

"What does Maganwetar know about its people?" I say.

She sneers. "Are you so easily swayed, Aza Ray? A moment ago, you were human. Now you speak as a Magonian."

"You talked about Magonia when you watched the squid. Who did you speak to after that? Who did you tell?"

I feel my spine freeze.

"How do you know about the squid?" The giant squid footage was a secret. Only Jason and I knew about it.

Heyward looks steadily at me for a moment, and then smiles. "I see why you like him," she says.

My heart pounds painfully in my chest.

"What do you mean?"

She looks at me, assessing. "He told me everything. And so will you. Who else on earth did you speak of Magonia to? Which parts of Captain Quel's plan are already in motion?"

"I'm not telling you anything," I say.

"Your boy gave me this," she says calmly, and hands me a piece of paper. I unfold it.

It's charred at one edge, but still readable.

I { } you more than [[[{{{ }}}]]].

I can't speak.

I can't—

"Where'd you get this?"

"He took it from your body," Heyward says. "When you died. But then you weren't dead. Or, I wasn't. He gave it back to me."

I feel all my blood rising—

"Well, perhaps he didn't *give* it to me," she says. "Perhaps I took it from him. The same way he took it from you."

My fingers and toes go numb.

Dead?

He—

I stare at her, this monster, and I lose control of my voice.

"NO!" I scream, the note smashed into my hand, and there's a blood-boiling shriek of answer from out of the dark above me.

Milekt emerges from the sky, a golden thorn shooting through the air, screaming rage for my disobedience. He drops into my chest and I sing the loudest, highest, most savage note I've ever sung. Rage and grief and disbelief—

NO.

A cloud of bats pour out of the night all around us, tugging shreds of dark onto the ship. They drop it over the Breath, blocking their sight as cleanly as if they'd been put under hoods.

NO.

"BOARD!" Dai shouts, out of the invisible, and I see an entire swath of Zal's starry-camouflage unwrap from around *Amina Pennarum*.

Dai dives into the rigging right above me, twirling a rope. He and Svilken are singing incredibly fast. There's a giant wind kicking up and the squallwhales are orbiting us, looking ready to sing a hurricane. Dai's shouting at me, and now, now I start singing. Singing like I've never sung.

Jason. Jason. JASON.

It's that song, that griefsong that slams into a Breath, yanking out his tubes. The Breath falls, clutching his chest, ropes twisting around him.

A boom, a big boom and the *Regalecus*

ShAkEs

And sags at one end, one sail half gone.

I see Jik slash at a Breath, stronger than I could have imagined, still on Zal's ship, but fighting for me. I'm screaming hard, this song roaring out of my throat. Because. I can't. I won't let this be true.

I sing the hummingbirds loose from the official ship's sail. They fly, darts of dark, fast, fast, into the sky.

My song rises up, Dai amplifying it, and one wasp detaches itself from the *Regalecus*'s other sail. Then another. A swarm spins up into the dark. The ship lurches, ponderously, a huge weight settling.

Heyward raises her chin in the air, inhales oxygen, and starts to launch herself to tackle me to the deck.

NO.

I dive at her instead with everything I have. Every memory. Every rage. Everything.

JASON.

I open my mouth and Milekt and Dai join with me. Sand forms in the space between Heyward and me. I sing the air solid. I sing it full.

Choke, I sing, and I think of her lungs, think of her gasping the way I gasped all my life, strangling on air.

I knock her down, but she's not that easy. She kicks herself forward, a knife in each hand, trying to get to my chest to cut Milekt out. She's trying to kill my canwr.

I sing harder, deeper. I feel things shattering on this ship, Breath helmets, and bits of rigging.

Heyward's knife slices my arm.

All I have is my voice, but it pushes her, twists her, wrings her.

All around us, my crew and Zal are fighting Breath.

Heyward's hurt. She grits her teeth, pure force of will, and launches herself at me again.

I roar, this shrill shrieking noise, and I feel it vibrate my vocal cords, feel my canwr with me, and there's Heyward in front of me, and a sound, a thundering sound.

JASON, I screamsing.

I can hear what I'm doing, calling to the sky and telling it to come to me. Telling it to empty itself for me.

The air's cracking. There are flashes of light all around us, the sky splitting, and I'm still making the noise, high and sweet and deadly.

I feel it in my fingers, in my tongue, in my teeth, the beginning of fire.

I'm making a storm now, making the air into it, making parts of our bodies into it.

It's a deathsong, and I'm not sure whose. If it's for Jason or Heyward or for the entire universe.

Inside my chest Milekt revolts, refusing, and I gasp, choking, trying to breathe.

In that pause, all the Breath dive off the ship, covering themselves in shadows.

Heyward is the last to abandon ship. She shouts in fury,

shoots me a look made of ice, and dives off the plank.

They're gone into the night faster than we can follow.

My song is broken by tears. I can't. I can't.

Jason.

I sag. I sing, and I don't know what I'm singing now, but it's only grief and after a minute, all I can do is sob.

My crew ransacks *Regalecus,* hanging in the sky now by a single sail. They open the closets, pushing through the vaults, taking provisions.

I'm with Dai, walking as though I'm asleep. I keep thinking squid. I keep thinking burned. I keep thinking gone.

Dead. Dead?

I feel a kind of blankness. I won't cry again in front of Dai. I won't cry at all.

If I do, I'll never stop.

Dai pulls the curtain off one of the portholes, and it's startling to see the room cloud lit, gray and piercing.

"I'm sorry," he says quietly.

"For what?"

"Your friend," he says.

He looks at me, his expression tight, his mouth a crooked line. "I know you loved him."

"I—"

"I know what it's like," he cuts in. "I know how it feels to lose someone you love."

I shut my eyes for a moment and stay in the dark. I stay there a while.

"What were you doing?" he finally asks me.

"When?"

"When you took off with Zal's heartbird," he says.

"Nothing," I say dumbly. "I made a mistake."

"You set the falcon free," he says.

"Yeah."

Dai nods. "Even if he betrayed Zal, he had no memory of it. It's better to set him free. He had no song, no use. He should have been released."

Dai opens a cabinet in the corner. I catch a glimpse of something pale, something fleshy. A body?

Oh god, what if it's—

"They're just skins," Dai says. "Same as the one you were in. Though impressive ones. New versions. Maganwetar must plan to go down among them now. Useful knowledge."

He rifles through them. They're each encased in their own bag. I shiver. Dai takes my hand. That does me no good. He pulls one of the skins out from inside the closet.

It's less than a body. Flat, deflated, almost a piece of clothing. She's pale and sad, her face peaceful. A lifelike doll-woman, hanging inside a clear sack, zipped into it. Her hair is long and blond. Her skin is pale, and her eyes are shut. Her lips are just slightly open.

"How do they even work?" I ask Dai, trying to distract myself from everything.

He tilts the skin inside its covering, showing me. There's an opening at its spine.

"You touch them and they wrap around you. They cover your skin, your organs. The one you had on down below would have made you indistinguishable from a drowner, though it should have degraded after a month or so. I don't know why it lasted so long."

All I want to do is wrap myself back up in my old skin, my familiar human self, the body I knew everything about, however flawed and Magonian it secretly was. But it's gone. I'm this thing that emerged from it, some kind of miserable phoenix.

I put my hand out to unzip the sack on another body: there are all kinds, male and female, and all ages. Dai grabs the casing around the one I have and pulls it away from me.

"Do you want to fall into it?" he warns. "Touch it, and it'll touch you."

Inside one of the bags, a skin opens its eyes and looks at us.

I yelp and step back. The girl staring at us is brown-skinned, her hair braided. A girl my age.

Dai shudders, then slings some skins over his arm. "It's empty. The skins just have reflexes."

We're taking treasure, I realize. Spoils for our defeat of the Breath ship. We're certainly pirates now, if we weren't before.

The skin watches me all the way out of the room as we carry her.

We load them onto *Amina Pennarum*, along with provisions, everything we can take.

Milekt and I quietly sing the remaining waspsail loose. It unspirals into the morning. It's dawn, and below us, ocean, white waves, and a dead Breath ship, falling through the sky, dropping into the sea.

It'll dissolve. That's what happens, or so I've been told. In the water, the leftover wrecks of many Magonian ships drift, hidden, barely visible.

If you were diving, I guess you'd never know. Skyship or seaship, they're just wrecks. And there are so many of them on the ocean floor.

"That's the last of it," Zal says. She's whispering, just to me. I can hear anger in her voice, but other things too. "Caru's gone. That's done now. You're forgiven for it. He wasn't mine in the first place, not if he betrayed me to Ley." She's struggling. "But that's your last mutiny. Agreed? It ends now."

My brain is blurred by sorrow, broken by grief.

"No more lies," Zal continues. "We're together, you and me, against Maganwetar." She tucks a strand of hair behind my ear and whispers gently. "No child was ever so wanted."

Even in the face of her display, I feel nothing. I'm gone inside.

She smiles at me. "You're loved, Aza," she says. "Very loved."

Loved. By Zal. It offers no comfort. But I'm back aboard *Amina Pennarum*.

Maganwetar hired the Breath that killed Jason.

And I'm at war.

Sunrise off the starboard, a white, brittle sunrise, stars still visible above the ship's rail, sun rising not over mountains or horizon, but over endless ice. Inside my chest, Milekt sings his own song, and I grieve and try to reconcile myself to the thing I thought I already knew—that I'll never see Jason again, never touch his hand again. I see him in my head for a second, not even looking at me, his intense concentration, the way he focused when he wanted something. I knew everything about him, every detail, every moment, but now I don't.

I thought I was the one who was gone.

I thought I was the one who would leave.

But now—

After a moment, I sing quietly with Milekt. We make a small whirl of white sand out of the moisture in the air above us. It hisses as it spins, and then we let it fall, sandsnow.

The icy world below us shines like an eggshell. We're near our destination. Close to our mission.

This is what I was born for. There's nothing else left for me.

I still don't fit. Heart half on earth, half in the clouds. I'm still different from everyone else. There's still no place I belong.

There are so many things so terribly wrong with the world below us—the way the rivers change colors from blue to green to brown. The way the smoke slips into the squallwhales and makes them sick, and the way Magonians starve, while earth eats.

I think about the way Maganwetar hoards what little we harvest, leaving Magonians like Dai's siblings to die of hunger, and sending mercenaries to innocents on earth—

Shh, Aza. Shh. Don't think about it.

The only solution is to wipe the slate clean. To abandon the old ways. To change everything.

I'm on my way to save not just my own life, but the lives of all of Magonia. And now I have more reason than ever.

A squallwhale from some other pod is off to the side, industriously making snow, eyeing me, before, startled by our speed, it torpedoes forward, pinging and whistling urgently back to us, informing us that we have no business moving at this rate.

Snowmaker! whistles the squallwhale. *Homesky! Sing and flee, sing and fly! Trouble the waters, trouble the rain! Shipstop.*

Other squallwhales join the song and for a moment, we're surrounded in every direction, an entire pod of them, calves and mothers and bulls, all of them singing furiously at us, *shipstop shipstop*, making clouds of snow and pouring them down upon the northern sea. They're singing a blizzard.

We pay them no heed.

I take a deep breath, pushing all the pain down.

I look out from the deck of *Amina Pennarum,* down into the ice, and apparently I own this for now. This sea. This sky. Captain's Daughter. I hear a bird calling from somewhere, a long and mournful call.

I could cry, but if I did, it would be black-blue ink tears, frozen ones. Icicles.

I think of Caru. Maybe he has a roost now, on some ship sailing south, or he's flying alone, singing his own song. He's free, and he's gone. I envy him.

Sleet ribbons pass my face in long, tearing streaks, and silver birdfish leap in the spray, throwing out tendrils of ice and flinging them downward.

I put my hand flat against the center of my chest, trying to keep my heart safe. It hurts.

Launches detach from the edges of the ship, and rise up beside us.

I see crew members rowing into the mist as we push through the clouds and gray to the edge of the sky, where the moon's turning color, and night's beginning to fall.

The deck is covered with ice, and I'm freezing, but I can't bring myself to go below. Dai's sitting beside me. Frozen.

I feel wrong. My heart. I miss. I miss.

I reach over and take Dai's hand. I look at our fingers twisted together. I sing a soft note, and he echoes it, quietly, gently magnifying it. We make a tiny cloud, and he makes it rain, a miniature storm. He looks at me, and blows the cloud away, and together we watch it drift off over the deck rail. He was born to this too. There's nothing else for him either.

Below us, I'm watching ice floes crashing against one another. I'm seeing the ocean, black between the white plains.

I hear another long call of mourning, from somewhere close.

Caru?

No. You get the canwr that's assigned to you, not the one

you choose. Milekt is mine. We're bonded. It's permanent. I think about what happens when it's not, and I don't want that for either of us.

Zal's pacing the deck, her own voice humming. All the crew is lit up with it—readiness, hunger.

We're stationing our ship above an old mine in a sandstone mountain, fitted out with everything to keep the world's seeds safe. Its location is its security. The mountain is its protection.

This is the vault the Breath talked about.

Down there are packets and packets of seeds, hundreds of thousands, sealed against moisture, on rows of shelves, almost a library. These are backups of almost all the edible plants on earth. Rice and apple seeds and broccoli and anything else you can imagine. There are walnuts in deep freeze, and down that old mine shaft, all kinds of tiny bins full of salvation.

Apparently, there are airplants here too. Or so Zal swears.

The vault is a reverse ark—plants not animals, under stone, not on the water. This isn't a military camp. There are no guns, no soldiers. What's there to keep the seeds safe is miles of rock.

And I'm the girl who can sing the rock into water. I'm the one who can bring the plants up.

I wonder for a moment what will happen once the rock shifts. Zal promised me again that this would be simple. But what does Zal's word mean?

I can't think about it. I'm in charge of myself, no matter what Zal may or may not want. I'll get the plants out, and we'll be done.

I feel Milekt singing again, a lullaby. *Loyalty.*

I wonder where Jik is. I realize I haven't seen her since we battled with the Breath. I don't know what she wanted me to do with Caru, or if I did it properly. I wonder if she's mad at me.

I look down again. The ice is breaking, and between the floes, something swims. A polar bear.

The spray from the Barents Sea splashes up onto our deck, and there are whitecaps on the edge of the rocks bordering Svalbard. I know there's a tiny town close by, a tiny airport, but the way we came there's been almost nothing below us but the sweep of ice hills. Now it's only snow and sea.

This is the closest I've been to the ground in a long time. How long exactly, Aza? It feels like forever. I don't belong down there anymore. But then, I guess I never did.

On the earth, I was never the person in charge of anything, not even my own body. But here, I'm important. Here, I'm the only one capable of doing *this*—the hard thing—the thing that will save my people.

And I have to do it now. I picture the airplants in Magonian skies again, fields and fields of them. No one starving. No more dying.

We're wheezing, all of us who aren't Rostrae. We can't stay this low for very long. My lungs are compacting and quivering, and inside them, everything's both cold and tight. That part's okay. That's accounted for. I'm not wearing a helmet. I have to sing, but in order to sing, I need to be able to breathe. I have a bottle of high Magonian air. I can gasp from it if I have to.

The batsail sings me a song that if I were human, I wouldn't be able to hear. There are no other bats here. It's too cold for them. Here it's Arctic foxes and polar bears. But the batsail isn't fussy about work. I think about how Zal told me it was just an animal. It isn't. It sings me comfort. It calms my soul.

The night gets a little darker, but it's all snow and ice down there, a kind of glowing gray.

Zal is beside me, looking hard at me. "Are you uncertain?" she says.

"No," I tell her. "I know what to do."

On cue, Milekt makes a golden sound from inside my chest.

Ready, ready, ready, Milekt sings. His claws are in my lung, holding on, and his beak is stabbing me.

Ready, I sing with Milekt. I zip up my suit, pull up my hood, walk out onto the deck, and stand at the rail. I catch my breath and it's not just this drowner air that makes me gasp. A tall gray shaft spikes right out of the permafrost. It's a splinter in the hillside. The repository entrance.

Milekt starts to sing the first notes of the song we've been practicing since Ley died. An old song, something Magonians sang hundreds of years ago.

When we get these plants back, the sky will be full of fields of epiphytes. Magonia will be self-sufficient. We can leave earth crops alone. And the capital will lose its power to deprive its people.

The song is full of hope, of green, of spring.

We'll harvest the clouds when we get them back. No more skysettlements will starve. And the rest of the things that are wrong here? They can be fixed. Hunger makes wars. Food ends them.

Green leaf, Milekt sings. *Skyblooms.*

I join him, light-fingered as a pickpocket at first, testing my techniques. Dai will sing too, but right now it's too delicate. We don't want to overwhelm the ice.

I sing a little harder to the rock below us, and to the metals of the entrance and the hidden building. For long seconds nothing happens. Then there's a low groan. Something in the earth moving.

(*Maganwetar's coming,* a voice in my head breaks in. *We broke every law. We're breaking more now. There's no way they're not going to find us.*)

I drive the thought away and focus, and the air starts to shine, a shimmering frozenness. Dai's opening his mouth—still silent, but ready, Svilken in his chest.

I reach out my hand and take his, and he squeezes my fingers. I sing a section of air into a sheet of ice.

The air is gleaming, a bright, knife-hardness, and I slam the ice, with my voice, into the ground.

I glance at Zal. Her face is lit up with excitement, her eyes trained only on the destruction I'm causing.

I sing one high note with Milekt, a piercing sound, and there's a scream from below, a shuddering lurch of stone. I watch the ground divide at the point into which I drove the ice. A crack in the snow, right outside the repository. Water wells out of the crevasse, melted and shifted, turned from stone into liquid.

I pant for a moment, dizzy. Dai holds me tighter. Milekt buzzes around in my lung, and I look over and see Jik. She's behind the captain, staring at me. Everyone is. Her feathers are standing up all over her shoulders.

"Open the rock!" Zal cries, exultant.

I take a breath from the bottle, and then sing deeper. I feel Dai's voice before I hear it. He joins his quiet note into my song, and things shift below us.

The change spreads quickly. The snow on the hillside

shudders into liquid and the great shaft of rock above the repository isn't stone now, no, it's a column of siltless, clear water. We hold it with our voices.

Zal maneuvers the ship directly above it; I can see through hundreds of feet of what was, a moment ago, a mountain. It's now a wide well, the rock receding deeper, and then deeper still until the stone at the bottom suddenly ends. The water wants to spill.

Yes, the water wants to flood, but I stop it, holding it in place with song. I feel Dai tense with the effort of keeping a world in motion motionless.

Through the swirling depths, we glimpse a room.

Shelves and shelves and shelves, lockers full of seeds. The vault.

The water wants to gush right into the corridors we've reached, but I manage to hold it where it is. Dai and I sing a few more taut notes, and the sinkhole grows wider. The entire surface of the island is churning now.

The crew is gasping, staring, at the force of this power. The hill's turning to a lake. Inside my chest, Milekt is frantic with effort, battering against me.

The water wants to fall more than I have strength to stop it, so I sing cold and turn acres of hill water into ice. Through it, we can see all the way down, clear as glass.

Room after room, chamber after chamber of cabinets, suddenly lit up. *Which seeds will we get? Which of the plants will we carry? There're too many.*

The strongest singers of the crew are starting their own notes now, and I can see cabinets bursting open, packets of seeds gusting into rooms, rising as if in high winds, each wrapped in their waterproofing. Floods have been planned for by the people who constructed this vault.

"Starboard!" Zal yells, and the ship moves, our Rostrae in the sky towing it. I look up and see Jik, her talons clasped on a rope. She's still staring down at me, but she's completely in bird form.

"Now, Aza," Zal says to me.

I sing a melthole in the ice, not so different from where a seal would rise to breathe.

Amina Pennarum's best fishers and hunters lean over the side. They tug the pulley from the back of our deck—the strong one we use for bringing up livestock—into position.

"Now!" Zal shouts, and the great weighted mass of hooks and snares plummets into the hole I've made. The pulley's flywheels spin and the gripper plunges into the shaft of water and into the center of the hill. Toward the seeds.

I expect it to reach the room we can see, grab what it can, ascend again, to repeat the fishing as long as I can hold the hill. But Zal orders me, "Go deeper."

Milekt directs our notes. He shrills, and I sing with Dai and Svilken. There are deeper rooms beneath the main vault. I stutter a second, confused, and a big chunk of the ice flickers for a moment back to stone. I steady my song as quickly as I can.

Lights, much lower in that storage facility than there should be, rooms of hydroponic rows deep in the mountain. Testing rooms with plants struggling into existence.

I sing, controlled, precise, but I feel as though something's wrong with me. It feels the same way it did when Dai and I accidentally sang that wave together, out of control.

I can feel him behind me, his quiet notes guiding my song, but they feel stronger than they should. My notes are tense and sharp.

At the bottom of the complex, the lowest of these clandestine levels, behind secure doors, guarded by cameras now breaking with sudden cold, are rooms full of secret seeds and plants. There's a whole level of them. I can only just make them out.

I didn't expect these. A chamber full of twitching root babies in pots. Mandrake roots. A vegetable lamb. Pumpkins fed by blood drips. Those, and more.

THERE. The things I'm looking for: the Magonian epiphytes. The plants from myth. They're as real as Magonia is.

The drowners have been hiding them.

My voice falters again, but Milekt, Svilken, and Dai are there, singing to me, singing hard into me, forcing me not to stop.

The plants are drifting in the air. They float like seaweed. Their leaves are long and silver. Their roots twist. They're rooted—in nothing.

Lost Magonian crops, still growing in midair. They're so beautiful I can barely believe it.

The hook plunges straight through the rooms of drowner crops. The crew moves fast, swiveling the hook. It oscillates in the room of eddying airplants, snags one, two, more on its teeth.

"Bring them up," Zal shouts.

They crank the handle of the pulley and the rope begins to ascend. It tugs the plants. They shake themselves loose of the air they've rooted in. They start to rise through the vault.

We only need enough to start a crop. This will change everything.

It's almost finished. I didn't know how afraid I was until the relief starts washing over me.

It's done, I think. I did it. I'm still singing, but it can ebb.

I glance at Zal for permission to stop, but she's not looking at me.

"Now," she says to Dai. "It's time."

There's a hunger and an anger in her voice that makes me feel frozen.

There's something wrong in the air suddenly. A hum, far away, a sound. My head jerks up to look around, but I can't see anything, only mist and clouds. Squallwhales.

What's happening?

I can't read Dai's expression. He steps back from me, but I still have his heat, the comfort of him next to me. Then Dai and Svilken join their song entirely to mine, at their peak volume. Our song surges, pouring out of me.

It's like I hit a trip wire. The need to sing is overwhelming.

Dai's notes blast into me. More than I can handle. I have no control. I try to silence my vocal cords.

I can't.

Power's pouring out of me, but I'm powerless. I'm being used as a tool in someone else's hands.

I scream and the scream is my song; Dai's notes are in my throat and roaring into my ears. In a moment, the song changes.

And what they're—what WE'RE singing is *Flood*.

This isn't the plan. The plan was the seeds. The plants. But the island starts breaking into pieces. Water rushing into and in from the sea.

Glacial ice batters against the edge of the island. The repository entrance shakes hard. The ice I've made from the hill's stone is shattering, turning into water, and starting to gush.

Zal stands beside me. "We will have our revenge, Aza Ray, on all who've wronged us, and all who've hurt you. Drown them. When the floods recede, we begin again with the true Magonia."

I blink, but I can't stop. My mouth is open and my voice is flying from it, like I'm Caru, like I have wings on every note.

Zal wants this, I realize. She's wanted it all along.

Below us, the rock island starts turning to ocean.

Flood, Milekt sings now, betraying me, acting against me, and Dai sings deeply with him, harmonizing, focusing the notes that Milekt sings into my whistling melody.

The corridors below are shaking and liquefying, and suddenly from one of them sprints a line of humans, uniformed. Soldiers from somewhere in the building, and *Amina Pennarum*'s hook is rising through the water I've made out of solid ground.

No. There weren't supposed to be people here.

Uninhabited, Zal told me. This wasn't supposed to happen—

The hill is shaking. The whole of Spitsbergen is trying to turn to water. I try again to stop, but Dai's song won't let me.

"Keep going," Zal shouts at him. Dai looks as terrified as I feel, but he's still singing.

Flood! screams Milekt, this tiny demon of yellow feathers, and I scream the song with him, helpless. *Drown.*

Zal is using me. As Ley warned she would, as Jik warned she would. I'm as much her slave as the Rostrae are. I fooled myself with the thought that I was special. I have no choice.

I calculate frantically, quickly. A few tons of matter is all it'll take. An island here, a mountain there, the seas will rise, and earth will flood.

Dai's song is right in me, moving with my own heart, my own lungs, my own body. I try to tell him NO, try to appeal to him with my eyes.

I can see his fear, but he's loyal to Zal. He warned me that he'd do anything she commanded. I didn't know this was what he meant.

A new sound mingles with our song. First a hum, but soon a deafening roar.

I see it rushing down out of the clouds. Something huge moving through the sky, something surrounded by wind. It's so enormous I can't see the size of it. Oh god. Oh my god. I see clouds and spinning, and ropes dangling from it.

MAGANWETAR.

Zal barks, "Bring the plants up now! Stations!" The pulley turns, and the rest of the crew starts whirling ropes and chains.

We're surrounded, out of nowhere, by the capital city and its twisting borders. And I'm still singing with Milekt in my chest—

The epiphytes are still rising up, and—

I'm losing myself. The song is singing me. I'm drunk with it, and some part of me thinks I don't care anymore.

I'll drown everyone, all of us, sing until my throat tears out, sing the sky open, sing everything into an abyss—

Another human runs out from near the repository, fighting the wind, shouting into the dark. It's snowing and hailing and I'm looking down at this person on this little island of ice, a tiny person seen from above.

We're maybe twenty feet up, hanging in the mist of our song, pulling up the plants, and the world's turning to water, and tears are streaming down my face, from rage and power-lessness, from grief, from desperation.

He's waving his arms.

I can't see him through the mist and flood. A person. A drowner.

"Finish it!" Zal bellows. *"Flood them."*

I see the world Zal wants. A sea made of the earth. A flash of a ship on a great sea, and of a bird above it all, a bird like Caru. Then gone. A flash of a flood rising up and covering over the world. The sea full of bodies. Drowned.

Someone near me screams. Someone above our ship screams louder.

An anchor drops onto our deck from the massive city above us.

Arrows zing by.

The whole time, Dai's singing *"Don't stop,"* and I'm singing *"FLOOD,"* even as our ship tilts.

Below, that flood is surging up for the person on the ground. He shifts and the mist moves away from him, the one person, the one drowner, his face suddenly visible, and—

A giant squid on a backlit screen.

An alligator at my birthday party.

A hoodie for the hospital.
Driving a car to fetch a hoax.
Together on my front steps.
JASON.

CHAPTER 26

{JASON}

I'm right below her. I can see her. I can see everything, at least every few seconds. It's like a bad connection.

I see a ship. More than a ship. I see something so insane up there, high in the sky, way above where the ship is.

There's a city in the clouds.

Mostly hidden, a huge, ponderous thing, buildings with spire tops, wind whirling around it. So, that's happening.

I'm alive. I didn't think I would be. The lightning struck me, leaving three burns—one in each hand, and one in the middle of my back.

When I opened my eyes, the groundskeeper was bending over me and saying "Son, you been struck. Should I restart your heart?"

"I think my heart's beating, thanks," I said.

Then my heart stopped.

He gave me CPR.

I was in the hospital for the next week. I was pretty much unconscious for four days, with people freaking out all around me. When I finally came to my senses, my body hurt like I'd been beaten up by a gang of giants, and I had long red burns branching down my arms and legs. But I was freakishly okay. In fact, I felt better than I've ever felt.

Magonian lightning? I don't know. I can see *things* now, no spyglass necessary.

Mr. Grimm was one of the first people who visited me, asking about the lightning, asking about how it felt, and I didn't know what to tell him, so I described everything. He went very pale. I felt bad for him. I probably sounded insane. I think he chalked it up to delirium.

The note un-Aza handed me, the one I'd given real-Aza, was gone.

So I knew where she was going. And I knew where Aza was going too.

Ergo, I knew where *I* was going.

That got me out of bed, even though I fell over when my feet touched the floor. But there was no version of my life in which I wasn't getting my ass to Svalbard.

You don't want to know how I got here, you don't want to know how much it cost, you don't want to know how gigantically in deep shit I am. I left a note for Carol and Eve. They'll never forgive me, except they love me, so they will.

I told them I'd be back and not to worry. I'm going to be explaining for the rest of my life. But hey. Some things you don't have time to explain in the moment.

The fact that I got here before she did is a miracle.

Forged documents. Hacked computer. Claiming of consular privileges. I called in favors. I accrued debts that I will be spending the rest of my life paying off. And I'm officially the biggest pain in the ass in the entirety of the dark side of the internet right now, but it was worth it. I'm here. So is she.

I can see her, every few seconds, a flash of her in a wet suit and a hood, on deck.

She doesn't look like herself, but I can hear her voice mixed with other voices. It'd be hard not to hear it. Everything else is birds.

There are screaming birds everywhere, but when I blink, I can see that they're not birds, really, not at all. Nope.

Human bird things. Some kind of hybrids.

I'm forcing myself not to pi, because I can't do it. I have to be here.

I can see her surrounded by people I can't understand—*"Something has happened above the clouds that man has not yet accounted for"*—and up in the sky right above her, there's this CITY, sending ropes down to her ship. She's right there in the middle of it.

Aza, Aza, Aza . . . !

I'm running from where I've been hiding, and out into the open space, because if she sees me, she can't—

She can. She keeps singing, and around me things are cracking open. The whole world's breaking into pieces.

This is some kind of earthquake, some kind of natural disaster, and somehow it's because of her singing. I feel her notes stabbing into the ice around me.

There's water pouring out of rock where there shouldn't be, and a hook rising up beside me, coming through the ground and attached to her ship. It's minus I don't even know how many degrees. It would be ironic, my brain informs me, to freeze to death, just after I was almost fried.

I shout her name. She doesn't respond. I shout harder, but the sky's full of ships now, and some kind of totally insane battle starts happening.

Cannonballs, arrows.

My vision goes in and out.

Blink. Blue sky.

Blink. Ship battle.

Blink. Clouds.

Blink. Cloud city.

Blink. Skysharks and skywhales.

I wave my arms.

"AZA!" I scream, and the water rises around my ankles. I look up at her and shout her name again, and I see her standing there, frozen, staring down at me, still singing.

I don't know anything. I can't tell anything.

Except that Aza's here, and she's alive. *I* might not be for much longer, but maybe that's okay as long as—the first part.

"AZA!" and I'm crying, but my tears are freezing, and I don't know what the hell I'm doing here, because up in that sky is her, and down here is me, and I'm without any kind of backup.

"3.141592653589793238462643383279502884197169399375105820974944592307816406286," I shout as though it's magic, as though pi is enough to summon her down, as fast as I can shout the numbers, the basic numbers, waving my arms frantically, and then, suddenly, she stops.

She sees me. I feel it happen. The whole island shakes. And something comes flying fast out of the sky above her.

NO!! I cover my mouth with my hands, clamping it shut, and Milekt screamsings inside my lung.

It's Jason! It's JASON.

Alive, alive alive!

Every note I sing is making the sea rise. Every second I sing is two hundred years of climate change. I stop my song,

But

I'm

Not

S

T

O

P

P

I

N

G

NO.

The sea's rising

and the song

is pouring out of me

WHY CAN'T I STOP?!

I look at Dai. He stares back at me, and he has no mercy. He and Zal are making me dissolve the world. I won't sing the world into a flood. I can't lose Jason again.

But I'm singing as hard as ever.

I'm looking down at Jason. I'm going to drown him. I'm going to drown everyone, and Dai's beside me magnifying my voice, and Zal's screaming at me, and Milekt's inside my chest, when everything—

Stops.

Out of the air above me, I hear a cry like only one thing I've heard before, a damaged opera, a sweetness so high and bright it hurts, discordant and ferocious, desolation and love twined into a song.

CARU.

He shoots down, black feathers and red wings. He hangs in the air above me, and there's fighting all around, ships and planes, and arrows and I—

SING! Caru screams. *SING NOW.*

I take a huge breath from the bottle and then rap hard on my own breastbone.

You will not! Milekt shrieks. *She's mine!*

Caru screams back at Milekt. *Never yours!*

I open the door in my chest, lay my lung bare to the cold and there's the bright yellow thorn inside it, shrilling at me.

This is my nest! whistles Milekt, and then he tries to force me back to the flood song, but he can't, because now I can see Caru.

Caru, who is loyal. Caru, who is no one's.

She chooses, he sings. *I choose.*

Caru, heartbird, chooses me.

He rises from the shadow of the ship where he's been flying, staying quiet against his own nature.

I grab Milekt, his tiny gold body, his screaming beak.

Traitor! he shrills, and I pry him out of my lung, where he's anchored his claws. I pull him out, and close the door. The yellow bird stares at me, his eyes glittering like jet.

TRAITOR!

But I'm not the traitor.

I hurl him out into the air, and he hangs there, shocked and enraged.

Caru's been here all along. I've been hearing scraps of his song. He's here to sing with me.

He stayed for me.

She would drown the earth! Caru shrieks. *She would kill them all. Kill the world. Drown the fields and the trees.*

Caru jabs his beak into my hand, and prods the ring on my finger. Zal's grabbing for him, but he dodges, glances off, and he screeches at her, too, and all around us, there are Magonians and Rostrae screaming, dying. There are Breath dropping down from above.

Svilken's out of Dai's chest and dive-bombing the falcon. Zal's aiming something at Caru, and I can see it. She's going to shoot him with her bow and arrow.

I look at Jason, this tiny figure on the ice. I can hear him shouting still, his voice, and I know what he's shouting. I know that number. It doesn't end.

Like {(( ))}. It never ends.

I know myself.

And I know what to do.

I open the door in my chest again, and I place Caru's ring inside it.

I hear Milekt scream a horrible scream. He shudders and tumbles to the deck at my feet.

I merge with Caru.

Heartbird.

I sing.

Separate but connected. By choice, his own and mine. We choose each other.

There's a huge quake, a change in everything. Caru looks at me and I look at him.

We're stronger together, I know, than anything else. Fiercer than everything else. He's both things, earth and Magonia and so am I.

Caru jerks in the air, those huge yellow eyes, his wings wide. He lifts up and hangs on the wind above me. His beak opens and he shrieks something that shifts the sky around us. I open my mouth and fling my voice out with his, and our notes wrap around each other.

I feel the whole sky respond. This isn't the way it is with Milekt, or even Dai. Caru and I—the two of us are one thing. Caru's voice comes out of my mouth, and mine out of his.

Caru and I sing waves of certainty. Stars blaze in the sky at our sound and fall in arcs on both sides. My voice is growing and so is Caru's. High-pitched sonar, singing out, singing out, singing out.

The world's flooding. I did it for Zal. I undo it for me.

It's overflowing, water against the vault, and Caru sings with my voice, changing it back, forcing me back to myself, making me able to sing my own song.

We un-sing the flood. We push the water back into shape, transform it back into rock.

"Up! Pull this ship up!" Zal's screaming commands at our Rostrae, but they're ignoring her.

I see Jik, her bright blue wings visible, her face half human. She's at a height where she can be in between. She's shrieking along with our song and, as I watch, the chains around her talons and ankles shatter. It's her own song, magnified, breaking whatever spell has been on the crew, destroying something. *Working from the inside.*

I see Wedda beside her. Wedda, who's always been loyal to Zal, perched on a mast. She spreads her wings too. I watch her chains dismantle themselves and fall to the deck, a glittering collapse.

I look at the batsail and see its wings folded in solidarity. It will not take Zal up. It won't save her.

We put the earth back together.

Moments ago Spitsbergen was water. It shudders as if with shame, and is stone all over again. The waves splash up and freeze into earth shapes, the water goes opaque, the island goes hard.

The hook with the epiphytes is only a few feet below the surface now. What if I gave Zal the plants? It would right an ancient wrong between earth and Magonia.

But my song with Caru isn't controlled. The earth is sealing up, and even as I think about it, it closes over the plants, locking them in the rock—the airplants, and the last few yards of line from *Amina Pennarum*.

The rope attached to our pulley is suddenly jutting up from the ground of Svalbard. The urgent whirring wheels aren't pulling the crops up anymore. They're yanking the ship down toward the earth's surface.

We list hard. The crew screams and stumbles. Dai's frantic voice stops as he slips across the deck. The ship veers, jostles and drops, and the crew are trying to cut the rope but it's too late, we've lost control. I'm clinging on but I'm not afraid.

Our song is strong enough that Caru and I can fly if we need to. I don't have to try it. I know it's true.

Now I do what some part of me knew I should always have done. This isn't a slave ship, not anymore. The Rostrae freed themselves, but the batsail is still trapped.

I use my song with Caru to cut the threads that bind *Amina Pennarum*'s batsail to the ship. I set it free. It sings a high note at me, *firefly*, and then it's gone, wings stretching out into the wind.

I watch the crew of Rostrae transform entirely, the sky suddenly filled with feathers. Wedda, an owl again, her wingspan tremendous. Jik, bright blue, rising up. Hummingbirds. The eagle.

Now I cut the enslaved canwr cote free, and the sky's flecked with gold, all of Milekt's siblings and students swooping out from the ship like motes of sun.

Fly, they trill.

Magonians fall out of the sky into the sea. There's gasping, and shuddering, and the water takes some of the crew.

We lurch downward, and at last, with a screaming splash and a shock akin to earthquake, *Amina Pennarum* drops into the ocean. The real ocean, not the sky we've been sailing in. We beach on the shore of Spitsbergen.

It takes me a second to get my bearings after the impact. I'm surrounded by cracking wood. Magonians are gasping and screaming, choking in the heavy air of earth. I don't even look.

I have to get to Jason.

I haul myself over the railing and drop a few feet onto the rock. I gasp air from my bottle.

Zal leaps over the rail behind me. Then she's in front of me on the ice, my screaming mother, this warrior, my captain. But down here she's not as strong as I am. I'm used to earth. I know how to walk here. I know how to survive on less than I need here.

The stakes have changed. I'm not the girl who came aboard *Amina Pennarum*, scared and delicate.

Zal reaches for my face, trying to grab my bottle for herself. I push her, and she falls backward.

Milekt flies at me and flutters around screaming ragesongs as Breath rappel down onto *Amina Pennarum* from Magan-wetar, and seize Zal.

Zal screams and fights, but she has no power over them. She

has no song. She's struggling to breathe but she battles hard. I sing her weapons into paralysis.

I wait for them to try to grab me too.

I sing a tiny note of warning, and Caru echoes it.

The Breath before me holds up a hand. Not Heyward. This is a Breath I've never seen before. He stares at me for a moment, and then turns back to Zal. They're not taking me. I don't know why, but they're not.

The note I sang with Caru echoes in the air, and all around me there's stillness. Protection. Strength.

Then he's gone, hauling Zal up into the Magonian command ship. Zal is flipped like a whale, choking on air. As, one by one, are her crew.

"BETRAYER!" Zal screams as she goes.

Dai is pulled up after her, unconscious from the fall. My heart clenches and my eyes fill, watching him hauled up. We're still attached; our bond isn't gone. Not gone at all. Though we didn't choose each other, we're supposed to sing together, no matter what.

I don't think this is the end of Dai and me.

I don't think I'm that lucky.

I see Milekt land on him as he rises, a dart of gold, abandoned by me. Dai has two birds now, one on each shoulder, one for each lung. Milekt shrills maddened bird loathing at me as he ascends.

Cut string! he screams. I feel a hideous racking inside me, guilt. I broke our bond. I had to.

Forget it, Aza. None of it matters.

I sprint across the snow, the tilting landscape.

I push into the repository entrance with Caru behind me, and it's dark, and still no one. Where is he? Gone? How can he be?

No, I hear footsteps. He runs into something and grunts. "Ow."

The simplest sound and it causes me to come to my senses. I'm not ready for this. I'm not the Aza he knew. I look—

I look like—

I feel my stomach drop. My legs go numb, my tongue trips in my mouth, my whole body crashes and burns with this insane feeling of falling from something so high there's no end. I feel everything tumble—comet meteor parachute wingless—into him.

"Aza," he says. He's coming toward me. "I know you're here."

I'm Magonian. He's human. There's no version of this that's okay. I can't be on earth. I can't let him see me. Not this way.

"Get off this island," I warn him, even though I feel my heart splintering. "Get away from here."

"Aza Ray. Do you know how hard it was to get into this place? I'm breaking laws in maybe five countries. You almost killed me. *They* almost killed me. And the Norwegians think I'm a curious and slightly stupid schoolboy on a trip to Longyearbyen."

I'm smiling inside my zipped-up hood because this is vintage Jason. He's alive. He's real. But I'm not Aza anymore. I have no idea who I am.

"And in order to get to Longyearbyen, I basically had to bribe God."

There's a silence.

"The airport's less than a mile away," he says. "If your clothes are warm enough you can walk. I had a tent with me. I think my tent sank. Where the water, you know. Was."

I say nothing.

"Come home with me," he whispers. "It's freezing. Whatever you're doing, you don't have to do it alone."

Caru sings in our voice, this terrifying screamsong voice, this nothing-is-inside-my-heart voice, and we turn the floor to water for a moment, because we're scared, I admit it, I admit it. Jason's eyes get huge, and he stumbles, splashes, sinks, recovers.

I can't be with him I can't be with him. Caru sings a high awful pitch, a shrill of despair, and agony, and Jason covers his ears in pain. Caru keeps singing with my mouth.

Jason's gasping, but he looks up again, and I see his face now. The furrow between his eyebrows is deeper than it was. He fidgets in his pockets and stuffs earplugs into his ears.

"Idiot," he says. "Do you really think I'm leaving without you? Do you really think I'm going back to my full-on meltdown? Reciting pi for three weeks? Talking in my sleep?"

He straightens up, wet to the thighs with water that, after it falls from him, goes back to being concrete. He doesn't seem to give a damn.

Caru arcs, *Leave leave leave go go go drowner*, but then Caru stops singing because I can't stop crying.

Jason's in front of me. Things have changed in him. Just like things have changed in me.

No no no. He's human. I keep reminding myself that I'm not. But oh my god oh my god, my heart. My heart feels human.

"You'll have to kill me if you want me to go," Jason says. "I'm not leaving you here."

"I thought you were dead already," I say.

He's got nothing for a minute.

"Then we're even," he finally says, and his voice breaks with an only slightly muffled sob.

I step out from behind the pillar. Covered completely. I'm wearing the clothes I had to wear to do Zal's bidding. A suit zipped up all the way to keep me safe from too much oxygen. Emergency war gear. Only my eyes are visible.

No one but me could ever tell that he's scared. No one but me has ever seen Jason Kerwin cry.

"I'm not going anywhere," Jason says. "You can keep trying to tell me to leave, but it's not going to work. I came for you. I'm not leaving without you."

"Aza's gone," I singsay.

Jason looks steadily at me. He takes a step toward me.

"Bullshit," he says.

I take a step back.

He steps. I step.

Another.

Rock wall behind me.

But.

I'm going to leave him.

But.

He reaches out his hand, and like he doesn't even notice it's a thing, he puts his hand on the hood of my suit, and unzips it, taking the panel away from my face.

My hair uncoils into the freezing air. It twists and moves toward him as though it's trying to bite his hands. My skin flares with electricity, storm sparks, too much oxygen.

I can't breathe this way for long.

I'm here in front of him, Magonian.

Jason doesn't even flinch.

I try one more time. This body, this person, this skin, this face, these red-gold eyes, the real, freaky version of the girl he knew. He's looking at me, at my insane Medusa hair, at my too-long fingers and everything not what it was, and I must be hideous to him.

"Do you get it now? I'm not Aza," I wheeze. "I'm not who you think I am—" and then Jason Kerwin takes one more fast step forward and—

He's kissing me.

He's got me in his arms. His human lips. My Magonian mouth. And it's weather, a surging storm breaking, a vast, warm expanse of sun and of rightness coming across the sky. I'm glowing with it, his skin, my fingertips, his jaw and—

He moves back from me so that we're not kissing for a second.

"Aza Ray," he says. "You hold no horrors for me."

He breathes me in, and I breathe him in, and when we breathe out the air freezes between us and falls. Snow.

I'm shaking and stupid, and for a second I think I'm not going to know what to do, but then I do.

I grab his face in my hands and kiss him until *he's* the one who can't breathe. I keep my eyes open. So does he. We've been not looking at each other for too long. Like, for our whole lives.

Real now.

No more parentheses. No more brackets.

I can hear new sounds out there. Engines, airplanes,

helicopters. Whatever we did, people are about to know about it.

"It's okay. I planned for something like this."

I look at Jason, and remember how even though I know what he is, I always underestimate him. He smiles at me.

I stagger into the broken, sideways hull of *Amina Pennarum*, singing camouflage all the way. I know I don't have long. They'll never let this wreck stay.

I run as fast as I can through corridors I once knew, past tangled hammocks and twisted ropes to find the skins that Dai took from the Breath ship. It's dark and smoky in here, and there's a sizzle not far away, a sting outside, the smell of ozone, but I tear off my uniform and grab the closest skin.

I unzip the cover. I put my hand on the skin, warm, soft, fragile, and I touch it. I feel it touch me. It wraps around me, pressing, crushing, melding to me, melting into me, and inside my body I feel the vibration of Caru, questioning, from outside the vessel.

Okay, I sing. *Calm,* and I feel him sing back. Feel rather than hear.

The skin closes over me, smooth, perfect, and new, and I tug my clothes back over it and run, run, as the ship collapses around me.

I fling myself out a porthole onto the ice. I look up, but Maganwetar is gone. The ships are gone. The sky and ground are clear of everything but squallwhales and human things, planes in the distance, and cars coming across the island. People are arriving, running across the frozen landscape.

Casually, me dressed in my Magonian uniform, breathing a little easier with these borrowed doll lungs, Jason and I walk away from the seed repository.

We walk away like we're two American teenagers on a field trip who saw something they shouldn't have seen, but only kind of saw it, officer, because we snuck away to make out.

CHAPTER 29

{JASON}

It takes some seriously heroic lying and bullshitting, and this is where having a little bit of money comes in handy, but in the end I get us on a plane home. Fake passport for her. I said heroic, didn't I? Yes. Heroic.

I'm not entirely well from the lightning, and I've been feeling sick the whole flight. It's weird and terrifying to be on a plane now, after all this. I don't know if Aza thinks so. She's so exhausted that she's been sleeping for nine hours. I can hear a familiar, ragged edge to her breathing, but it's much better than it has any right to be.

The skin she's wearing now is stronger, a new version of what she had before. She has some time, we hope, before things start to fail.

The skin. I think about that. It makes no sense. Aza tried to explain it to me, but finally gave up after she said it was a combination of camouflage and Aqua-Lung. I told her to stop because she wasn't helping make any sense of this, and she said, "Fine, Jason. It's magic. I can't help you. I don't get it either."

I think back to that night when Aza and I watched the giant squid—the creature that also seemed fact and fantasy, real and imaginary. That day, we were uncomplicated. I mean, relatively, compared to today. Even that's something we're never going to have again.

I'm not looping.

Okay, fine, I'm looping.

Looping as in: this won't work, this can't work, what's coming for us?

As in maybe she isn't who she was, maybe I'm not who I was, maybe nothing about this is right at all.

As in, maybe she'll die again. Maybe it will be worse this time than it was last time, except that this time she'll *really* be dead.

Loop. Worry. Panic attack quelled by breathing and a pill and a tiny, tiny dose of pi. Shh. Aza not awake and not noticing, and me in the bathroom of the airplane, trying not to fall apart now, after all the weeks of fervent *NOT* falling apart I've done.

This is completely insane. This was love at first sight. And now, she's here with me, and I'm here with her, and the whole sky's full of angry people who want her dead.

And is she even staying down here? Can she?

But it doesn't matter. I can't imagine a universe in which I try to unlove her.

What if one day she looks at me and says, "I want to go back up"?

What if I'm an anchor, snagged, holding her to the rocks?

This isn't just Jason and Aza. It's not me racing against death to save her anymore. It's us racing against impossible.

I think about my moms. I think about how there was a moment in which they thought they'd never be able to be together. Their families panicked. Two women? No men? They did it anyway. My birth certificate has both of them on it, and they did I-don't-even-know-what to make that happen.

They were brave. I can't be less brave than they are.

But even Eve would be scared of what we saw in Svalbard. And maybe of the girl beside me.

At the beginning of the flight, I saw a formation of geese passing our plane, going the other way, and so did Aza. She pressed her face against the glass.

"You okay?"

"Yeah," she said. Her hand was on the glass, too, as though she was greeting them, but also like she was getting ready to do something. The air felt gritty. After a moment, the geese passed the plane, and she relaxed.

"What just happened?"

"I wasn't sure what they were doing," she said, and looked at me with a kind of sheepish expression on this new face I'm still getting used to. "I thought they might be coming for us."

"Explain," I said.

"We're near a Magonian ship right now," she said. "The Rostrae were in formation around the hull. I don't know how we got out of there. I don't know how they let us go."

I look at her. I don't know either. We've been over everything. Heyward. The ship in the air. This Dai, her *partner*.

She explained. It wasn't a happy explanation, hearing her talk about how she was magnetized to him. We compared notes on everything that happened in the past month and a half, and we still have gaps.

There's nothing hitting the news about what just went down at the vault. I've been tracking it the whole flight. About the breach of the seed repository—about the massive earthquake—nothing.

Which means that just beneath the surface, *everyone's* freaking out. This can only have been an international incident.

I make sure Aza's sleeping, and then I pull out the business card I was given on the tarmac at Longyearbyen.

She was in the bathroom. A guy came up, black suit, dark glasses, two words, card, gone. I keep nearly, but not quite, telling her about the agent, who only said, "Thank you."

Now I wonder how long the feds were following me. I keep thinking Aza doesn't need to know. Maybe no one needs to know.

If I were them, I wouldn't hire me. I know more than I should. I think if I were in their shoes, I'd kill me.

I look over again at Aza sleeping beside me. I listen to her breathing. We're going home, but who knows how long we're going to be able to stay there?

In this skin, Aza looks like a new person. She isn't. She's still entirely Aza. Example: when we got onto the plane, she looked at me and said:

"What're you looking at?"

"You," I said.

"Don't get used to this. I think this skin's gonna fall apart. That'll be pretty. I'll look all rotten corpse and then we'll see if you want to hold my hand."

Which is not true. She'll turn more and more blue, and have a harder and harder time breathing, and eventually what happened before will happen again. And I'll still want to hold her hand. We're just hoping this version is better than what she had before.

She's got braided black hair and brown skin. Her body's the same, because the skin shrinks to fit. But other than the obvious changes, because I know she's Aza, she looks like Aza to me.

Same wide mouth. Same amazing strange eyes. Her voice is Aza's voice. Her words are Aza's words.

If I handed her a piece of paper and some scissors, she'd cut out the Empire State Building in three minutes. If I asked her what she thought about anything, she'd instantly have an opinion. Whether majorly wrong or not, she'd never hesitate to tell me what she thought. She's always been this way. She still is.

"How long was I sleeping?"

"Whole flight," I say.

"Am I still alive?"

"Of course you are."

"Because it feels like I'm dreaming, coming back here."

"We're going to make this work."

I wish I believed myself. I've been the King of Certainty the whole time I've known her, but about a lot of things I was faking. I'm faking right now. I don't know anything. I feel broken and messed up, terrified and convinced I'm about to watch her get shot down by airport security.

Aza kisses me as we're getting off the plane, full-on enough that I'm pretty sure everyone else in the jetway is blushing, and I'm blushing too. That doesn't keep me from picking her up and carrying her into the airport, over the threshold that separates this country in the air from home.

Everyone's laughing, all the people around us. They think we're cute. Maybe they think we're a little pukey.

People actually, amazingly, think we're normal teenagers in love. And for a moment, we are.

I'm expecting a hole where my house was. My family gone. Or it'll be surrounded by police, or Breath, someone waiting to take me away and lock me up, in a brig or a cell, same difference. My neighborhood looks wrong. No sky around us. No snow. No ice. The ground stable.

I turn the corner toward my address, expecting retribution. Maganwetar knows where I came from. Zal knows where I'll go. Someone's got to be hunting me.

Except for that Breath, willfully letting me go. It must have been on someone's orders. Whose? It makes me wonder if maybe, *maybe* we have some time. If Magonian officials want me down here somehow. I don't know. I can't figure it out.

I'm not what I should be. I'm illegal. I'm an alien. In all senses of that word. My mother is an assassin and a criminal and probably in jail in Magonia. Maybe I'm an assassin and a criminal too. I wonder about my father. Do I even have one? No one ever said. How come I never asked?

It's quiet on my street, but not too quiet. A few birds, none of them speaking. All they do is sing.

The sky's clear. The sun's shining. There's nothing up there that would suggest anyone knows I'm down here. I could almost (if I was insane) forget about Magonia.

Not even a breeze. It's cold, but not as cold as Svalbard.

And there—my house is there. In front of me, itself. Yellow front door. Blue car in the driveway. Dented side.

It's the dent that starts me crying. Maybe none of this happened. Maybe I'm just coming home after school, getting out of Jason's car, probably gasping a little. Normal. Except that I have Jason beside me holding my hand, and that would never have happened before all this. There was no official version of Jason and me before.

There's a rip in the neckline of his shirt, and he has a smudge on his face. I want to laugh, because a smudge? After everything? Only a smudge?

The world isn't over, though, and here we are.

I look up at Jason. I can feel the sides of his fingers against mine. I can feel his heart beating through his thumb.

"What do you think?" he asks me, like he doesn't know already.

"My parents are home," I say.

"You ready?"

"Not even."

"Maybe we should jump off the garage," he says.

"Maybe we should fly in," I say, which almost makes me sob, because. There are losses to this. Big ones.

I don't have a plan. Where else in the world would I go but here? Home. Not home. ~~Home~~.

I turn around and start walking in the opposite direction of my house. Nope. I can't see my parents, not this way. Look at me. I'm not me—

"Do you know," Jason says, his voice tense as mine, talking fast, a definite sign of barely hidden anxiety. "Do you know about the Ganzfeld Effect?"

"No," I say. I'm listening, but I'm not stopping. He's not going to seduce me with factoids. I walk faster.

"It's the brain amplifying neural noise in order to look for missing signals. For example, if you look at a clear blue sky without context, you start to hallucinate. Look at snow too long, and you'll see cities."

"That's not what Magonia is," I interrupt, irritated that he can even remotely say this after all he's just seen.

"The students of Pythagoras used to go into dark caves and stay there in order to bring it on. Wisdom out of nothing. Astronauts say they see the same thing. And Arctic explorers."

I feel his fingers lace through mine. He keeps talking without stopping. He's not letting me get away.

"Prisoners in solitary. There's a term for that version. Prisoners' cinema. Colors at the edge of night, figures and forms. Some people think the cave paintings in Lascaux were done in the dark, someone painting the things they saw when there was nothing else to see. Hands out, dipping fingers in pigment and painting in pitch-black, from visions. You could only see them if you stayed there long enough, looking."

I stare up at Jason. He's looking at me too now.

"No one knows, really, why the brain makes these visions. It wants to see something. All these beautiful things came out of the blue," he says. "And out of the black. The same way you did. Your country in the sky is the most beautiful thing I've ever seen. I believe you. I saw it. I see it now, little bits." He points up. There's a small sailing vessel, no threat, moving fast across the sky.

"Even people who've never seen a miracle can believe in miracles, Aza Ray. Even people who've never seen the light, people who've been kept in the dark, people who've gone snow-blind, or sky-blind? Even those people can believe in fantastic things. I believe you. Your family's going to believe you too."

"But I'm not me," I tell him.

"You ARE you." We pause. "Also, Aza, I'm scared too."

"You are?" This makes me feel weirdly better.

"Yeah," he says. "But at least we're not scared of each other."

I look at him.

"Are you sure?"

He hesitates for a little too long. "Nope. I mean, I'm not unscary. Maybe you're scared of me."

I smile at him. "I am deeply, deeply scared of you."

We go up the walk to my house.

I think about the day I don't remember, the day I came here fifteen years ago, newborn and no one, tucked into a bed not mine, in a body not mine, meant to die, and living because of these people who kept me safe without even knowing what I was. Who worked so hard to keep something broken going. Who loved me.

I think about my mom, apparently coming into my bed-room with a needle full of her serum, or so Jason tells me, and what was she then? Scared, and clueless. She thought I was human. She thought I was dying of something no one would understand. So she taught herself to understand it. She made me medicine. She put it into my bloodstream and hoped. When no one else could help me, she gave me everything she had.

Because of her, I'm still here.

I can feel my chest rattling.

Being home is better than breathing, I tell myself.

I ring the doorbell. And they're coming down the hall. I can hear them, my dad, footsteps, shoes on even though they shouldn't be, my mom murmuring to him.

Jason's kind of bouncing in place, like he might take off running, like we're some other kind of couple on the way to the prom.

I suddenly think nothing bad can ever happen again, which is not smart, Aza, not smart, but I don't care.

The door opens.

It's my parents.

I have to fight really hard not to freak them out by crying, this stranger bursting into tears. But I sure as hell make some kind of noise. And they're {???} and I'm {&,&,&} and they look at me like they don't know me, which makes sense but feels like everything wrong ever and so I say, "Mom?"

I look completely different. I knew this would happen, but I'm not ready. It hurts.

"What?" she says. "What did you say?"

"Nothing."

I discover I'm ready to reverse course and run from this, some kind of total coward. No one will know me down here. Not my parents. No one.

I start to stutter, start to stammer, and Jason steps forward.

"Hey, guys," he says. "This is going to be weird, but hear me out."

"Jason," my mom says. "Are you okay? You seem not so hot. Should I call Carol? I heard about what happened."

"Lightning," Jason says. "I don't recommend it. I'm mostly fine."

I feel a pounding in my chest. Caru, above me, in a tree opening his wings. I hear a song inside me, Caru singing comfort.

"Jason," says my dad, and I can see he's trying to smile, but he's startled to see Jason with someone who isn't me. "Who's this?"

"This is—"

I put my hand up to touch my hair. I don't look the way I looked. They can't possibly know.

"Hi," I manage, whispering. "It's good to see you."

Eli runs down the stairs behind my parents, and stops in her tracks.

"Whoa," she says. "I heard your voice, and for a second, I—" She looks closer. Her brow furrows. Confusion. "Jason?"

My parents are looking hard at me now. It's the voice. I forgot. It's the same. My voice belongs to me.

"Who are you?" my dad says. "I don't think I—"

"I don't know I don't know I don't know—" says my mom, her voice getting higher and higher.

"This isn't funny," says my dad.

"No," says Jason. "I'm not trying to be funny. She has to show you something, okay?"

My mom stares hard at me. My dad is crying. I can almost not stand it.

Jason hands me a piece of paper and a pen. "Right?" he says. "This is what you do. You know what to do."

"This is an apology list," I say, louder than is strictly necessary.

I put the paper against the wall and start writing. I know whose handwriting I'm writing in. It hasn't changed. There are all these things that don't change, ever, no matter what.

"I'm sorry," I say. "For not knowing what you were. All the times we did normal things. All the times you came into my room when I was scared and you told me you loved me."

"Wait," my mom says. "What is this? Jason. This isn't okay—"

"I'm sorry," I say to my dad. "For making you come to my school over and over to get me loose from the principal's office. I'm sorry for not appreciating it when you held my toes as I went into the MRI machine, and for saying I wasn't scared. I was scared. You made me less scared. You told me you'd fight Big Bird for me."

My dad's expression is crumbling. He lets out a strangled sob.

"I'm sorry you suck at backflips and strained your back showing me who was boss."

He snorts suddenly and looks up at me, his face shifting.

"I'm sorry I died when you were with me, and you couldn't keep me from dying. It wasn't your fault. I can explain it."

I look at Eli.

"I'm sorry for—"

"Stop," she says. She looks at me hard. "You don't need to. I can see you in there, Aza."

"I never even gave you a real I Love You list," I manage to say, because I'm not far from crying right now, "let alone a real apology list. I put everything stupid in your list, and none of the real things."

Eli looks at me. "Also, you underestimated me," she says, and grins, a very Eli grin. "I notice everything."

"What are you saying?" My mom. I take her in. Her blond-gray ponytail. Her face. Her eyes are shining, wild.

"I'm sorry," I say. "For not seeing you. I didn't know how lucky I was. You worked late and I slept late. We never saw each other. I made fun of your war-mice. I told you that nothing you did ever helped. I complained. I crashed the car into the garage, twice, and then pretended you did it with your bike. The last thing you said to me was on the phone, when I was in the ambulance, and you told me it was okay to go."

The corners of my mom's mouth wobble.

How do you prove you're not gone? How do you prove you're alive, when your whole family saw you dead? How do you prove you're even human, after all that, after everything that's happened, and everything that's probably still going to happen? I don't know how you prove it. I only know you have to have faith in people.

My family's around me. There's a moment of not knowing, of not loving, of not caring.

Then my sister reaches out her arms. My dad does too. Then my mom. I hear Caru whirring from the tree outside the front door. I reach out my hands to them and throw myself in. Jason's on the outside for a moment, and then I grab him and pull him into us, and we are like

( )

like [[[[[[[[[[[   ]]]]]]]]]]]]

like

H O M E

O   M

M   O

E M O H

For as long as it lasts.

They'll come for me. Zal isn't dead. Magonia isn't gone. And Dai—there's Dai. There's Heyward and the Breath. There's a whole world of trouble out there.

But right now, Jason and me and my family are holding on to each other. All of us in this kitchen.

However much time there is? I'll take it. I feel my strange, beautiful bird in my heart, and the unflooded world all around me.

Aza Ray, human and not, Magonian and not, Aza Ray, whose history is hospitals, and whose future is more interesting than her past. Aza Ray, who was born in the sky. Aza Ray, who's in love with a boy from earth.

If I have to fly, he's flying with me. If I have to sail, he's on my ship. I lace my fingers into Jason's. I hold on tight.

I breathe in. I breathe out.

NOTES AND ACKNOWLEDGMENTS

Magonia as depicted in this book is largely my own invention, but the historical basis is accurate. In the source and inspiration department, thanks are emphatically due to Miceal Ross, author of the terrific paper on anchors tethering the earth, sky, and sea to one another, *Anchors in the Three-Decker World*, which is where I initially ran across mention of Magonia. The research Jason and Aza do into *The Annals of Ulster*, etc., is real. There's a lot of other material out there as well, including the passages written by Jacob Grimm and others by the nineteenth-century folklorist Charles Leland, often dealing with weather witchery and harvests. It was a small step from that into this book.

My gratitude to my agent at the Gernert Company, Stephanie Cabot, as well as Ellen Goodson, Will Roberts, Seth Fishman, and Sarah Burnes for additional advice and thoughts. Sally Willcox at CAA for notes and intrepid voyaging.

At HarperCollins, my editor, Kristen Pettit, for seeing all of the Magonian sky in the first wild-eyed version of the manuscript, and for insisting on more stormsharks and bigger battles. I'm tremendously grateful *Magonia* ended up in her hands. Elizabeth Lynch, editorial assistant, for additional brainy notes, and the entire spectacular Harper team: Susan Katz, Kate Morgan Jackson, Jen Klonsky, Alexei Esikoff, Veronica Ambrose, Charles Annis, Alison Klapthor, Barb Fitzsimmons, Christina Colangelo, Elizabeth Ward, Gina Rizzo, Alison Donalty, and Craig Shields for the beautiful cover art. Also at Harper, Rosemary Brosnan, with whom I worked on *Unnatural Creatures*, which was my first Harper experience. Elsewhere in the publishing world, the excellent Kathy Dawson, who gave early and generous feedback that greatly improved this book.

Early readers Kat Howard and Molly Headley, whose suggestions made the monsters brighter and the singing stronger. John Joseph Adams, Sarah Alden, Libba Bray, Mark Bemesderfer, Nathan Dunbar, Kelley Eskridge & Nicola Griffith, Neil Gaiman, Barry Goldblatt, Liz Gorinsky, Mark Headley & Meghan Koch, Adriane Headley, Ben Loory, Sarah McCarry, Francesca Myman, Sxip Shirey, Jared Shurin, Nova Ren Suma, Michael Damian Thomas, Lynne Thomas & Christie Yant, for writeworld enthusiasm, whooping and empathy, all of which definitely kept me writing this book even when I gnashed. My dear ones Zay Amsbury, Jess Benko & Kate Czajkowski for late-night shoutings, laughings, and life-savings, much of which climbed into this story. Timothy & Kira Don for letting me live in their house and listen to their garden of birds. Patrick Farrell for getting me through storms with grace and petting. My kids, Sarah Schenkkan and Joshua Schenkkan, who didn't get to have this book written for them when they were small, but who definitely helped teach me how to write it. My dear friend and fellow traveler Matthew Power, who died as I was finishing this book, and whose adventurous spirit is all over it. I miss the everything out of him.

Finally, China Miéville, who never lets me thank him, and

without whose imagination, intellect and stone-cold genius large portions of this book wouldn't exist. He's been more generous with me than I can possibly repay in this lifetime, scribbling edits, notes, and brilliant suggestions on every draft from the first pages to the tenth maddened edit, assessing plot flaws and analyzing them into ferocious spreadsheets, bringing me oddity treasures from his own vaults, sending me obscure bestiaries, essays about songbirds, and gorgeous ink pens configured for the left-handed. He generally makes me feel so fortunate to be alive and writing alongside him that I can hardly stand it.

I am beyond lucky to have such extraordinary shipmates.

1. Where are you right now?

I'm in a house set into the side of a volcanic island off the coast of Sicily! I'm looking at two live volcanoes as I type this.

2. Why are you there? What are you doing?

I'm here because I'm writing a book, and it turns out that the perfect place to write a book if you're a person obsessed with hanging out with other people is a place where, you know, there aren't any other people. Or at least, only a few. I hunted around on the internet until I found this chain of islands, the Aeolians, and then I looked up houses for rent here. My island has no cars, only mules, and it also has a colony of falcons, which I think is very auspicious given that I've also been finishing copyedits on *Aerie*, the sequel to *Magonia*! Out in the sea off my terrace, I've seen a couple of spouting pilot whales—also very relevant to the contents of this book. The only other traffic is fishing boats and ferry boats. It's basically like I'm in Magonia, albeit the Earth version. The only sounds out here are birds singing, wind, and rain.

3. Do you always have to be in an exotic or inspiring location when you write?

No, but it's nice when I am! Usually I write in coffee shops in New York City (also inspiring, frankly), or in my house, which is actually both exotic and inspiring given that it's full of things I've collected in order to inspire me. I've definitely found that my first drafts are benefitted by going off to a place where there's literally nothing to do but write. I am an exceedingly distractable person, and when there are interesting people around me all I want to do is learn their stories. A couple years ago, I decided to combine ferocious writing and ferocious living as well as I could, and so I started finding places like this to write in, so that at least I didn't feel like I was missing out on being alive. Being a writer requires a lot of solitude, so you might as well make it gorgeous solitude.

4. *Magonia* is a fantastical flight of fancy, yet you've said it's autobiographical. How?

The part of *Magonia* that is autobiographical is Aza's journey through life and death illness, into a new version of herself. I'm a type 1 diabetic, and when I was a teenager, and was diagnosed with this disease, I was sick for months, and ultimately had a near-death experience. When I returned to school the next year after that happened, I was the girl who'd died—I felt like everything had changed invisibly inside me. It was as though I'd gone to an imaginary kingdom for a year, as though I was an alien. So, though Magonia is an invented country based on some fabulous folklore, the emotions and journey Aza experiences are very much like things that actually happened in my life.

5. Jason is our imaginary boyfriend! Do Jasons exist in real life?

Yes. Jason is partially based on someone I know very well, my main collaborator as a writer and my best friend. There's nothing better than finding someone whose brain inspires you so much that you want to invent universes in order to entertain it! I think everyone can meet their brain-match, and when you do, if you can, hold onto that person in whatever capacity. The writing I've done in the past few years has been very much inspired by the fact that I could always tell my friend about it, and get his thoughts, which have always made me a better thinker and writer. I think there are people like that out there for all of us, and you can find them at any moment. Usually you meet them across a crowded room and feel like you've known them since you were five. In this case, I just made that the reality of Aza and Jason.

6. Aza is a human girl who's never belonged on Earth, then she's a Magonian who has no idea what to do in the sky. Where do you think Aza really belongs? Where is her true home?

Everywhere. ☺ I don't know if I really believe in true homes. I believe you can make a true home wherever you are, as long as there are people you love around. So, as far as Aza is concerned . . . there are lots of possibilities.

7. Where did you get the idea for people who make weather and live in the sky?

That comes from some old lore, eighth and eleventh century things, which are actually depicted in *Magonia* as the research Aza and Jason do. All that information about Magonia is right out of the history books. I departed from there and made an entire kingdom, but I grabbed lots of things from folklore, weather myth, and history. There's a pretty significant history of people on the ground believing that weather was made by people in the sky, and those things have always been very interesting to me, whether I found them in fairy tales or in miracle books, where the weather is sometimes depicted as things like, for example, showers of flying fish and birds.

8. The book has a distinctly environmentalist tone. Are environmental issues important to you?

Of course, as they should be to everyone. We're in a place of major fail right now, and it's because we've been in denial for years. The idea of human-created climate change is something that's been talked about since I was a little kid, and it's not folklore, though some people still persist in thinking it is. We have to do so much better. The place where I'm writing right now basically lives like we're hundreds of years in the past, fishing, growing food, using every element of the things that are available. People are very careful about not wasting things. It's not so hard to live that way, actually; we're just spoiled out of it in America. America and the way American culture works is a big part of the world's problem. We sell new and shiny to everyone, when really, we should be selling things that last.

9. What's your advice for a YA reader who wants to someday be a writer?

Being a writer is, first and entirely foremost, a matter of writing. So, write. Write all the time. When you have an extra hour, write. You can write a book in an hour of writing a day. Success is never overnight. It's work, like anything else, and so, my advice is write as much as you can and stop worrying that you're failing. You're not. You're making something. It might not sell, but the next one will be better. And the next one. Eventually, you'll know what kinds of stories you need to tell, and you'll know how to capture them in words. That's the goal for all of us, and, for most writers, we learn it over again with each new project. But it's actually majorly fun to keep learning. There's nothing else I'd rather do for a living.

10. What can we look forward to in your sequel, _Aerie_?
Well, there's a major new character that some of you will be wondering about after reading _Magonia_! That's one of the big things. Love, betrayal, bad decisions on the part of good people. Wild journeys through the sky for Aza. And, as I said in the question above, learning. Aza isn't done figuring out what and who she is, and she's not done figuring out how to live in this multilayered world. There will be war and pain, and Aza will be tested, reaching the limits of her voice and heart at the same time.

Turn the page for a sneak peek
at the sequel to *Magonia*

I wake to the sound of someone trying to sound like no one,
my bedroom window opening, a scratching creak. I'm
reaching my arm down to grab the telescope beside the bed—
a telescope, Kerwin, really?!—when . . .

My girlfriend (fine, fine, this still sounds impossible to me,
still sounds like far more than I could ever deserve in any universe not science fictional) tumbles head over heels onto my
floor, and lands in a pile of knees and elbows. She's managed to
climb my drainpipe in the middle of December. It's not everyone who can shinny straight up two stories.

Aza Ray, of course, isn't everyone.

Aza Ray is the *only* one.

I clamp my mouth shut because 1) She's trying to surprise
me and 2) Every time I even glance at her I want to grab both of
her hands and never let go.

This is what happens when you lose someone once. You
never really feel safe again. Complication: having that someone
be a girl who is always running as fast as she can, not necessarily away from me, but in nine directions at once. Three of them
straight up. Causes anxieties.

She mutters a string of colorful swear words as my window shuts on her forgotten-on-the-sill foot, but she's fine. She's just Aza, the superspy version. Yep, she hums a scrap of *Pink Panther* theme. She can't help herself. Triumph makes her talkative.

I pretend I'm beyond asleep so she can have the satisfaction of sneaking up on me.

Not that I ever sleep. Would anyone?

Imagine your girlfriend making the water rise up out of a wading pool, and turning it midair into rocks. Imagine her singing a piece of the sidewalk into a sudden lake, and then imagine that lake has no bottom. Imagine this amazing, not-of-this-earth mind, this girl who tells me casually about silver tentacles reaching out of clouds, who sings me notes of Magonian song, who one day made me something out of rain that shimmered green and gray. It wasn't a gemstone, nor anything I'd ever seen before, and when I asked, Aza shrugged, and said, "Minor meteor, blah-de-blah."

Imagine loving *her*.

Imagine losing her.

Everyone thought she was dead. Everyone but me. Someone like Aza couldn't die.

I was right, in the end. She hadn't. She'd become—already was—something else. Something *more*.

Now imagine being the guy who has to worry about that, about losing her all over again to a country in the sky.

My eyes are open to slits. I watch Aza tiptoe across my bedroom. She shakes her hair out of her hat, and tries to silently unzip her—what is she wearing?—and get out of her boots at the same time, which results in another near collapse of tangled limbs. Aza's failing to navigate her new skin. She's still not used to this version of herself.

"Damn it," she says, bending over me, her clothes half off, her hair standing straight up. "You're totally awake now, aren't you?"

I laugh. "When have I ever not been totally awake?"

"There was that one time you slept through the night five years ago."

"An aberration."

She puts an icy, questing hand on my skin, clearly considering jabbing it into my armpit, and so I grab it and roll her under the covers with me, until I can wrap her up completely.

I get her into my arms, face-to-face, and she's cracking up.

"You could've come in the front door, you know." I hide my twitchiness over her being out at night alone (during a storm, no less) with no one watching her, no one even knowing where she is.

Aza doesn't ever follow rules. If I try to point out even basic things, she transgresses double time. Storms make me nervous. Every time the sky darkens, I think it's Aza's last day of this life, and the first day of something much worse.

"It's not like my parents don't know you sleep over."

"It isn't like Magonians like to use the front door," she protests, and puts her frozen nose into my neck. "It was a misjudge, though. It's icy out there. And disgusting. Like, sleet city disgusting." She shivers. "I don't have toes anymore."

I hold her despite her cold feet trying to sap all the warmth from my body. Like I care about cold feet. Like I care about anything beyond Aza in my bed. Even a year later, I'm still in shock every time. All those years of me being lamentably, silently, secretly in love. All those years of not knowing. She clamps around my ankle bones.

"Nope, don't worry, you still have toes," I say. I feel her smiling into my skin. She wriggles closer. I kiss her, forehead, nose, mouth. I run a hand down her spine and feel the familiar lines of her shoulders, her rib cage, the bones beneath the skin the same ones as ever. Different body, same girl. Same voice.

Same Aza.

Why am I so stressed out then? There's a list of give or take fifty terrible things I keep expecting, chief among them anchors falling out of the sky and a crew of warriors bringing Aza straight back up to Magonia.

Maybe everyone spends a big part of their time afraid they're about to lose the love of their life. Maybe most people live like that and it never shows.

Not everyone's hiding an alien in their skin, obviously, but everyone's hiding something. I try to convince myself that it's normal to be this paranoid, but my life feels like I'm standing on a cliff, the camera panning out to discover Niagara Falls.

I mean, I'm okay. I'm not saying I'm not. *Pi* has been largely backgrounded in the last few months, due to a better regimen of pills. They manage anxiety loops efficiently, so I don't end up spending half of every day caught in a spiral of infinite digit recitation. I still have the kind of mind I have, though, which means I have to map out every bad eventuality and then make plans to evade said eventualities.

I used to know that the only person I'd ever love was going to die at any moment.

Now I have hope. Hope, it turns out, is problematic.

"*Hope is the thing with feathers*," says Emily Dickinson

inside my head. *"That perches in the soul—and sings the tune without the words—and never stops at all—"*

Yeah, *the thing with feathers*. I want hope to have zero feathers. No feathers, or plumage of any sort, anywhere.

When we got back from Svalbard last year, I tried to hire someone to guard Aza's house. I wanted protection, surveillance, but that costs like $3,500 a day. I'm serious. Just for some low-rent service, the kind of thing you hire to see if someone's husband is cheating, or if someone is stealing from someone else's business. So THAT was obviously impossible. I had to do other things.

Those things are what have me sleepless these days.

In theoretical math there's a concept called the pea and sun paradox. The Banach-Tarski paradox, if official is what you want. Basically, it's the idea that you could reorganize the molecules of a pea into something the size of the sun, or the sun into something the size of a pea. The universe is elastic.

Aza is elastic.

I want her pea-close, like she is right now. But there are forces that want to turn her into the sun.

I glance at the clock. Midnight. I pull out a book of matches. "Shut your eyes," I tell her.

She does, though she makes a patented Aza Ray face at me that says I can never surprise her, because *hello*, she knows everything about everything.

Not this time.

"Hold on to this." I put something in her hand. "Over the floor, not the bed."

I strike the match, and then there's sizzling and spitting. "Open."

She opens her eyes. She's holding a sparkler in the shape of an ampersand.

"Happy birthday, Aza Ray," I say.

It sends off tiny "&" fireworks in the dark of the bedroom. The look on her face says I got it right.

&, is what I want. & more. &, &, &.

I hand Aza a little package and she opens it. A compass. A really good one, engraved with a tiny winged ship. I don't fool around when it comes to birthdays.

"It goes all directions."

"All?"

"Should work down here," I tell her. "AND up there. Just in case." It has a spinning orb in the center, with arrows pointing every possible way.

She points it at me.

She smiles. "Seriously, Kerwin?"

Yeah. So maybe I had a high-tech modification put in. So maybe north is not actually north, but *me*, all the time.

It took some doing.

Minor sensor installed under my skin.

I know, I know. Untested hackology. But once I learned I could do something like that, was I really *not* going to do it? I scoured all the clandestine message boards, and I was willing to pay for it. It was already reality, just not in the larger world.

"Just in case," I say. She looks at me. Her eyes, even in the dark, are ridiculous, ink with fire underneath.

"Where do you think I'm going?" Aza asks.

What if she just decides to go out yondering (I don't care, it should be a word) into the wild blue?

"Nowhere, but you never know. It also has a flashlight inside it," I say. "And other things. It's like . . . one of those multi-tools."

"So if I'm lost in the dark, I can always point north, turn on the flashlight, and find you?" she says.

"Correct," I say.

I've run the stats on catastrophe, and I've run the stats on love. Lost love, smashed love, messed-up love, star-crossed love. And finally, love *as* catastrophe. I'm trying to determine if the two are inevitably, inextricably linked. Thus far, my studies are inconclusive.

"So . . . ," I say.

"So," she says, and smiles at me.

"So, do you hate it?"

"Are you real right now?" she asks. "How could I hate it? In what universe could I possibly hate it?"

"Because I can return it," I say. I try to take it back. She grabs it from me.

"How do you return a compass that has YOU programmed into it as north? Do you think I want other people northing at you, Kerwin?" She looks into my face, and smiles.

"Maybe not," I say.

She kisses me hard and presses herself so close to me that there's no space between us at all. We're like two pieces of a very particular puzzle.

Optimistic data to counteract the catastrophic data: my parents are still madly in love. They chose it every day for years, even when the world felt impossible, or at least, that's what Carol said when I asked her a few months ago. Carol isn't the romantic one of my moms. Carol's the realist. Eve would tell me romantic things about how love saves you from the rest of the darkness of living. Carol would never go there.

"Eve has my back," Carol told me. "Even when I'm at the hospital twenty hours a day, even when my patients are so sick that I feel like I'm failing, and I'm worrying about you at the same time—"

She gave me a Significant Look. It was ignored. I can't deal with my moms being worried about me at the same time I'm worried about the fate of the world and more particularly, the fate of Aza.

"—she can make me crazy. I can make her crazy too. But we're still here. Nobody better on earth for either of us, far as I can tell."

Carol, of course, was saying this with no knowledge of anything that'd gone on lately.

This is a universe of choosing. Aza chose me. That was a year ago, but here she still is, choosing me, climbing in my window in the middle of a dark and stormy night.

She sings very quietly, a little scrap of Magonian song. In my bedroom a tiny star appears, floating overhead. It's blue at the center and red around the edges. It's so bright I kind of can't look, except that all I want is to look at it forever.

I pull out my phone and video her song and the little star. I'm compiling records of the ways her notes bend the air, the ways Magonian sonics can shift matter.

Seems unreal at first, till you know about breaking glass with a high note, for example. You can also put out a fire with a certain kind of loud note, which displaces all the oxygen in the air. Truth.

For now, Aza's song isn't shaking the world. It's just a tiny star in my bedroom. She's getting better at singing and controlling her song.

"Why do you look like that?" she asks me.

"Because I'm in love with you, stupid," I tell her.

She runs a hand down my side, and kisses me again. After a moment, I kiss her back. I try to live in that for the moment. It turns out, I can.

"I'm in love with you stupid too," she says.

I roll over and feel her underneath me, her hip bones and ribs and elbows. I can smell the smoke from the ampersand star I gave her, and I can see her face in the light of the Magonian star she's sung into being.

I kiss this girl who is mine because of some miracle. I keep my back to the star.

I only want to look at Aza, and try to forget she might belong somewhere that isn't with me.